WHAT CJ DIDN'T THINK TO ASK

"MOM?" I SAID, touching the heart shape on the softest part of my cheek. "Why's it called a 'cherish'?"

My mom was quiet at first, and for a second I worried that she really had been drawn Far Away. But then Aunt Nic reached out across the ugly corduroy couch and gently unwrapped the towel from my hair. Eased my curls down to my shoulders. Picked up the hair cream and began working it through my hair, just like she did every night.

"Because you are so loved, CJ Ames," she told me as she coaxed my curls into perfect spirals, "so cherished, that it shows up on your very skin."

The funny thing was, I asked my mom the question, but it was my aunt who answered. But I guess I liked what she said too much to ask why.

To Beans

Also by Lisa Graff

FAR AWAY

Lisa Graff

PUFFIN BOOKS

PUFFIN BOOKS
An imprint of Penguin Random House LLC, New York

First published in the United States of America by Philomel Books, 2019
Published by Puffin Books, an imprint of Penguin Random House LLC, 2020

Visit us online at penguinrandomhouse.com

THE LIBRARY OF CONGRESS HAS CATALOGED THE PHILOMEL BOOKS EDITION AS FOLLOWS:
Names: Graff, Lisa (Lisa Colleen), 1981– author.
Title: Far away / Lisa Graff. | Description: New York, NY : Philomel Books, [2019]
Summary: Twelve-year-old CJ believes her mom is dead and that she can only
communicate with her through her aunt, who is a medium, but when CJ finds out
that her mother is actually alive, she goes on a journey to find her. | Identifiers:
LCCN 2018006766 | ISBN 9781524738594 (hardcover) | ISBN 9781524738600
(e-book) | Subjects: | CYAC: Mothers and daughters—Fiction. | Aunts—Fiction. |
Mediums—Fiction. | Spirits—Fiction. | Classification: LCC PZ7.G751577 Far 2019 |
DDC [Fic]—dc23 | LC record available at https://lccn.loc.gov/2018006766

Puffin Books ISBN 9781524738617

Printed in the United States of America

1 3 5 7 9 10 8 6 4 2

Edited by Jill Santopolo.
Design by Jennifer Chung.
Text set in Legacy Serif ITC Pro.

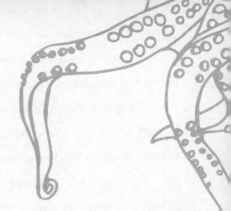

PROLOGUE

PEOPLE ALWAYS TRY to feel sorry for me when they find out my mom died, but I like to look on the bright side. Like, she never stops me from eating extra cookies, or forces me to study when I don't want to. She's never scolded me for staying up past my bedtime, either—although she usually tells Aunt Nic to scold me later.

"Where is she right now?" I used to ask Aunt Nic. I asked that practically once an hour when I was a little kid. "She hasn't been drawn Far Away, has she?" I was terrified of the idea of my mother going Far Away for good, like my grandparents had before I was born. Once a spirit takes up permanent residence Far Away, it's nearly impossible to communicate with them anymore, and I like to talk to my mom as much as I can.

But Aunt Nic would assure me every time.

"Don't worry, CJ," she'd say. "She's still here on Earth, keeping an eye on you—and she's Far Away, too, with Grandma and Grandpa Ames and all the other spirits. She's in both places at the same time."

But I would never feel *really* satisfied until my mother told me herself. She usually did that at night, after dinner, while I was sitting in a folding chair scooched up against our motor home's kitchen sink and Aunt Nic was massaging shampoo into my curls under the just-right warm water.

"I'm right here, CJ, darling," she would say. It was always Aunt Nic's voice, of course, but the words were my mom's. You can tell when Aunt Nic's talking to Spirit, because her words get softer, slower, like she's listening at the same time she's talking. I may have been dealt a bad hand, being born to a mom who was going to die four hours later, but at least I got lucky enough to have an aunt who could communicate with her. A "medium," that's what most folks call her—because Aunt Nic can deliver messages from both sides.

"But *where* are you?" I asked my mom once. "I mean, *exactly*." It was my fifth birthday—I remember, because Aunt Nic was taking ages washing my hair, and I was wondering if we were ever going to get to birthday cake. "Are you sitting on the couch?" Our motor home, back then, had an ugly brown corduroy couch that was our seat for the table, and my bed, too. "Are you swimming in the sink?"

"Sweet seedling," my mom replied. I always love when she calls me "seedling." It makes me feel warm, like being wrapped up in a blanket. *"I'm everywhere and nowhere all at once."*

And I guess that answer must've done it for me, because I

pulled my head out of the sink to ask an even more important question.

"Can you tell Aunt Nic I'm ready for my birthday cake?"

My mom just laughed, right through Aunt Nic. *"I helped your aunt find something even better this year,"* she told me as Aunt Nic squeezed the water out of my curls. The shower in our motor home was nearly as busted as the engine, so Aunt Nic washed my hair in the sink every night and helped me work cream through it after so the curls stayed bouncy.

"Nothing's better than birthday cake," I told my mom and my aunt together.

I guess they didn't agree, because Aunt Nic only wrapped a towel snug around my hair and walked over to the motor home fridge. I watched as she poked around the leftover rice and macaroni salad, and the ketchup bottle that had tipped over so many times the rim was red with goo. Finally she pulled out two tiny Styrofoam containers and set them on the table in front of the couch. I came over to see.

When Aunt Nic peeled the lid off the first container, I wrinkled my nose right up on my face. Light brown glop with curved dark sprinkles—that's what my mom and Aunt Nic had gotten me instead of birthday cake. I was about to say it didn't look like anything I wanted to eat when my mom started in with one of her stories.

"I was young when you were born," she said, and I could tell

right away that this was a story I was going to want to listen to. *"Just nearly twenty."*

Aunt Nic jumped in then, only she didn't say anything to me. She started talking directly to my mom. That happened sometimes.

"Yes, Jennie June," Aunt Nic said. " 'Young *and* gorgeous.' I was gonna add that part."

I tucked my feet under my butt to get comfortable.

"I was excited to meet you," my mom went on, *"but I'm not gonna pretend I had my act together. For one thing, I'd lost track of your dad before he was lucky enough to know he was having a daughter."*

My mom and Aunt Nic always say that I'm the product of a "whirlwind romance"—but I never figure I miss out much, not having a dad. Two grown-ups who care about you is as much as most kids get.

"And then the morning of December sixth came," my mom said, *"and I hadn't even picked out a name for you yet, but it was clear you were coming, and quick."*

Aunt Nic raised her eyebrows at me then. "CJ," she said, "your mom wants me to tell you she was cool as a cucumber the whole time at the hospital, but—Jennie June, I'm not gonna lie to the girl. I was there!" When Aunt Nic's eyes went wide, I could tell my mom had words for her. "Well!" Aunt Nic chirped. "I'm not gonna repeat *that.*"

"What happened after I was born?" I asked, to remind

them to keep going with the story. I had a feeling the next part was important.

"What happened, my seedling, was that you were gorgeous." My mom gave me a look then, through Aunt Nic, like the image had stayed with her, even though her body hadn't. *"Tiniest thing I'd ever seen, with dark, thick curls. And that birthmark!"* Through Aunt Nic, she reached out and pressed one thumb soft against my cheek, to the dark heart-shaped spot. *"That's called a 'cherish,' you know, that sort of mark."*

When I put my own hand to the spot, I could feel the memory of my mom's touch there, warm and gentle. I kept my hand like that for a long time.

"As soon as we were alone in the room," my mom continued, *"just us three Ames ladies—well, your aunt pulls a cooler out of her purse."*

"A cooler?" I asked.

"She'd brought it with her to the hospital! Had it on her the whole time, only I hadn't noticed."

Aunt Nic tilted her head to respond. "You were busy, Jennie June," she said.

"True," my mom replied.

"What was in the cooler?" I asked. Because sometimes they'd get so busy talking to each other they'd forget anyone else was listening.

It was Aunt Nic who answered that one. "Back where

Grandma Ames's family came from, in Lebanon," she said, peeling back the lid of the second Styrofoam cup, "whenever a new baby comes into the world, they serve caraway pudding. For good luck."

Peering down into that little white cup, I felt like I might be starting to understand. Those dark skinny curls on top of the pudding, I realized, were caraway seeds. Suddenly it didn't look so disgusting after all. My mom picked up the story as I dipped the tip of my spoon into the container.

"It only took a single bite of that pudding," she said, *"for me to know. I looked at you, tiny thing curled in my arms like a seed, and I told your aunt, 'Her name is Caraway.'"*

Maybe I'd heard the story before. But that day, on my fifth birthday, was the first time I remembered. It was definitely the day I realized that caraway pudding tasted a whole lot better than it looked. It became a tradition after that. Every year on my birthday, no matter what city we happen to be in, no matter how busy Aunt Nic is, my mom helps her track down some caraway pudding, and the three of us celebrate together. Even after Aunt Nic got to be "big potatoes" on the psychic medium circuit, and she hired Oscar and Cyrus to travel with us for extra help, and we swapped our busted motor home for the new tour bus with the fancy shower so I didn't need help washing my hair in the sink anymore—even after all that, Aunt Nic and my mom find time and pudding for my birthday. Every year.

I still remember the way that first bite tasted on my tongue, sweet and silky, as they told me the rest of the story. They left in every detail, even the ones so sad they made my throat tight with tears.

Like how, just minutes after she gave me my name, the hospital machines started beeping out of control and the nurses rushed in all panicked.

And how they tried and tried and tried to save her.

And—throat-clenchingest of all—how she died, right there in the bed beside me, from a sickness no one had known to look for.

But they told me the happy details, too.

Like how she visited Aunt Nic just days after she died, because she knew her sister had the Gift and could hear her when she spoke.

How she told Aunt Nic to be my guardian here on Earth while she cared for me in Spirit.

And how, since she'd left the world before giving me a middle name, my mom asked Aunt Nic to pick it.

"*You* picked June?" I asked Aunt Nic. "After my mom?"

Aunt Nic nodded. "Caraway June. 'Cause you're my sunshine in December."

The story was so filling—sweet like pudding, but with some bite to it, too—that it wasn't till I was scraping the last of my birthday dessert out of its cup that I thought to ask.

"Mom?" I said, touching the heart shape on the softest part of my cheek. "Why's it called a 'cherish'?"

My mom was quiet at first, and for a second I worried that she really had been drawn Far Away. But then Aunt Nic reached out across the ugly corduroy couch and gently unwrapped the towel from my hair. Eased my curls down to my shoulders. Picked up the hair cream and began working it through my hair, just like she did every night.

"Because you are so loved, CJ Ames," she told me as she coaxed my curls into perfect spirals, "so cherished, that it shows up on your very skin."

The funny thing was, I asked my mom the question, but it was my aunt who answered. But I guess I liked what she said too much to ask why.

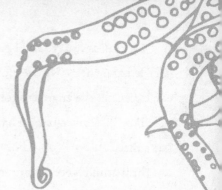

ONE

AUNT NIC'S NOT joking when she says that dead people pay our bills. My whole life, Spirit has been nothing but kind to me.

Still, I don't plan on crossing realms anytime soon.

So when I'm nearly mowed down by the white pickup truck crossing the parking lot of the Santa Barbara Community Theater on the morning of my twelfth birthday, I'm more than a little peeved.

"Hey!" I shout as the truck lurches to a stop. It sputters for a quick second before dying completely, inches from where I'm bundled in my puffy blue coat. "What gives?" At first I think it must be Cyrus inside—except Cyrus isn't here. And he also wouldn't try to murder me.

But when the head pops out of the driver's window, it all starts to make sense. "Oh, *man!*" the driver shouts. "That could've been, like, *super* bad."

He's a teenager—sixteen, max—wearing a navy baseball jacket and way too much gel in his hair.

"So I guess you're Jax," I greet him.

He barely nods. He tries to start the truck up again, but he can't even get the engine to roll over.

"I'm CJ," I say, waving a hand at him. "Caraway June Ames. Nic's niece."

"You mind getting out of the way?" Jax calls out the window. "Uncle Oscar told me I have to practice, and I don't want you to get hurt." There's a loud screech of metal meeting metal as he grinds the gears.

"The only thing you're gonna hurt is that truck," I tell him. I glance at the tour bus parked at the far end of the lot, then back to Jax, who's busy murdering Cyrus's beloved vehicle. I whip open the passenger's door.

"What are you doing?" Jax asks. His dark eyes are huge, like he's afraid of me, even though *he's* the one who nearly just killed a person.

I hop inside, slam the door shut, and readjust my headband to push my curls out of my eyes.

"I'm teaching you to drive stick," I say.

"How do *you* know how to drive stick?" Jax's knuckles are gripped tight around the steering wheel. "You're, like, ten."

"I'm twelve," I reply. "Today's my birthday. And your uncle taught me stick, same as he taught you." I pause. "Well, way better than he taught you, obviously. You're not giving it enough clutch. You gotta press all the way to the floor."

Jax's eyes somehow go even wider, like he can't take in the whole *one* piece of information I've just thrown at him.

"Here." I grab the gearshift between us. "I'll do the shifting. You just worry about your feet. Try starting her up."

All Jax does is blink. Seriously. I'm not even sure if he's breathing. I don't know if he's confused about driving or worried that I'm about to mug him for bus money. Maybe both.

"I'm only trying to help you," I tell him. "The way you're mutilating this truck, I'm surprised Cyrus hasn't leapt out of his hospital bed in Toledo to rescue it already." Jax continues to blink at me, silent. "Look, I know Oscar hired you 'cause you're his nephew and we're in a major pinch right now." When one of the key members of your four-person crew decides to roll an ATV over his leg in the middle of your sixty-city tour, it turns out you can't be too picky about finding a replacement. "But you probably also know that Oscar's not, like, the most *forgiving* person, so if you wanna last on this crew for more than five minutes, you might want to take my help."

I guess that last part reboots him or something, because he finally says, "Uncle Oscar didn't tell me it was your birthday."

I've known Oscar for over two years, and I know he cares about me in the way that, like, he wouldn't ever hope I got botulism, but still. "Your uncle's not too big on celebrations," I tell Jax. "Last year for Christmas, he gave me a high five."

"Sounds like Uncle Oscar," Jax replies. And a crack of a smile breaks through his face. "Anyway, happy birthday."

"Thanks." I point to Jax's foot on the clutch, my left hand still firm on the shifter. "When you're ready for me to shift, say go."

It takes seventeen tries, and once Jax gets so confused he grabs my left arm like he thinks he's going to shift *me*, but he does get it, eventually. He manages to start up the truck, drive one whole length of parking spots, and even shut down the vehicle without a single sputter. 'Course, I had to be working the shifter the whole time, but, you know, baby steps.

"Hey!" I congratulate him. "That wasn't terrible!"

"Right?" he says, pretty proud of himself. "I might even make it all the way to L.A. tonight without breaking down."

"You're gonna need a *lot* more practice to go a hundred miles on the 101 by yourself," I say. And just like that, Jax's grin vanishes. I feel a little bad, but not *too* much. The kid needs a reality check. "No offense, but why'd Oscar even hire you if you don't know stick? Besides working the floor during the show, splitting the driving is like half your job."

Jax has pushed up the left sleeve of his jacket and is scratching his lower arm with his right hand. "I'm working spotlight," he replies. "Not the floor. And I'll get better at stick shift. I mean, I have to, right? If I want to keep this job."

I examine the side of Jax's face as he pretends to study

super-important displays on the truck's dash. Scratching his arm like it's a lotto ticket he's sure is gonna cash in huge.

"Try it again," I say, nodding toward Jax's clutch foot. I grip the gearshift.

He looks up at me. "Yeah?"

"Sure," I say. "Ready? And . . . *clutch!*"

Jax presses down the clutch once more, I shift us into first, and we drive about as fast as a sloth in slow motion.

"You sure you don't have somewhere better to be?" Jax asks, after we've moved all of ten feet. "Birthday party? Homework?"

"Aunt Nic and I aren't celebrating until later," I tell him. "And I finished my worksheets hours ago." All I have left to do before the show is to compile the email list for the monthly newsletter and plan our route for the weekend, but I've got plenty of time. "Rev her up a little faster so you can practice shifting into second." Jax speeds up. "Hear that?" I ask. "That's the truck telling you to shift. Ready? And . . . *clutch!*" Together we transition to second gear, then celebrate with a mini seat dance party.

We're shifting back into first when Jax asks, "You like being homeschooled? Uncle Oscar's supposed to tutor me too now."

I point out a parking spot near the theater's back entrance, across from where Oscar unloaded the sound equipment before picking up Jax at the airport. "Pull in here. We'll work on reversing." Jax inches into the spot. "Oscar's a great tutor," I tell him. "Even better than Cyrus. Oscar never checks *anything*. Like, I used to mess with Cyrus sometimes, add extra letters into my spelling tests and stuff, just to see if he'd notice. But last week I turned in a social studies report all about our first president, George Watermelon, and Oscar gave me full credit. Ready? And . . . *clutch!*"

Jax eases to a stop in the parking spot, doesn't even hiccup on the clutch as I shift us into park. "He did not," he says.

I put my hand over my heart. "No joke! I added lots of good details, too, about President Watermelon's wooden ears, and how he led his troops across the Potato Salad. It was awful. I got an A."

I can tell Jax does not understand what a great situation he's lucked into, because he asks me, "But don't you want to *learn* stuff?"

"I know plenty of stuff. I *do*," I say when he looks skeptical. "I'm in charge of all the navigation for the entire tour, for one thing. I can plan the fastest route to any stop, no tolls, accounting for weather and elevation. I *know* stuff. Anyway, I read the book about George Washington. I just did a joke report, for Oscar."

"Mmm," Jax replies.

I don't like that *"Mmm."* There's all sorts of judgment in it.

"Ready for reverse?" I ask, and together we slowly back up. "How'd you land spotlight duty, anyway?" Oscar said there was no way I could run spotlight, because we couldn't afford the medical bills if I fell out of the bay. Still, way up above the audience, where the spot operator works, is my favorite place to be during a show. It's the closest you can get to Spirit. All I ever get to do is gopher duty—*"CJ, go for coffee." "Go for cable ties." "Go for electrical tape." "Go for . . ." "Go for . . ."*

Jax adjusts his rearview mirror as he continues backing up. "I told Uncle Oscar I'd rather work up in the spotlight bay than down in the audience," he explains. "So he said as long as I was *super* careful—"

There aren't a ton of crash sounds that are good news, but the enormous *CRACK-CRUNCH!* that jolts the truck then seems especially bad.

"Uh-oh," Jax says as the engine coughs and dies.

I whip around in my seat. "I think maybe there's a better word for it than 'uh-oh,'" I tell him when I see what we've hit.

The sound equipment that Oscar unloaded is flat on the ground. Pieces of the mixing console are scattered across the parking lot.

"Jax Delgado!" comes Oscar's howl as he storms out of the theater. Just in the few steps it takes him to get to us, his hair somehow gets grayer. "I am going to *strangle . . .*"

Within thirty seconds, Jax is off spotlight duty.

"But—" Jax tries to argue, which makes me wonder if he's ever met his uncle before.

"No buts," Oscar snaps. "You're lucky I don't ship you back to Miami this second. One more screwup—I mean *one*, Jax— and you're gone. I obviously can't trust anyone on the spotlight but myself." He turns to me. "CJ, I need you working the floor tonight with Jax. You'll handle mics while he's on camera. Keep an eye on him so he doesn't cost us *another* thousand bucks." He picks up a chunk of the mixing console and growls. "Never thought my nephew would need an eleven-year-old babysitter."

"No prob," I reply. Jax is back to scratching at that arm. I wish there was more I could do to help the poor kid, but the truth is, if he's gonna last on this crew he's going to have to grow a backbone all on his own. "And I'm twelve now, by the way," I remind Oscar.

"Oh, yeah," Oscar says. And on my way to the tour bus, he gives me a birthday high five.

. . .

The loft above the tour bus driver's seat is small, but it's all mine. My bed takes up most of the space, with its midnight-blue bedspread. All up the walls and on the ceiling are glow-in-the-dark stars. I've got a photo of my mom beside my window, and a glowy bird lamp, and a shelf on the far wall with drawers for my clothes and knickknacks and atlas. It's exactly as much room as I've ever needed.

As soon as I reach the top of the ladder, I flop onto my bed and pull the atlas out of its drawer, flipping till I find the map of our current location: Santa Barbara, California. Then I turn onto my belly and begin to plot our route.

I've been Aunt Nic's navigator since I was seven years old. That was the year I found an honest-to-goodness road atlas at a garage sale in Bangor, Maine, marked for five bucks. The man whose house it was said, "You sure you want that, little girl? Everyone uses GPS these days." And I said, "Oh, really?" like that was news to me. Then I haggled him down to one dollar.

I like to plan out our route a few days in advance, adjusting for any unexpected delays or complications. Our crew travels at night, after loading out a show. Me and Aunt Nic mainly drive in the tour bus, with Cyrus and Oscar in the truck, and the grown-ups split driving shifts when needed. We don't sleep till we arrive at our next location—me and Aunt Nic on the bus, Cyrus and Oscar in a nearby motel.

Luckily, this week's leg of the tour is an easy one, driving-wise. For the next few days we're skirting the coast of Southern California—Santa Barbara today, then L.A. on Friday and Oceanside on Saturday. We won't have more than a two-hour drive till we head east to Phoenix Saturday night. That will give Jax plenty of time to practice before his shift-splitting becomes crucial.

I always do my route plotting in pencil, drawing careful

lines across the roads our wheels will spin over in just a few hours, only pulling out my tablet to check the week's weather forecast.

Two years ago, Cyrus convinced me it would be "a hoot" to be in charge of Aunt Nic's mailing list. It is not a hoot. Mostly it's boring. Each theater's box office sends us the contact info that people plug in when they buy tickets, and I merge the email addresses into our database so we can send out Aunt Nic's monthly newsletter. But at least the job came with a tablet I can use for web surfing. Cyrus disabled the tablet's phone capabilities for some reason, even though I told him that everyone I know either lives on the road with me or died a while ago.

As my pencil skims over tonight's route, it hovers above one particular city.

Bakersfield, California, is nearly 150 miles northeast of here. Definitely *not* on our route to L.A. tonight. But it's close enough that we could make a stop if we wanted to, without hardly losing any time.

We won't, though.

"Bakersfield is not a place people stop, seedling." That's what my mom says every time we travel this way. *"It's a place people pass through."*

Aunt Nic always agrees. "We ought to know, your mom and I," she tells me. "We lived there nearly twenty years each, with only a few years off for good behavior. And it's not like there's anything left to see."

That's the thing, though. The house might not be there anymore, but there's still plenty in the town I'd love to visit. The miniature golf course where Aunt Nic first connected with Grandpa Ames's spirit, before he went Far Away for good. The art room of East Bakersfield High, where my mom staged her legendary sit-in after the school laid off her favorite teacher. The "dumpster fire of a Dairy Queen," where Aunt Nic and my mom co-won Employee of the Month in high school because their boss never knew they got the Oreo Blizzard stuck in the ceiling grate to begin with. The Walmart where Aunt Nic worked after she left college to take care of Grandma Ames in the final stages of her Alzheimer's. The used RV lot where my mom led Aunt Nic two weeks after she died, forcing her to "get off your sad butt and use your Gift to *help* people already!" I've got my pencil pressed so hard on the spot where the 101 meets the 126 toward Bakersfield that I poke a hole in the atlas.

That's when the tour bus door opens down below. "Hello?" Aunt Nic calls. "Ceej? I want you to meet someone."

I poke my head through the curtain separating my loft from the rest of the bus. "Hey!" I shout down.

Aunt Nic's face brightens as soon as she sees me. "You know, you *look* twelve," she says, and I grin.

There's a man standing beside her, tall and skinny, with a knobby Adam's apple and more gray hair than Oscar, even though he seems lots younger. "Welcome to our humble abode," I greet him. That's my joke with Aunt Nic, since the tour bus is so much fancier than our old motor home, with plush armchair driving seats, two flat-screen TVs, and a fridge so smart it announces when we're low on ice cream. "I'm CJ."

"I recognize you from your photos," the man tells me, putting one hand to his cheek to indicate my cherish. "I'm Roger Milmond. It's lovely to meet you, CJ."

"Thanks," I say. Then, before creeping back behind the curtain, I tell him, "And don't worry about Spirit getting distracted during your reading. They're used to me up here." The past few years we've been working bigger and bigger venues, so Aunt Nic doesn't do house calls anymore. But some spirits are shy about connecting in groups, so most afternoons before shows Aunt Nic squeezes in a few people for private readings at our dining table.

"Actually, CJ," Aunt Nic says slowly, "I . . . have some news." Her face is happy-worried, and for a second I think maybe she's about to tell me Roger is her new boyfriend—even though she always says, "Spirit hardly leaves me time to eat a sandwich, let alone *date*."

But then Roger tells me, "I'm the lead producer for the LCM Network," and my squeal fills the whole bus.

"You got the show!" I holler, leaping down the ladder to hug Aunt Nic. "This is *amazing!*"

Aunt Nic's been in talks for over a year to see if she'd be a "good fit" for the subject of a reality TV show, and up till now it's been hard to get her to say more than five words about it. She won't blink an eye when it comes to talking with Spirit, but for some reason being on TV makes her nervous.

"Don't get excited yet," Aunt Nic says, pulling out of the hug. "It's not quite final."

"My crew's here to take footage," Roger explains. "If all goes well tonight, the big kahunas in L.A. will catch tomorrow's show—so that's when your aunt *really* needs to bring her A game."

"She always brings her A game," I tell Roger. Every night, Aunt Nic changes people's lives. Gives folks hope after they thought they'd lost it forever. Every night, I watch a woman's face light up as she's reconnected with her dead father. Or I see a man break down when he hears his daughter's words, years after she left him. "She's the best in the business."

Roger smiles at that, big and toothy. "I agree," he says. But the happiness doesn't quite reach his eyes.

"Will the whole crew be in the reality show?" I ask. "Do I get my own cameraperson to follow me around, or do I have to split one with Oscar and Jax?" *If Jax makes it through the week,* I don't say out loud.

Roger glances at Aunt Nic like she's going to answer that, but when she doesn't, he says, "We're mainly focused on the lady talking to Spirit. Unless . . ." He pauses, like something's just occurring to him. "You've got the Gift, too?"

People always ask me that. I guess they figure it must be in my genes or something. "I used to try all the time when I was little," I say with a shrug. "But nope."

"Shame." Roger grins. "Aunt-and-niece mediums would make a really great show."

"I need to discuss a few details with you, CJ," Aunt Nic jumps in. So I plop myself down in the passenger's seat to listen.

But no one discusses.

"Well," Roger says after a weird moment of silence. "I should be off. CJ . . ." He takes a step toward me, but instead of shaking my hand like I think he's going to do, he ends up clutching both my hands together super awkwardly. "I'll see you at the show."

"Nice to meet you," I tell him.

I readjust my headband as the bus door closes behind Roger. As hard as I try, I can never get my curls as smooth as Aunt Nic can. Somehow, I always end up with more product on one side than the other, so half my curls are crunchy and the other half are limp.

"You're not still nervous about the reality show, are you?"

I ask Aunt Nic as she settles into the driver's seat beside me. "You know you'll be amazing."

Aunt Nic spins in her seat and reaches for something beside her. "First things first," she says, then hands me a blue gift box. "Happy birthday, Ceej."

I open the box.

Inside is a leather bag—not quite a purse but not a brief-case, either. It's a deep, luscious brown, with a large flap over the front with a brass clasp and one long, long strap. It's not frilly or fancy but sturdy and plain, with tiny stitches around every seam, and the leather is so soft that I can't stop smooth-ing my hands over it.

"It's a messenger bag," Aunt Nic says. "I saw it way back in Missoula, and I knew you had to have it. I thought it would be just the right size for an atlas."

I jump up to grab my atlas from the loft. Sure enough, it tucks perfectly inside. "I love it," I say. "Thank you."

Aunt Nic grins big.

"Is my mom ready for pudding now?" I ask, but I'm already halfway to the fridge. Aunt Nic's been so busy lately that it's been eons since I've talked to my mom, and I have tons of ques-tions stored up for her. Like what she thinks of my new blue coat, and if she thought I made a smart decision about our route out of Toledo, and if she agrees with me that Aunt Nic needs to change the line in her intro about the Vicks VapoRub.

I don't know when Aunt Nic managed to sneak out and find a Lebanese restaurant, but there are two small Styrofoam containers on the top shelf of the fridge. I'm grabbing two spoons when Aunt Nic says, "Before the pudding . . ."

She's holding a second gift box.

I head to my seat, set down the two pudding cups and spoons on the center console, and reach for the box, excited.

Only, when I open it, I'm all sorts of confused.

It's an outfit. Bright-yellow skirt, short and pleated, made of thick, stiff material. Matching yellow blazer. Two identical button-down white shirts and a pair of yellow socks.

"It's . . ." I say. "Nice."

It's not.

"It's a uniform," Aunt Nic tells me.

I am not less confused. "A uniform for what?"

"The Plemmons Academy." Aunt Nic leans over and unfolds one side of the blazer to show me a patch. "Boarding school."

I feel a bit like I'm swimming inside a bowl of oatmeal. "I don't . . ." I start, but I can't suck in enough air to finish the thought.

Aunt Nic sighs then. Rolls her shoulders like she's resetting herself. "I'm sorry, CJ, I'm doing this badly. I thought you'd be excited. I should've . . . I've enrolled you at the Plemmons Academy, in Vermont. You start in January."

I drop the box and the uniform with it. "Vermont? Next

month?" Suddenly my words come out pinched and quiet. "Don't you want me here anymore?"

"Oh, Ceej." Aunt Nic reaches over to squeeze my arm. "Of *course* I do. I *love* having you here. But this is going to be so good for you. It's a world-class institution. They have an enormous library. A beautiful atrium!"

"When have I ever said I wanted to go to boarding school?" I ask seriously. "And I don't even know what an atrium *is*."

"See?" Aunt Nic says. "That's half the trouble." But she keeps a tight grip on my left arm, like she's not so ready to let me go. "It's my job to make sure you're getting a good education, and you're definitely . . . *not*."

"I get a fine education."

Aunt Nic raises an eyebrow. "George Watermelon?" she says.

"That was *one* report."

"Last month you filled in a test about the water cycle with the names of Pokémon characters."

That's true. Cyrus gave me an A-plus on that one.

"What are you even going to do without me here?" I ask. "You *need* me. Cyrus is out for months, and Oscar says we can't afford more temp guys, 'cause they're all union. And have you *met* Jax? If I'm gone, how are you going to—?"

"CJ." Aunt Nic sinks back in her seat and takes a long breath. I wait. My skin is tingling just thinking about living anywhere else. I can't. I won't. "You're the backbone of this whole crew. Honestly. It's going to be next to impossible without you. I'm going to miss you so—" Her voice catches. She takes another breath. "But I need to think about what's best for you, not just this business. It isn't normal for a girl your age, traveling all over. Being surrounded by dead folks every night."

I frown at that. "Who wants to be normal?"

"Not everything that's normal is so bad, Ceej. It'll be good to get to know more kids your age. You could join the softball team. Get a crush."

"Dress like a lemon," I add, nodding toward the box in my lap.

She cracks a smile. "I know you already like the school," she says. "Remember? After our show in Montpelier in September, we drove by that little stone campus. All the leaves were changing? You said how beautiful it was, and your mother started whispering in my ear. Wouldn't shut up about it, actually."

I look up from the horrible yellow blazer. "My mom . . . ?"

"She told me to look into it," Aunt Nic replies. "So I did. And sure enough, they had one spot open for the spring semester."

I lift the blazer again, feeling the bulk of the material. It's hard to argue with Spirit. When they tell you to do something, you're always better off doing whatever it is right away, because Spirit knows things humans can't possibly understand. Still. I don't want to be a Plemmons Lemon. I don't want to leave the crew.

"Can I talk to her?" I say. My voice is a squeak.

Aunt Nic squeezes my arm one last time, then lets go to make the connection. While I wait, I grab one of the Styrofoam cups. Peel off the lid.

The pudding is chilly and silky and sweet, and the dash of caraway seeds sprinkled on top gives it the exact right amount of crunch. I take another bite and let the taste settle on my tongue.

"*Happy birthday, seedling,*" my mother greets me.

I swallow quick. "Hi, Mom," I say.

I'm choked up already.

"*You're growing up into such a beautiful young lady, CJ. I'm so proud of you, every day.*" And she reaches out, through Aunt Nic, and touches my cheek. My cherish. I hold her hand there, tight, as she goes on. "*I know the road ahead will be hard, seedling, but this is the best course for you—I'm sure of it. Do you understand?*"

I want to argue, but she knows I can't. She's a spirit now, so she has all the wisdom of Earth and Spirit, too.

"I understand," I tell her. Even though it hurts to say it.

My mom's touch lingers on my cheek, Aunt Nic's hand under mine. "*I need to tell you something else, seedling,*" she says. "*Something very difficult. But I know you're strong enough to hear it.*"

Aunt Nic's voice is shaky as the words come out, and I don't know which one of them is upset by what I'm about to hear. I clutch the hand tighter to my cheek.

"*I'm not going to be able to visit you anymore, seedling.*" The words scratch at my ears. "*This is going to be our last visit on Earth. I'm being drawn Far Away.*"

It is everything I've ever feared.

"No," I tell her. Because she's wrong. About this, I'm certain she's wrong. "No."

"*I've waited until I could tell you myself,*" she says. "*But I can't fight it anymore. When Spirit draws you, there's no way to stop it.*"

"No."

The way things are now, my mom can talk to me whenever she wants, as long as Aunt Nic's there to translate. But once she's Far Away for good, she'll be gone—and the only way back, even for a brief visit, is if she's *pulled* here, and "I don't have a tether," I tell her. "How will I pull you here when I need you?"

"*Spirit wouldn't take me if you truly needed me,*" my mom says. Her words are getting fainter, like she's already drifting away.

"Stop it!" I screech. I don't know when Aunt Nic wrapped her arms around me, but now she squeezes tight.

"*I'll be watching you, from Far Away,*" my mom goes on, her words thin like tissue. "*I love you, my sweet seedling. Goodbye.*"

"Mom! Stop. You can't—"

I feel it, when she goes. Aunt Nic's body drops into mine, her muscles loose. When I look, I see that her face is sickly yellow, her cheeks wet, and I remember that she just lost someone, too.

"I'm so sorry, CJ," Aunt Nic whispers into my hair.

"We don't have anything?" I say. "Nothing that might be her tether?"

When Aunt Nic shakes her head, I feel it across my whole body.

"I'm so sorry, CJ," she says again.

. . .

When a spirit is drawn permanently Far Away, they can still send messages to their loved ones on Earth through other spirits—but it's difficult for them to cross back into our realm to speak for themselves.

Difficult, but not impossible.

In order to do it, they need to be pulled back momentarily, by a tether—a physical object that the spirit treasured during their time on Earth, the item that contains their strongest source of emotional energy. In her years as a medium, Aunt Nic's used all sorts of tethers to help draw back spirits—rings, belt buckles, diaries. Even a dog bowl once. I saw it.

For my mom, there is nothing at all.

I was three months old when my mom came to give us the news that the house they'd grown up in had burned to the ground. We were thousands of miles away already, in Milwaukee, and Aunt Nic says she took it as a sign that there was no turning back on our old life.

"Why don't you rest tonight?" Aunt Nic asks gently. I don't know how long we've been weeping, but it feels like an eternity. "I'm sure Jax can handle things without you."

I shake my head. "He can't." Besides, I'd rather be surrounded by spirits in the theater than by myself on the bus.

"If you're sure," Aunt Nic says, standing. She checks the clock on the dash. It's past time for sound check, but she doesn't head out, she just stands there, watching me. "Ceej?" I look up. Wipe my nose. "I know it's hard, but . . . the longer we hang on to things we'll never get, the more hurt we end up. Do you . . . ? Can you understand that, CJ?"

"I understand," I tell her.

But after the door creaks shut behind her, I wipe my eyes as dry as they'll go. I turn my attention upward, to any spirit who might be able to reach my mom.

"If there's anything I can do," I tell them—I don't ask, I beg—"*anything* to draw her back, I'll do it. Give me a sign, and I'll do whatever you say."

If Aunt Nic's worried about getting hurt, fine. I know she's suffered plenty, losing her sister twice. But me—I can't get more hurt than I already am.

I wait and I wait for Spirit's response, but all I hear is a car horn outside. The low buzz of nearby traffic. No sign about my mom's tether.

My chest heavy, I walk to the bus door. Stretch out my arm

for the handle. And that's when I see it. There's a stain on my arm, poking out from the bottom of my left sleeve. A thin line of dark-blue ink, curling across my wrist.

I push up my sleeve to discover that it's not an ink stain at all. It's an image. A stamp, maybe, or a drawing.

An octopus.

A deep inky-blue octopus with its legs splayed wide, one letter formed in each of its eight tentacles. A message. I bring my face close to read it.

"What—?" I whisper, looking to Spirit as my sleeve falls back over the image. I tug it back up quick.

But even as I do, the dark ink begins to crumble like ash. And by the time my sleeve is rolled up to my elbow, there is nothing to see but skin.

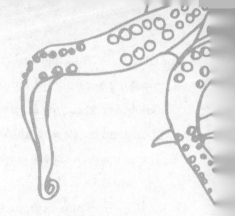

TWO

"AN OCTOPUS?" JAX asks, examining my arm, even though I *told* him there's nothing there anymore. Just a few traces of inky-blue ash. We're backstage, in the wings of the theater, before Aunt Nic goes on, and I'm helping Jax balance the shoulder rig so he can get a steady live feed with the camera. Across the darkened stage, I can see Aunt Nic doing her pre-show stretch in her "teal Thursday" tracksuit. "You sure you didn't imagine it?" he says as he snaps in the battery pack.

"Yeah, that's the thing that makes the most sense," I say. "I *imagined* I saw an octopus appear on my arm with letters inside it. Who *hasn't* imagined that?"

Jax's face is still scrunched up like he's worried I have some sort of octopus-hallucinating fever. "It's just so weird," he says.

That's the first thing he's said that I agree with. "Definitely. But signs from Spirit don't always make sense right away. Spirit's as clear as they can be, but it's our job to figure out what they mean." One by one, I pull the three handheld mics from the nearby table and check that they're flicked to STANDBY before tucking them into my mic belt. I had to poke an extra hole in the belt just to cinch it, because it was custom built for Cyrus, and he's got at least a hundred pounds on me. "Like, once," I go on, "Aunt Nic was doing a reading for this woman whose dog kept barking at this tree in her backyard, and Aunt Nic said, 'It's a sign from Spirit, you gotta pay attention.' And then a year later, the woman told Aunt Nic that same tree crashed through her house during a storm—right onto her bed. The only reason she wasn't sleeping was 'cause she was up early walking the dog."

"Huh," Jax says. But I can tell he's only half listening. He's staring out toward the stage, scratching at his arm again.

"You're not freaking out, are you?" I ask him. I really hope not, because any second now the audience lights will dim, and then it's officially showtime—although for a while it's just Aunt Nic and the spotlight on the stage alone. She always spends at least twelve minutes—thirteen, if it's a laugh-heavy crowd—introducing herself and explaining how readings work. But as soon as Spirit leads her into the audience, that's when me and Jax will have to *move*.

Jax scratches harder, then stops when he notices me watching. "I might be a little freaked," he admits.

"You sure you don't want to swap?" I ask. "Cyrus lets me play around with the camera all the time. I know how to focus and steady it and everything."

Jax only squints at me, like that's the dumbest thing he's ever heard. "You can't run all over with this thing on," he says, shrugging his shoulder under the rig to lift the enormous camera up and down. "It weighs a ton." Okay, so maybe he has a point. "Anyway, I know how to use it. I took Media and Tech at my old school."

Then he stares out at the stage again, and I realize what's *really* freaking him out.

"It's not creepy," I tell him, securing the last mic in my belt. "When Aunt Nic talks with Spirit, I mean. You'll see. It's not like in the movies, where little kids' heads spin around on their necks. In real life, spirits act basically the same way they acted here on Earth." Then I say, "'Take heed' means 'be careful,' right? It's, like, a warning?"

"More like 'pay attention.'" Jax isn't actually scratching at the moment, but that might only be because it's hard to balance the rig with one hand. I honestly don't know how Cyrus manages that thing and the mic belt every night. "If it really is a sign from Spirit," Jax says, yanking his gaze away from the stage, "then what do you think you're supposed pay attention *to*?"

I shrug. "Octopuses?" I say.

"I think the plural of 'octopus' is 'octopi,'" Jax tells me. Like that's the thing to focus on.

"Maybe Spirit's saying I can pull my mom back with an octopus," I say, thinking it over. I never knew my mom had emotional energy stored up in octopuses, but . . . "I could take the bus to the L.A. aquarium tomorrow, before the show."

"Or maybe you're supposed to go to a sushi bar," Jax says. "Or learn how to scuba dive."

I think he's joking, but he has a point. "I guess I just have to figure it out," I reply.

That's when the lights go down. The roar of the audience drops to a hush. And after Oscar's canned announcement about cell phones and recording devices, Aunt Nic strides onto the stage to loud applause.

"Good evening, Santa Barbara!" she calls out cheerfully. No matter what's going on offstage, Aunt Nic always puts it aside when the spotlight's shining. "Welcome, friends, alive and deceased!" There is another roar of applause.

Beside me, Jax has turned his arm into a scratching post again. "Spirit is friendly, I promise," I whisper.

He nods but does not stop scratching.

"Any of you fine folks ever been to a medium before?" Aunt Nic continues. Light applause. "I bet it was some stuffy old lady with a crystal ball who stunk like Vicks VapoRub, am I right?" The audience responds with chuckles, but I swear she could get a bigger laugh there. I told her nobody knows what VapoRub is. "Well, I'm a little different." Aunt Nic gives a kick then, showing off her sneakers under her tracksuit. She has seven different tracksuits, one for every night of the week.

"What you see is what you get with me. No fake tarot cards or crystal balls or hocus-pocus. Just you, me, and your loved ones. Whatever they say to me, I pass it directly to you, bad words and all." That's always a bigger laugh.

While Jax works on scratching his arm off, Aunt Nic explains about her Gift—how it works, when she first realized she had it, and how my mom pushed her to share it with others after she died. I've heard her give this speech so often, sometimes I actually say it in my sleep. So I'm mostly thinking about octopuses—*octopi?*—until Aunt Nic calls out, "Now, who's the one with the sister? Died of cancer?"

"Come on, newbie!" I whisper, tugging Jax so we can follow Aunt Nic into the crowd, where she's searching for the person Spirit's directing her to. We whip across the stage just as the projection screen drops down behind us, missing Jax's head by inches.

"I'm getting a name," Aunt Nic goes on. "Starts with 'M.' Marie, maybe, or Mary?"

"I'm Mary!" comes a shout. A woman jumps out of her seat, and just like that I rush over with my mics, Jax following with his camera. "That's my sister Eliza!"

Mary is about fifty, thin, with a bright-green blouse and short hair. As we reach her, Mary's handing a purple scarf to Aunt Nic. Jax takes it all in with the camera, and the live feed transmits to the screen onstage, so that everyone can see and hear what the lady and Aunt Nic have to say. That was one of Cyrus's innovations, when we started booking bigger venues, and it's definitely made our whole operation seem more professional.

I pass a microphone to Mary, who takes it without hardly glancing at me. Her attention is on Aunt Nic, who's tilting her head, purple scarf in her hand. Mary looks terrified about whatever it is she's about to hear—or not hear.

"Eliza hasn't been drawn Far Away," Aunt Nic says after a beat, and Mary lets out a breath so huge it sounds like a storm over the handheld. "So you don't need a tether. But Eliza's thrilled you brought this scarf anyway. She says, *That one looked real good on me!*"

Mary cries around a breathy laugh. "That's Liza, all right," she says, and suddenly it hits me all over again that I may really never hear any more of my mother's words.

I only get to worry about that for a second, though, before I notice that Jax has the camera focused on me instead of Aunt Nic and Mary. I tug it in the right direction.

"She was smart, your sister, huh?" Aunt Nic is saying. "Used lots of big words?"

Mary thinks about it. "Sometimes, yeah."

"But she didn't like to show off. Didn't want everyone else to feel bad, knowing they weren't as smart as she was. She was always looking out for other people."

That gets a huge nod from Mary. "Oh, yeah. Always."

Aunt Nic smiles back, and I sideways glance at the screen to make sure everything's in focus. "She's still looking out for you now," Aunt Nic continues. "Every day. She wants you to know that. She says, *I've always got your back, sis, same as before. You and the—* You got kids? Eliza's mentioning kids."

"Yeah. Just had my first grandbaby."

Aunt Nic spends a few more minutes with Mary and Eliza before a spirit calls her from a different side of the audience and she races over to make the connection.

It's hard work keeping up with Spirit. Aunt Nic always ends up darting between one side of the audience and another, like a tennis player chasing a ball. But so far, Jax is handling himself pretty well, especially since there are more obstacles to dodge than normal tonight, with Roger and his two camera-people grabbing footage of their own.

When Aunt Nic is called to three grown-up sisters, at first my heart aches for them, because Aunt Nic tells them right away their dad was drawn Far Away long ago, and she can't pull him into our realm to make the connection. But then one of the sisters shows her a doorknob and says, "Will this help? It's from the door to his den. That's where he spent most of his time."

And as soon as Aunt Nic grips it, he is pulled down to Earth.

"Which one of you just got married?" Aunt Nic asks the sisters. "He's telling me, *My daughter looked gorgeous in that dress.*" One of the women is so overwhelmed that another sister has to hold her up. "He was there," Aunt Nic tells the women. "You sensed him, didn't you?"

While I'm passing out mics to the sisters so they can answer, Aunt Nic tells the crowd, "A lot of folks ask me about tethers— how to know which one thing, of all the *stuff* you might have, is filled with enough emotional energy to pull your loved one back."

I tighten my jaw, thinking about families with whole houses of items to sift through. All I have of my mother's are photos. But those aren't things she touched and loved and cared about.

"Sometimes it's hard," Aunt Nic goes on. "Because the object really can be anything. Jewelry, clothing— Is that a lamp, sir?" She shades her eyes with her hand to peer out across the audience and receives a hoot in response. "Sometimes people walk in here, think we're having a garage sale after the show." She pauses for chuckles. "When you find the right object, you *feel* it, okay? Maybe you're not a medium like me, you weren't born with the Gift." She puts a hand on her hip. "Being honest? Sometimes it's a gift I'd like to give back." More laughter. "But even if you can't hear the words your loved one's saying, the way I can, you can *feel* the emotional energy in their tether. It might be a strong, warm *sense* that overtakes you, or even"—she turns to the sisters again—"what is that smell I'm getting? It's so *him*. It's a weird smell, right? Like chemical-y, or . . . ?" She sniffs the air. "What *is* that?"

"The burning?" one of the sisters chimes in, straight into the mic I handed her.

Aunt Nic nods, a fast up and down. "Yes!"

And the older sister laugh-cries. "That's his model trains. The whole den always smelled like ozone from his trains."

"It's *awful*!" Aunt Nic says, and the women all laugh again. She tilts her head. "He's saying it's not awful, but—I'm sorry, sir, it really is!"

I wonder what it would've been for my mom, her tether. A favorite paintbrush? That pair of orange ballet flats she's wearing in six different photos I have of her? *What am I supposed to take heed of?* I think at Spirit as we rush to another loved one. *And what does the octopus mean?*

The next person Aunt Nic is called to is a woman with her army husband's dog tags, and after that it's a young couple who lost a baby. I hate the ones where they lost a baby. I think Aunt Nic does, too, although she's never said as much. But she usually goes quick with those ones.

"He was so little," the dad says when Aunt Nic asks about the blanket the baby is mentioning. Only, the man is sobbing so hard he's having trouble getting words out. "We never even got to hold him before he . . . We couldn't . . . We didn't . . ."

As Aunt Nic talks to the boy, a sweet smile crosses her face. "He says, *Don't worry, Daddy, I'm safe and warm here with Spirit. I left that blanket so you and Mommy could be warm, too.*"

The woman sob-snots, completely overwhelmed by the message, and before she lets Aunt Nic move on to the next connection, she makes her wait for an enormous hug. The dad, too.

"Hey," I whisper to Jax as we hustle across the floor. Because he still looks a little freaked. "You're actually doing really great."

"Yeah?" He grins.

"I bet by the end of the week, Oscar'll even let you work the floor all by your—"

That's when Jax bangs shoulder-first into one of Roger's camera guys, and the whole audience *oohs* in horror as they both crash to the ground. We get a close-up shot up Jax's nose, too, giant on the screen. I swear I can hear Oscar cursing from up on the spot bay.

"Maybe by the end of *next* week," I say, helping him to his feet.

As soon as Aunt Nic is positive everyone is okay, she returns to translating for Spirit. "Who had the car accident?" she calls out.

It's another couple we reach next—older this time, grand-parent age. A huge truck of a man with dark skin who doesn't look too comfortable with the mic I push under his nose. His wife is a kind-looking white woman, short and fat, with an enormous chest.

"It was our daughter," the woman says. "Ashlynne." She's shaking as she holds out an envelope for Aunt Nic. "That was her wedding invitation. We lost her before the wedding."

Her husband puts an arm around her. "We don't have to do this, Meg," he tells her, then pulls his mic away when his words get picked up for the whole audience to hear. "We should go home."

Jax zooms in on the envelope in Aunt Nic's hand, and I watch on the screen to make sure everything's in focus. The letters tower six feet tall.

> *Mr. & Mrs. Grant & Margaret Ezold*
> *877 Lake Forest Drive*
> *Bakersfield, CA 93301*

I hold my gaze on the last line of the address.

Bakersfield.

And just as it hits me that this couple is from my mom's hometown, the woman says, "Ashlynne knew you, actually. Do you remember her, from high school? Ashlynne Ezold?"

"I think I—" Aunt Nic begins, studying the envelope.

"She was two years behind you in school. I'm sure you

remember. She and Jennie June were practically joined at the hip senior year."

I whip my head back to look at the couple. "My mom?" I say. I'm not supposed to talk to the loved ones. "You knew my mom?"

"You look so much like her," the woman, Meg, tells me then, with that sadness-smile I always get from folks who know my mom has died. "We were so sorry to hear she'd—" She chokes up again, then finds different words to push out. "I brought something." She digs through her purse while, beside her, her husband, Grant, slow-blinks toward the sky. I wait for Aunt Nic to relay Ashlynne's message, because they usually come through right away, but she's tilting her head like whatever station she's listening to isn't tuned properly. At last, Meg pulls out a photograph, a printed-out one, with a crease in one corner. She tries to show it to Aunt Nic, but Aunt Nic's still tuning, so Meg hands it to me instead. "The girls painted that together, in Ashlynne's bedroom. Isn't it gorgeous? She was so talented, your mother."

I'm looking at a photograph of a long wall with an enormous mural painted on it, floor to ceiling. The side that covers the closet door is a sand dune, with strange skinny flowers reaching toward a blue sky. Seagulls soar above toward a deep, dark ocean, with all sorts of creatures swimming in the water. Fish. Sharks.

An octopus.

"*Take heed,*" I whisper.

"What's that?" Meg says.

But before I get a chance to reply, Aunt Nic speaks into her own mic, loudly. "I'm so sorry," she tells the couple. "It wasn't your daughter." And she hands back the wedding invitation.

"I don't—" Meg begins.

"The spirit reaching out to me is a man," Aunt Nic clarifies. "I'm sorry." She takes back their microphones, hands them to me as I fumble, confused. Then she calls out to the wider audience, "Who's the man, in the car accident? There were no passengers, only him?" A man jumps up, waving his hand, and Aunt Nic bolts off to talk to him, leaving Meg and Grant to sink sorrowfully into their seats.

"CJ?" Jax says when he realizes I'm not following Aunt Nic.

I glance at my aunt, plowing ahead into the audience, and then at the Ezolds, still clutching that photograph with the octopus in it. And as much as I don't want to, I tell Jax, "Coming!" and hurry off behind him. I just have to trust that if Spirit has gotten me this far, they can get me the rest of the way.

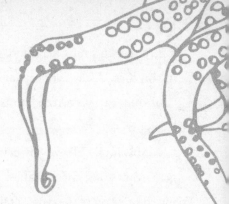

THREE

"HOW ARE YOU going to have time for schoolwork if you're out driving?" Aunt Nic asks me. She's sitting at the table in the middle of the tour bus, sipping her coffee, still in her pajamas. "Plemmons is going to be a real shock, you know, if you're not prepared."

I bounce from foot to foot in the doorway. It's not even seven a.m., but I'm buzzing with energy.

"It'll just be a couple hours." I point to Oscar and Jax's hotel at the far end of the parking lot. "Jax really needs the practice, and Oscar said he was too busy to do it. Please? Next month I won't be around to help anybody at all."

As soon as the show was over last night, I rushed to the Ezolds' seats, but they'd already gone. Then I spent the whole trip from Santa Barbara to L.A. trying to find their email addresses in my contact list—till I realized they must be the sort of old folks who don't have any. I was starting to worry I'd messed up Spirit's whole plan until this morning, when I figured out what they must've wanted me to do all along.

Aunt Nic wraps her hands around her coffee mug, studying my face. "Okay," she says at last, and I leap with excitement. "But only surface streets, no freeways. And be back by lunch, all right?"

"Absolutely." I grab my new messenger bag off the passenger's seat. Atlas, check. Tablet, check. I drape the strap across my chest. "You're the best," I tell Aunt Nic, standing on my tiptoes to give her a hug. It takes everything in me not to tell her where I'm really going, and what I'm going to bring back for her. But with Spirit guiding me, I know she'll hear her sister's voice again soon. I can't wait to see her face light up when she does.

I can't wait for my face to light up, either.

. . .

"This seems like an awful lot of practice," Jax says as we zoom along the 101 North. "I thought we'd just stick to, like, parking lots."

"Nah," I say. When Jax picks up speed, I shout, "Ready? And . . . *clutch!*" And together we shift into fourth. "Aunt Nic specifically said she wants you to practice freeway driving. It's six hours from Oceanside to Phoenix tomorrow night."

It's not like I *want* to be lying. And I'll tell Jax the truth eventually, when it's too late for him to turn around. But if I tell him now, he'll only call Aunt Nic. Get her worried about me all over again.

Anyway, I am helping with his driving, so it's only partially a lie.

"I guess that makes sense." Jax nods toward the cup holder, where his cell phone is resting. "You mind calling my uncle? I want to double-check when he needs me back to help set up."

"Eyes on the road!" I scold. "This is a cell-free driving environment."

Jax scrunches his mouth. "But if *you*—"

"Chill out. We'll be fine on time." It's a little over two hours to Bakersfield without traffic and two hours back, so we have to hustle if we want to make it back for lunch. But once I bring Aunt Nic my mom's tether, I figure she'll forgive me for being a few minutes late. "Keep your eyes peeled for the 5 North."

That gets another mouth-scrunch from Jax. "You lost or something?"

"I've traveled to all forty-eight continental states," I tell him, "at *least* three times each, and I've navigated the whole way myself. I've never once been lost." I point out the windshield to the sign for the 5. "The exit'll be on your right."

"If you're up to something, you have to tell me. I can't get in trouble with Uncle Oscar. I can't lose this job."

"All I'm up to is helping you out. Like Oscar asked me to." Technically, Oscar said I *could* help. "Or do you think you're ready to shift by yourself already?"

Jax lets out a sigh. "Whatever you say, Miss Navigator," he replies. He checks his blind spot, then switches lanes.

. . .

The 5 is by far the quickest route to cut through California, but it's incredibly boring. Desert all around. Dirt and highway and highway and dirt. Every once in a while, there's a tiny speck of a farm.

We drive in silence for twenty minutes or so, until I can't take it anymore.

"Do you know how to play Horse?" I ask Jax.

"Like H.O.R.S.E. the basketball game?"

"Horse the car game," I specify.

"Oh. No."

"Okay, I'm going to tell you the rules. It's really complicated. You listening?"

"I'm listening."

"All right, here it is. When you see a horse, you yell, '*HORSE!*'" I shout at the top of my lungs. "You got it?"

He blinks at me. Once. Twice. "That's it? That's the whole game? You yell the word 'Horse'?"

"Yeah," I say. "I think Aunt Nic might've made it up. We drive a lot. We get bored."

"How do you win, though? You yell 'Horse' the most?"

"You don't win. You just yell 'Horse.'"

More blinking. "Or we could just, like, *not* do that."

I cross my arms over my chest. "You'll see," I tell him. "It's awesome. You just don't get it, because you haven't played before."

"Mmm."

I do not reply to the "Mmm." There aren't any horses around right now anyway. "How 'bout Twenty Questions?"

At that, Jax perks up a little. "Sure. You pick first."

Jax guesses my pick—a tree—in only five questions, then stumps me completely with Alexander Graham Bell.

"That's the guy who invented the light bulb, right?" I ask after I lose.

Jax pulls one hand from the ten-and-two position to smack himself in the forehead. "The *telephone*, CJ. Alexander Graham Bell invented the *telephone*." I only shrug. "I think probably your mom and Nic are right about boarding school."

"At least I know how to drive stick," I snap back. "Anyway, it's my pick again. I'm going to really get you with this one."

Jax guesses in four.

"You keep picking things just 'cause you can see them," he says.

"*No,*" I reply, even though I picked my atlas. "Anyway, I'll get yours this time. Is it a person?"

"No. Nineteen questions left."

"A place?"

"No. Eighteen questions."

"Okay, so it's a thing, then."

"Is that a question?" Jax asks.

Even though I'm sure I'm walking into a trap somehow, I ask, "Is it a thing?"

"No. Seventeen questions."

"How can it not be a person, place, or thing? What the heck it is, then? You're cheating."

"I'm not cheating. You wanna keep playing or what?"

I huff and slouch in my seat.

"Don't you think we should turn around soon?" Jax asks while I try to figure out what *isn't* a person, place, or thing.

"Nah. Oscar said not to come back till you were a highway-driving expert. I say we stay on the 5 for at least"—I check the atlas—"thirty-five more miles."

Jax gets this *look* on his face, like he might be bad at stick but he is not a dummy, and he says, "Cough it up, CJ."

"Cough what up?"

"I know you're not hauling me all the way out here to practice stick. You're trying to get somewhere. And I think I should get to know where."

I think over my options. On the one hand, even if Jax did want to turn around now, he probably couldn't without me helping to shift. On the other hand . . . My gaze drifts to his cell phone in the cup holder.

"You promise not to tell Aunt Nic?" I ask.

"Uh, *no*," he says. "Actually, the fact that you asked me that makes me think I probably *will* want to tell her." And when I scowl at him, he continues, "Look. Maybe I'll agree to keep going, maybe I'll flip a U on the highway and call your aunt right away. I won't know which till I hear the truth. But you could at least tell me what crime I'm helping you commit."

"It's not a crime," I say at last.

"Okay. So." He nods. "Tell me the truth. And I promise, no matter what, I'll always tell you the truth, too. Where are you taking me, CJ Ames?"

I take a deep breath.

"Bakersfield," I say.

And suddenly, it's like I can hear the gears clicking in his brain.

"That couple from last night?" he asks. "The ones who knew your mom?"

I nod. "I need to get to that mural, the one my mom helped paint. That's her tether—I know it. It's my only way to draw her back to Earth."

"O . . . *kay*," Jax says slowly. Like he's thinking things through. "Only. Okay, say that really is her tether."

"It is."

"Say it is, and we get there, and you see the mural, and you have the feeling or whatever." I nod, not sure what he's so confused about. "I mean, then what? Every time you want to talk to your mom, you and your aunt have to drive to Bakersfield and touch a mural? Wouldn't it be easier if you had a doorknob or something?"

"I don't have a doorknob," I say. I'm feeling grumpy toward Jax, and I'm not totally sure why. "I have a mural. Anyway, you know what's better than a doorknob? A whole door."

"A door?"

"The mural covers the closet," I explain. "I saw it in the photo. The closet has a sliding door. And closet doors"—I sit up a little higher in my seat, growing more sure of my plan as I say the words out loud—"come off their tracks. So I don't need to bring Aunt Nic to Bakersfield every time she wants to talk to my mom. I can bring the door to her."

Jax takes his eyes off the road long enough to give me another *look*. "How do you know these people will even let you *see* the mural, let alone take the closet door off?"

"They'll let me," I say. Spirit sent me this far. I know they're not going to give up on me till I get what I need.

When Jax darts his gaze to me again, his face is softer. "Are you sure this is what you want to do, CJ?" he asks.

"I don't have a choice," I reply. "Spirit's telling me what to do. I'm just going where they say."

Jax doesn't answer for a few minutes. But he doesn't reach for his phone, either.

Finally, he says, "Can I tell you something I don't get? How do you know when Spirit's sending you a message and when it's just a coincidence? I mean, with that story you told me last night, with the lady and her dog. Maybe that was Spirit, warning her about the tree, but maybe, like, the dog kept smelling a squirrel."

I just raise an eyebrow at him. Because Jax Delgado definitely isn't the first person to try to tell me that the signs Spirit sends aren't really signs at all. "Fine," I tell him, to let him think he's won the argument—just for a second. "Say the dog *was* smelling a squirrel." And then I turn it on him. "How can you know it wasn't Spirit who *put* the squirrel there, to make the dog bark?"

Jax opens his mouth, like he wants to argue, then closes it again, like he can't.

Point: CJ.

"Here's how I think of it," I say, to try to make it all clearer. Because I was raised around Spirit—to me, it's like breathing. But I know all this is new to Jax. "Me and Aunt Nic were outside of Cleveland once, when we had our old motor home, and we had to call this repairman. Aunt Nic was mad 'cause she hated to pay for repairs—we used to fix everything ourselves back then. Mostly with duct tape." Jax snorts. "But this time, we needed help, 'cause there was this *hissing*."

"Hissing?" Jax repeats.

I nod. "It'd been there for days, but we couldn't figure out where it was coming from. It was *so annoying*."

"Sure," Jax says. I can tell he's waiting for me to get to the point, so I hurry it along.

"But then this repair guy, I swear, the *second* he walks into the motor home, he goes right over to the sink in the kitchen, and he takes this big ol' wrench, and he just whacks the wall with it. Busts a hole"—I show Jax how big, with both my hands together—"right through the wallpaper."

"I bet your aunt was thrilled about that," Jax says.

"Right?" I reply. "Only then, the guy steps back, and we see behind the wall, and there's this pipe with a gash in it, shooting water out the side, exactly where he busted the hole. That whole time, we'd had a burst pipe, *hissing* at us right behind the wall, and we had no idea. But this total stranger walks in and *bam!* He knows exactly where to look. And you know what he said when I asked him how he knew that?" Jax doesn't shrug or anything, but I can tell he's listening. "He pointed to these little specks of mold over the faucet, and these tiny bubbles in the wallpaper, and he goes, 'I followed the signs.'"

I lean back in my seat and fold my arms over my chest, pretty proud of myself for making my point so clear, with a cool little story and everything.

Only Jax just squints into the sunlight. "So . . ." he says

slowly, "the lady with the dog is the wrench? Or the mold?"

I sigh. Obviously my story wasn't as clear as I thought.

"Spirit is like the pipes in our walls," I explain. "When we lose people we love here on Earth, we can't see them anymore, but they're still around, right? They watch over us. They help us out. They're around us all the time, just like when you're in a house or a motor home, the pipes are there, too. Only you don't usually *see* them, you know? Most people don't even *think* about them. They don't think about where the water travels through to come out of the faucet, and they don't think about Spirit, either, taking care of them so they can be safe and happy. You don't have to know the pipes are in the walls for them to work, and you don't have to know about Spirit, either. But either way, they're there. And if you pay attention, and you know how to read the signs, you can figure out where they've been, and what they're doing."

Jax thinks on that. "Maybe," he says at last. But I can tell I haven't really convinced him.

I give up. I don't have any other cool stories. "Wait till someone you love dies," I tell him. "Then you'll get it."

As soon as I say that, I see Jax's face fall, and I know. I've seen that look a hundred times a night.

"Who was it?" I ask. My voice is softer.

It takes him a moment to answer. Not like he's thinking about what to say, but like he needs time to get the words out.

"My grandpa," he says. "My dad's dad. We were really close. He died in April."

"I'm sorry," I tell him. I know from experience that's the only real thing to say.

"That's part of the reason my mom thought it might be good for me to work here. She thought your aunt could talk to him for me. But then when I got here, I wasn't so sure I wanted her to."

"It's not scary," I say, suddenly understanding why he was so freaked out last night. "Your grandpa is just as nice as a spirit as he was when he was alive."

Jax snorts. "Uh, Abuelo was awesome," he says, "but he was never *nice*. Once when my sister was five or something, she showed him this picture of a horse she'd made in school, and he was like, 'I could do better.'" He laughs a little snot-laugh, then darts a sideways glance at me. I pretend not to have noticed. "He was pretty great, though."

I'm quiet for a minute, letting Jax think. I know what it's like to miss somebody. Sometimes you just need space.

But too much space can be bad, too.

"You didn't tell me you had a sister," I say.

"Yeah," Jax replies. "She's a year and a half younger. She's super annoying. At some point she decided I should pretend to be an 'international pop sensation'"—he says the phrase like it's a curse word—"because she thinks if she's related to a famous person, she can cut in line at the Cinnabon." I laugh.

"Sometimes my mom makes me take her and her friends to the mall, and they spend the whole time trying to teach me poses." He hunches into the collar of his jacket, then gives me what I'm guessing is supposed to be a cool-guy sideways smirk. "Mari and her friends call me 'Jackson Gato.'"

"You look *just* like a pop sensation," I tell him.

He does not.

"Once while I was doing it, the woman at the fro-yo shop gave Mari a mini sprinkle cup," he says, "but I'm pretty sure it was just a promotion."

When he goes quiet after that, I ask, "Is it weird being on the road? Away from your family, I mean?" Living on a bus is all I've ever known, but I can imagine it might be hard, for someone who's used to staying put.

Jax thinks for a minute. "So, for Christmas, right?" he tells me. "While dinner's cooking, we always go to the park on the water to watch the boat parade. It's awesome because everyone decorates their boats with Christmas lights and there's fireworks and everything." He drums his fingers—*thump, thump*—on the wheel. "And Abuelo makes this huge deal, every year, about how no one can eat anything from the food trucks so we won't ruin our appetites, but then the two of us always sneak off when no one's looking and grab something." He laughs, but then he clears his throat, like he's embarrassed he's told me something so personal.

I give Jax as much space as he needs.

"Anyway," he goes on, straightening his back a little, "I'm always in charge of making the relleno for Christmas dinner." He glances at me and clarifies. "It's a side dish. Like, Ecuadorian stuffing, basically. And one year when we came back from the park I found out Mari had dumped in, like, an entire jar of extra olives when I wasn't looking, just to mess with me. So now my main cooking job, every year, is to hide all the olives." He *thump-thump*s on the wheel again.

Thump-thump.

Thump-thump.

"I just keep thinking how this year she'll probably get away with it," he says, his voice heavy. "And then the relleno will be ruined for everyone."

I look out the window instead of at Jax.

"We usually order pizza for Christmas," I say at last. "And we play poker for pretzels. I kick everyone's butts."

"I believe it," Jax replies seriously.

I lean forward in my seat, finally looking over at him. "If you want," I tell Jax, "I'll dump a jar of olives on your pizza so you feel like you're at home."

And at that, Jax laughs. "That's very thoughtful of you."

I smile back at him. "You know," I say, "I'm glad you're the one I tricked into driving me to Bakersfield. I don't think Oscar would've been nearly as fun." Jax laughs again.

"You don't have brothers or sisters or anything?" he asks me. "It's just you and your aunt?"

"And my mom, yeah."

"No dad?"

"Nah. Well"—I adjust my headband—"I *have* one, obviously, but no one knows who he is. My mom met him when she was traveling through Europe, but she never even found out his last name or anything." I move on to something more serious. "Is it a watermelon?"

Jax snot-laughs so hard he has to wipe his nose. "A watermelon is a *thing*!" he shouts.

"Well, just tell me what it is, then."

He shakes his head. "You're down to sixteen questions."

"Potato?"

"No. Fifteen."

"Cactus?"

"Are you just guessing stuff so you'll lose and I'll tell you what it is?"

"Maybe. Is it a haircut?"

"This is *so* not how you play this game, CJ."

"Is it that stuffing stuff? Relleno?"

"No. Thirteen questions."

"Hey, Jax?" I say. He darts his eyes at me again. "Thanks for not turning around after I told you where we were going."

He nods. "But if your aunt gets mad at me for helping you,

you have to have my back, okay? Because, seriously, I *cannot*—"

"I know, I know. You love this job more than anything. Don't worry, okay? Aunt Nic won't be mad when we get back with the tether." When he opens his mouth to protest, I say, "And if she *is* mad, I'll swear on a Bible that it was all my fault, and that I kidnapped you. Now." I slap my hands on my thighs. "Is it an alligator?"

"You are *so* bad at this—"

"Wait, I've got it!" I shout suddenly.

"You do *not* have it."

"I do." I'm serious now. "I know what it is." I shift in my seat because I want to see the look on Jax's face when I get it. "It's Spirit."

"Spirit?" He wrinkles up his nose like he smells something awful, which is not exactly the look I was hoping for.

But I *know* I must be right. "Yeah," I say. "Spirit with a capital 'S.' All the souls that have left Earth, whether they're drawn Far Away or still passing back and forth. That's got to be it, because it's not a person, place, or thing. I guessed it."

Jax does that scrunchy-mouth thing he's so good at. "No," he says. "Although that would've been a great pick. I wish I'd picked that."

I throw my hands in the air. "I give up. For real. Just tell me. I can't take it anymore. What is it?"

"Photosynthesis," Jax replies. When I glare at him, he says,

"That's how plants make their food, using light from the sun."

"You could've picked anything in the world," I say slowly, "and you picked *photosynthesis*? Anyway, isn't that a 'thing'? I think photosynthesis counts as a 'thing.'"

"Oh, no."

"It is," I say. "It totally is, which means I'm right and you lose."

He shakes his head at me, and suddenly I realize he's not thinking about Twenty Questions. "I meant 'Oh, no, there's something wrong with the truck.' Look."

There's a blinking light on the dash—a circle around an exclamation point. I've lived on the road my whole life, and if there's one thing I know, it's that blinking exclamation points are never good.

"Get off at the next exit," I say. "We'll find a gas station. I bet someone can help us figure out what's wrong." I try to sound confident, but there's one thing I'm worried about—is this detour a part of Spirit's plan, or are we off course before we've barely even begun?

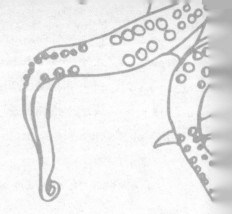

FOUR

"OH, YEAH, DEFINITELY a simple fix," says the super-friendly trucker I met coming out of the food court with a handful of lotto tickets. He's sitting in the passenger's seat of our truck, checking out the blinking exclamation point, and I'm standing beside him, trying to listen so we can get back on the road.

Jax, however, is being less than helpful.

"I can't believe you let some *stranger* climb in the truck," he hisses at me. Jax is supposed to be pumping gas, but the pump is doing all the work. What *Jax* is doing is scratching his arm and being even weirder than normal. "That guy is going to drive off and steal our truck, and then what will we do?"

I roll my eyes. "*That guy*'s name is Gerald," I say, and I don't even bother to lower my voice, either. "And how's he gonna drive off while you've got the gas pump in there, huh?" Jax has no response for that.

Gerald, who has obviously heard everything we've been saying, nods to his own rig across the way. "My truck's nicer'n yours anyway," he says. "So stealing this one wouldn't make a whole lot of sense, economically speaking."

I turn back to Jax. "See?"

"You can't just walk up to any person you meet at a rest stop," he hisses. "Didn't your aunt teach you about stranger danger?" He is *peeved*, but if you ask me, I'm the one who should be in the bad mood. At least I'm doing something to solve our problem.

"What were you gonna do?" I reply. "Cross your fingers till the light went away?"

"What if he's a *murderer*?" Jax whispers.

I'm getting a headache from all my eye rolling. I point to Gerald's left arm, where a huge panda bear tattoo is exposed beneath his T-shirt sleeve. "I'm pretty sure most murderers don't have cutesy tattoos," I tell Jax.

Beside me, Gerald clears his throat. When I turn back to him, he is waiting patiently for us to stop squabbling.

"So," he says, and Jax and I both straighten up, very serious. "Like I said, it's no biggie. Low tire pressure." When we both stare at him blankly, he explains, "You gotta refill the air in one of your tires. I'm guessing neither of you knows how to figure out which tire it is?"

"Uh . . ." I start. I know how to *change* a tire, and I'm a whiz with jumper cables, but somehow I don't know anything about tire pressure. I glance at Jax like maybe he'll be helpful, but he's busy avoiding eye contact.

"Well, I'm happy to show you, if you want," Gerald says. "And how to fill it with air, too. Then you'll know how to do it yourselves for next time."

"That'd be awesome," I say.

Jax, of course, says nothing.

"Great. Air pump's back there." Gerald points to a row of metal machines near the rear of the station. "Takes quarters. You kids got quarters?" I nod. Jax scratches. "Well, that's one thing, at least. Pull up to the pump, and I'll meet you over there."

"You're a lifesaver, Gerald, seriously," I say, just as the gas pump clunks, letting us know our tank is full. I wait for Jax to pull the pump out, but he doesn't. "Need help?" I ask him. His hand is on the pump, but he's stone-still, eyes on Gerald in the passenger seat. Finally, I figure out that he's waiting for Gerald to hop out before he removes the pump.

"For Pete's sake," I say, rolling my eyes again.

Gerald is watching us. "You know," he says slowly, "this is awfully rough road for a joyride. You kids sure you don't need me to call someone?"

"Huh?" Jax asks, hand still on the pump.

"He thinks we're dumb kids who stole their parents' truck," I tell Jax. Then I tell Gerald, "We are not dumb kids. Jax is official driver of my aunt's business." I leave out the part about how we kind-of-sort-of *are* driving off where we're not supposed to. "Just 'cause we don't know how to put air in tires doesn't mean we're imbeciles. It means we need help."

"Well," Gerald says. "I stand corrected. I'm happy to help you not-imbeciles get back on the road."

"Thank you," I tell him. And he hops out of the truck.

. . .

When we get to the air hoses, Jax sits in the driver's seat while Gerald shows me where to find the info about our truck's required tire pressure. It's located on a sticker like two inches from Jax's elbow, but Jax won't even look at us as we inspect it. Gerald hands me his pressure gauge, which is this tiny tool with a top shaped like a diving helmet, and he demonstrates how to attach it to each tire and let out just a hiss of air, so the gauge pops out and gives the reading. I do two of the tires by myself, and I'm the one who figures out that our left front tire is super low.

"Feed the quarters into the machine," Gerald instructs me while Jax remains useless. "Great. Now we're gonna hook the hose to the air valve, same as we did with the gauge."

"Are you *sure* you don't want to try?" I ask Jax as I cross his side with the hissing air hose. "It'd probably be good if you knew how to do it."

Jax shakes his head, eyes straight ahead.

Scratch-scratch-scratch.

"And always remember to replace the stem cap," Gerald tells me when the tire is properly inflated. He hands me the tiny black cap and waits while I screw it back onto the valve. "Perfect. You guys are good to go."

"We owe you one for sure," I tell Gerald. "Can we buy you a Twinkie or something?"

"Nah," he says, patting his belly. "I don't like to eat right before I go out murdering people."

Over in the truck, Jax's eyes go wide, even though it's *obvious* Gerald is messing with him.

"Sorry," Gerald says, "bad joke." Then he leans a little toward me. "Is he okay?"

I shrug. "Who knows?" Yesterday, during Aunt Nic's show, I thought he was jumpy because he was freaked out by Spirit, but as far as I can tell, Gerald's not a spirit, so I don't know what gives.

"Tell you what," Gerald goes on. "Next time I find myself in the same town as you and your aunt, you get me discount tickets to one of her shows. I gotta see this lady for myself."

"I'll get you in for *free*," I tell him, and we shake on it.

And that's when I see it—the tattoo poking out of Gerald's right shirtsleeve. It's inky and blue, a skinny curved tentacle.

I grip Gerald's hand tighter. "Let me see that," I say, trying to tug his arm closer.

"This old thing?" Gerald asks, pushing up his sleeve with his other hand.

The octopus on Gerald's arm is nearly identical to the one I found on my wrist, only slightly larger. Nearly the exact same shape. Same profile, same image, same color. And just like the one on my wrist, there's a message inside it, one letter in each of the eight tentacles.

"Jax!" I holler to the bozo in the truck. This time I need somebody else to see what I'm seeing. *"Jax!"*

"I see it," Jax says. He's already leapt out of the truck. He's not scratching anymore. "Where did you get that?" he asks Gerald.

Gerald snorts. "You kids are definitely too young for tattoo parlors."

"It's a sign," I explain. "For me." *Slow down.* Why does Spirit want me to slow down?

But Gerald only pushes his sleeve down to hide the tattoo again. "Sorry, CJ," he says. "This one was meant for me."

He's wrong, obviously, but it doesn't really matter as long as I get the message. Only, there's one thing I'm wondering.

"How come yours didn't disappear?" I ask Gerald. "The octopus I got didn't even last a minute."

As soon as I say that, something on Gerald's face changes.

"So you've been Charmed, too," he says, eyebrows raised. Only he says "Charmed" with a soft *ch* sound, like "chandelier" or "chef."

"Charmed?" Jax and I repeat.

"Haven't figured it out yet?" I get the sense that Gerald is enjoying leaving us in the dark. "Took me a while, too. And it did disappear, same as yours. I just had my buddy re-create it in ink. What'd yours say?"

"Take heed," I tell him.

He nods, thoughtful. "Good advice. You follow it?"

"Trying to. When did—?"

But Gerald cuts me off. "This is a mystery you're going to have to solve on your own, CJ," he tells me.

And with that, he's off, tipping an imaginary hat at us as he heads back to his truck.

"Uh, *that* was weird," Jax says, hoisting himself back into the driver's seat. He spends a second checking the dashboard and seat and shifter, like he thinks maybe Gerald sabotaged us somehow. "What do you think 'Charmed' means?"

"No idea. Why do you think Spirit needed to send me

another sign? I mean, I think we're on the right path, because they didn't say 'Turn around' or 'Stop what you're doing!' but . . ."

"Well, none of those messages would fit inside an octopus," Jax replies. He slams his door shut, concentrating so hard on starting up the truck that he doesn't notice me giving him the stink eye. "Uh, you gonna help me shift or what?"

I shut my own door. "Ready? And . . . *clutch*," I tell him, and we start up the truck together. Make our way back toward the 5 together.

Only, obviously, one of us is taking this trip a whole lot more seriously than the other one.

"You're not even going to *try* to help me figure out what this new sign means?" I ask.

"It's not a sign," Jax says. He's lots more sure of himself now that Gerald the Not a Murderer is gone. "It's just a coincidence."

I cannot narrow my eyes more than I currently am. "You honestly think that what happened back there—*Ready-and-clutch!*—was a coincidence? Three octopuses in two days? That's not just a random thing that happens. *Ready-and-clutch!*" We merge back onto the freeway.

Jax checks over his shoulder, then switches into the middle lane. "Maybe there's been tons of octopi all over the place, your whole life, only you never started noticing them till yesterday."

I was wrong. My eyes can narrow even further. "Doesn't it seem a little more likely that Spirit's *putting* the octopuses there for me to find?"

"All I'm saying is you *want* them to be signs, so you think they are."

"And you want them to be coincidences," I reply.

Jax nods at that, like *fair point.* "Help me shift into fourth?"

I put my hand on the stick shift, then realize what I'm about to do. I pull away. "Slow down," I say, repeating the message from Gerald's tattoo.

"Wait, what?" Jax asks. Then, realizing what I mean, he lets out a huff. "CJ, seriously? We're supposed to drive with the flow of traffic. Traffic is going more than forty miles an hour. I need to upshift."

"Sorry," I tell him. I raise both my hands in the air. "Just following orders from Spirit."

"You are the most annoying human, CJ Ames," he says. But he merges back into the right lane, where traffic is moving more slowly.

"*I'm* annoying? What about you, Mr. Freaked-Out-For-No-Reason? What was that back there? Gerald was being totally helpful, and you were being weird."

"I was *not* being weird," Jax argues. But he lifts his right hand from the steering wheel to scratch under his left sleeve again. When he sees me noticing, he pulls his hand away and slaps it back on the wheel. "It's not weird to not want to get murdered, CJ."

His words are angry, but there's something else there. He's like a porcupine, with his quills up, trying to keep me from getting at something tender.

I slouch back in my seat, arms over my chest, gazing out the window at the cars zooming around us. "You want to play the Geography Game?" I ask.

I kick Jax's butt at the Geography Game, obviously. He seriously thinks he's gonna stump me with "Phoenix," like I can't come up with any places that start with "X."

"Xenia," I say immediately.

"Uh, where's that?" Jax replies. "You made that one up."

"Xenia is a city in Ohio. I've been there." There's one in Illinois, too, but I've never been to that one. "Want to see it in the atlas?"

"No," he says. "What letter do I have? 'A'?"

"'A,'" I agree. Then Jax goes silent for approximately fifteen minutes. "You are *so* bad at this game."

"I'm *thinking*! There aren't that many places that start with 'A.'"

I count off on my fingers. "Anaheim, Azusa, Apple Valley, Arcadia . . . And that's just within two hours of here."

"All right, all right," Jax grumbles. But there's a laugh in there, I can hear it. "I give up. You win."

"Yeah?" I sit up in my seat, excited. I mean, I *knew* I was gonna win, but still, it feels nice. "You gotta say, 'CJ Ames is the Geography Game Champ of the Universe.'"

"I don't know about the *universe*," he says. "Definitely this truck, though."

"Say it," I instruct him, very seriously. "Say 'Universe,' or I'll make you play another round."

At that, he rolls down his window, sticks his head out as the wind zips past. And he shouts, "*CJ Ames is the Geography Game Champ of the—!* Whoa."

As we crest the hill ahead, that's when we see the accident. Major crash, three cars all smashed together in the middle lane.

"Holy . . ." Jax begins. It is *ugly*.

Together we downshift to second, then inch past the wreck in silence. Crushed metal. Scared people on the side of the road. The sound of sirens approaching.

"I hope everyone is okay," Jax says in a hush.

And I don't say anything, but here's what I think.

Slow down.

That could've been us in that accident. And it wasn't, because I followed the sign.

I lift my eyes and send up a thank-you. Obviously Spirit wants me to get to Bakersfield in one piece.

All I need to do is pay attention.

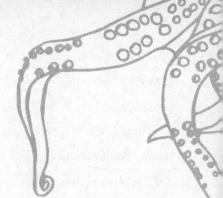

FIVE

"YOU REALLY THINK it's a good idea to just knock on the door?" Jax asks as we climb the porch steps. I told him he could wait in the car, but he said if I went in alone I'd probably get myself murdered, and then he'd lose his job for sure. "What if they won't let you in? What if they're not home, or this isn't even their house, or they're mean?"

"Their car is here," I say. "And this is definitely their house." I point to a wooden sign beside the door—THE EZOLDS. "And they seemed nice last night."

"But what are you going to say? 'Hello, people I don't know. I want to go into your dead daughter's bedroom to look at an old mur—'"

Ding-dong! I ring the bell.

"Don't worry," I tell him. "Spirit wouldn't lead me here if it wasn't going to work."

Meg whips open the door before I even hear her coming. "You kids selling gift wrap?" she greets us. Then she checks the sky like she's figuring out what time it is. "Shouldn't you be in school?"

I stick out my hand, very polite. "Hi, Mrs. Ezold," I say. "I'm CJ Ames. Monica Ames's niece? From last night. This is Jax Delgado."

All at once, Meg recognizes us. But she does not shake my hand. "You drove all this way to see me?" she says. I can't tell if she's about to burst into tears or shout at us. "Why?"

And that's where I get stuck. Because I figured this part would be easy—Spirit got us this far, after all. But I guess I need to figure the rest out for myself.

So I say the first thing I can think of that I know will get us in the door.

"Ashlynne told us to come," I lie.

. . .

"Seriously, what is *wrong* with you?" Jax hisses at me from the other end of the kitchen table. Meg is upstairs getting her husband. "I can't believe you said that."

The entire kitchen is decorated in a "climbing ivy" theme. Ivy on the wallpaper, ivy on the tiles behind the kitchen counter, ivy on the curtains. There are even ivy patterns on the backs of the chairs we're sitting in.

I'm trying to avoid looking at Jax because I'm not exactly thrilled with myself at the moment, either. But still. "I got us inside, didn't I?" I ask. Meg practically yanked our arms off pulling us in here, she was so excited. "That's what Spirit wanted."

Jax doesn't seem convinced. "Did you see her face? She was so . . . *happy*."

"Since when is it a bad thing to make someone happy?" I ask.

"But what are you even going to tell them? They're expecting you to give them a message from their daughter. Are you just gonna make something up?"

I have no idea what I'm going to do. I'm trying not to think about it. "I'm sure Spirit will help me out, when I need them," I say. But Jax won't stop giving me his I'm-so-disappointed-in-you glare. "Oh, why don't you just go back to scratching your arm and leave me alone?" I snap at him.

And that shuts him up, at least. Jax darts his eyes to the table, and I can tell he *wants* to scratch but won't because I said something. For a second, I feel bad, but he's *sixteen*—he shouldn't be getting his feelings hurt by a twelve-year-old.

Anyway, that's when the Ezolds come in.

"You know how I can tell you kids are lying about talking to my daughter?" That's what Grant Ezold asks when he enters the room. He's a huge man, fills the whole doorframe.

I don't answer. I can tell I'm not supposed to.

Grant nears the table, one heavy footstep at a time. "Because my Ashlynne," he booms, "would *never* disrupt my crossword puzzle."

Scratch-scratch-scratch.

"Oh, lay off, grumpus," Meg tells her husband. She shakes her head in our direction. "He's just . . . like that," she explains. "You kids've had a long drive. You drink coffee? Pot's already made." She heads to the coffee maker on the counter without letting us answer. "For the love of god, Grant, sit down and stop acting so goofy." She makes angry eyes at her husband until he gives in and sits in the chair between me and Jax. I sort of wish he hadn't. "Grant has trouble with mediums and stuff," Meg explains as she gathers mugs from the cupboard.

"I don't have trouble with it," he replies, folding his arms over his chest. "It's hooey."

Beside me, Jax is on a major scratching spree, but I try to act normal. "Men usually take longer to accept the presence of Spirit," I say, mostly to Meg, because I can tell Grant doesn't exactly want to talk to me. "Aunt Nic says that's because women are naturally attuned to emotional frequencies."

Grant snorts, but Meg ignores him, pouring steaming coffee into one mug, then another. I get the feeling she has a lot of practice ignoring Grant's snorts. "You'll come around," she tells her husband, setting down one mug for me and another for Jax. "Soon as we hear what Ashlynne wants to tell us." I wrap my hands around my warm mug, breathe it in. The smell is strong, inviting. Almost enough to settle the sour feeling that's growing in my stomach.

Meg slides herself into the seat beside me with two more coffees. Jax takes a sip of his, then immediately jerks his head up, eyes bulging, and gives me a look that clearly says, *Don't drink it.*

"So," Meg says, pouring cream into her mug. Despite her cheerful tone, she's shaking. She dabs at some spilled cream with a paper towel while I clench my stomach tighter. "I knew Ashlynne was trying to reach us. Last night with your aunt, I said, didn't I say, Grant? I said, 'Ashlynne's here, I *know* it, she's trying to speak to us, this lady's got it wrong.' And the whole time, she was talking to *you.*" She picks up her mug. It's white with maroon letters that say DON'T BOTHER ME—I'M RETIRED. "Who knew you had the Gift, too?" She smiles at me, sad-happy. "Your mother would've been so proud of you, you know. I always knew she was a special one, that Jennie June. She and Ashlynne were such good friends, in school, and then afterward they lost touch. It wasn't till a couple years ago we heard your mom had died. All of us, we were just heartbroken. And when Ashlynne . . ." She chokes up. Can't even finish the sentence.

Scratch-scratch-scratch.

I do not look at Jax. I do *not.*

Suddenly Meg sets her mug down, liquid sloshing over the top. "Okay, I can't take it anymore!" she says, too loud. She is nervous laughing. "Just tell me, CJ. What's Ashlynne saying?"

Scratch-scratch-scratch.

"Well, Mrs. Ezold—"

"Please, call me Meg. And the grumpy one is Grant."

"Meg," I say. And I wait for a sign from Spirit, but nothing comes.

Scratch-scratch-scratch.

Somewhere, a clock is ticking.

"Your daughter . . ." I begin. But I don't know how to finish.

"This is nonsense," Grant says. "This kid can't talk to Ashlynne." But Meg shushes him quick.

"Let's just listen," she tells her husband.

Tighter, tighter, I clench my stomach. If Spirit thinks I can do this all on my own, they must be right.

"Ashlynne says she loves you," I tell them at last. Because what could be wrong with that? Meg brings her hand to her mouth, eyes welling up. "And she's safe," I go on, *not* looking at Jax. "She's happy to connect with her other relatives Far Aw—"

Grant slaps his hand on the table so hard that more coffee goes sloshing. "I can't," he says. "This whole thing is some scam. This kid and her aunt scope out the biggest rubes, then she comes here to steal our—"

I put my hands up in the air. "I just want—"

"We know you're not going to rob anyone, sweetie," Meg says, handing me a paper towel. "Grant's just terrified of what you're going to say, that's all." And she shoots him a look like *Enough.* He harrumphs but stays quiet.

Scratch-scratch-scratch.

I've felt this sour feeling in my stomach exactly once before—back when I was five, and I thought it would be a good idea to eat an entire mega-bag of gummy peach rings in one sitting. But unlike that time, I can't just yack the feeling away.

Meg reaches out and grabs my hand. Squeezes it gently. "We can take it, CJ," she says. "I promise. Just tell us." She takes a big, shaky breath. "Does Ashlynne forgive us?"

"Forgive you?" I ask. I wasn't expecting that. Absolutely everyone is watching me, waiting to hear what I'll say. I'm sure Spirit is watching me, too.

Scratch-scratch-scratch.

What do I tell I them? I think up to Spirit. *What if I get the answer wrong?*

But if Spirit sends a message back, I don't get it.

I drink a sip of my coffee, to give myself an extra second to think, then make exactly the same face Jax did. It is *not* good.

"I . . ." I say slowly.

I could make an excuse and leave right now, that's what I'm thinking.

I pour cream into my coffee, and sugar. Three spoonfuls.

Or I could find a way to do what Spirit sent me here for.

"Meg," I say. "Grant."

I take a long, slow sip of coffee. Still disgusting.

"Ashlynne is telling me she would like to see her bedroom."

. . .

The upstairs hallway is painted beige, but the door Meg reaches for is bright purple. It even says ASHLYNNE on it, scrawled there in pink, from when their daughter was just a kid, I bet. Meg's hand shakes as she grips the door, like she's not sure what she's going to find when she opens it. Behind me I can hear Grant's stompy footsteps and Jax's scratching. My stomach is still sour—but I'm excited, too.

This is it, I think. *My mother's tether is right behind this door.*

Only, it isn't.

"This isn't right," I say, spinning around the room. Suddenly, my body is ice. "Where's . . . ? This isn't her room."

"What do you mean?" Meg's voice is shaking now, too. "Of course this is her room." She turns to Grant, desperate, like he'll understand. "Why would Ashlynne say this isn't her room?"

"Where's the mural?" I ask. Jax is behind me, *scratch-scratch-scratch*ing, but I don't care if he's freaking out. *I'm* freaking out. "In the picture . . ."

It's gone. The room is the same as the one in the photo, but the mural isn't here. The wall is beige now, just like the other walls. The closet door is beige, too.

Meg sinks onto the bed, toppling a pile of folded clothes. "Ashlynne doesn't know about the mural?" First her jaw shakes, then it all turns to weeping—deep, uncontrollable sobs. It's awful, watching her sob like that.

I look away, to where the mural should be. "I thought—" I begin.

When I catch sight of the look Grant shoots me then, I know I'm done talking. He is *mad*—but somehow when he sits down beside his wife, he's nothing but gentle. "Megs," he says. Just that. He puts one big arm around her.

"*CJ,*" Jax whispers to me from across the room. I can tell he wants to leave, but I can't. I don't have anything to leave with.

"There was an earthquake," Meg finally squeezes out between sobs. "Will you tell Ashlynne that? A waste pipe in the ceiling burst. Back in August. We had to gut half this room, couldn't save hardly anything. It was like"—she gulps down another sob, and Grant brings her in closer—"losing her all over again."

The only thing stopping me from crumbling to dust is knowing that if I give up now, that's it. The last word I'll ever hear from my mom is "*Goodbye.*"

"But even the closet door . . . ?" I ask.

Meg answers with another sob.

"We've had enough," Grant tells me. His voice is firm. "We don't want what you're selling. You can both leave now."

"I'm really sorry," I say softly. Because I am. I've obviously done things all wrong. I know Spirit wouldn't have wanted Meg and Grant to be so upset. I know I should probably go, like Grant asked.

Only I can't seem to make myself leave the room.

I rub the spot on my wrist, where I found the octopus. *Take heed.* That's what the message said. And "take heed" means to pay attention.

So I look around—at Meg crying, at Grant comforting her, at poor Jax scratching in the doorway.

I need to find a way to make this right.

"I'm sorry," I say again. Because all I have to fix things is the truth. "I messed up. I . . ." Big gulp. Small words. "I lied." I look down at my feet, but there's no help there. I look back at Meg and Grant on the bed. "I don't have the Gift. Ashlynne didn't tell me anything at all. I'm sorry." I have to say that part again, because Meg's sobbing has grown even louder, and I want to make sure she hears. "I thought if I could see the mural, I could use it to pull back my mom. I thought the mural was her tether," I explain. "If I don't find something to pull her back, I'll never talk to her again." Meg's face is wet with tears. Grant's just looks like fire. I don't dare look at Jax. "I thought Spirit was telling me to come here and—" But my voice breaks then, and I know I won't say any more.

"CJ?"

When I turn to Jax in the doorway, he doesn't look mad or disappointed. He looks like he feels sorry for me.

"Come on," he says softly. He gestures toward the door. "We'll stop for pancakes or something before we head back."

I nod, because I don't have any words to say back. But just as we're heading out, another voice pipes up.

"We could whip you up some pancakes here, if you'd like."

It's Grant who says it. He still has his arm wrapped around Meg. I meet his eyes, surprised to find something forgiving in them.

"You must miss your mom every day, huh?" he asks. And he doesn't wait for any sort of response before he tells me, "I know how you feel."

. . .

"Here we go," Grant says, flipping through a photo album. He's being a lot friendlier now that he doesn't think we're trying to rob him. We're back at the kitchen table—me, Grant, and Jax—and Meg is stirring up pancake batter at the counter. "I'm sure there are some of your mom in this one." He pushes the album a little closer to me so I can see. It's the old kind, with thin, filmy pockets for the photos to slide into. I glance at Jax to see if he wants to look, too, but he's more interested in watching Meg stir.

"There's got to be a million photos in here," I say, scanning the pages. I've seen lots of pictures of my mom before, but now that I know there are new ones, it's like learning there's a sequel to my favorite book, and everyone's read it but me.

This album has photos of everything—people, buildings, weird close-ups of flowers and shoes and a bowl of pretzels.

"Ashlynne took her first picture when she was three years old." Grant taps the edge of one photo gently to make it even with the others. "We've got all her albums in the den. Must be about a hundred of them."

"Closer to two hundred, I'd say," Meg calls from the counter. "Everyone's eating pancakes, right?"

And when I look over to shout, "Yes, thanks!" that's when I notice Jax is no longer sitting beside me. At some point, he got up, super quiet, and now he's standing beside Meg at the counter. He watches her measure out milk for the batter.

"Got any ginger?" he asks her. I think it's the first thing he's said to either of them since we walked in the door.

Meg startles a bit when he says that, like she wasn't totally sure Jax could talk. But she just raises one eyebrow and says, "Ginger in pancakes?"

Jax nods. "Fresh ginger's best, obviously, but ground is good, too, if you have it. Just a pinch. And don't, um"—he reaches one hand out to the bowl, then jerks back like he's afraid to touch anything—"don't overmix the batter. You're actually supposed to keep some lumps in there."

Meg smiles and pushes the whole bowl his way. "Work your magic," she tells him.

While Meg searches the spice rack for ginger, Jax stirs. "Vinegar's a good trick, too," he says. "I know it sounds weird, but you don't taste it. It just makes the pancakes extra fluffy." The way he taps the spatula just so on the edge of the bowl makes him look like some sort of pro.

Huh.

I turn back to the photo album.

Ashlynne was a very pretty teenager. Not a twig-tiny teen, I see as I flip the pages, but chubbier and tall, with dark skin like Grant and braids that swoop around her head. She's probably only around Jax's age in these photos, but she seems like she's ready to take on the world.

Even as I'm thinking that, Grant smooths a hand over the plastic pocket and says, "God, she was such a kid." He keeps his hand on the page. Won't move it.

I'm trying to think of something to say when Grant tells me, "I didn't talk to her for a whole year before she died. She was . . . I didn't like her boyfriend. Her fiancé. And I got mad, and she said some things, and . . ." He darts his eyes over to Meg at the counter, who's putting flour back in the cupboard, pretending not to listen. Grant lifts his hand and turns the page. "Ah!" His voice is suddenly clear of sadness. "Your mother!"

Sure enough, there's a photo with my mom in it. I recognize her right away.

My mom looks young in an old way, just like Ashlynne, but very different, too. Where Ashlynne's hair is carefully braided, my mom's is wild. She's got dark curls like mine, but hers are long and frizzy. In this photo her hair is in a high ponytail on top of her head, the curls sprayed out like she's a feather duster. Her clothes are wild, too—a too-short teal sundress with bright-red shorts underneath and canary-yellow sandals. None of it matches, but somehow it works. My mom has one arm around Ashlynne, and she's kicking toward the camera, like she thinks she's a ninja or something, who knows.

She looks happy. They both look so happy.

Grant and I flip through the pages some more, looking at photos. There are lots of my mom. Laughing, shouting. She was apparently in at least one school play, which I didn't know.

"There's a truckload more photos in the den," Grant tells me. "You want to look?"

"Sure," I say, rising out of my seat. "Jax, you wanna come?"

Jax is heating up a pan on the stove now. "Nah, I'm good," he calls over his shoulder. Meg gives us a thumbs-up. I shrug and follow Grant.

Grant flips on the lights as we enter the den, and I suck in my breath. There are cardboard boxes piled up against every wall—dozens and dozens of them. A few have their lids cut open but most are taped closed.

"These aren't all filled with photo albums, are they?" I ask. I thought Meg was kidding about the two hundred thing.

"And these are just precollege," Grant replies. "Vin kept all the later ones. That's Ash's boyfriend. *Fiancé*," he corrects himself. Then he nods toward a row of boxes. "The albums are all labeled. Look for 'high school.'"

And we get to work.

"You're a lot like your mom, you know," Grant says as we dig through boxes on opposite sides of the room. I wonder if I'll get the chance to ask my mom about the school play. About Ashlynne. I wonder why Spirit sent me here, if it wasn't for the mural.

"Yeah?" I reply. I'm not surprised, exactly—Aunt Nic and my mom have both told me that before, how much we look alike—but it's more real, somehow, when a stranger says it. "I have her hair, for sure."

"Right, but also . . . She was impetuous, your mother."

"Impetuous?"

"Strong-willed. The kind of kid who'd steal a truck to drive two hours to lie to total strangers."

"I didn't *steal* the truck," I argue.

Grant only snorts. "Just like your mom." He pulls out an

album, looks at the spine, then puts it on top of a stack on the floor. "I used to drive them around, sometimes."

I find one album labeled STREET SHOTS, then glance at the next one. ZOOS/MUSEUMS.

"When I had someone in my limo finished early," Grant goes on, "I'd pick up Ashlynne and some of her friends, drive them around in the back. They liked to go through drive-throughs or roll up at soccer games like little movie stars." He chuckles. "Ashlynne had a lot of friends, but your mom stands out. Meg and I used to look at them, bouncing around like they owned the world, and think, 'Those two are going places.'"

I don't know what it's like to lose a daughter, but I know how it feels to miss someone, so my stomach goes sour again at the thought that I'm responsible for some of the sadness Grant's feeling right now.

"I'm really sorry for lying before," I tell Grant again. I try to find the exact words for what I mean. "I didn't think it would hurt anybody, I guess, to tell a lie about someone who had already died."

Grant is so quiet for so long that I figure he must be looking at an album. But when I glance over, he's just staring into an empty box.

"You okay?" I ask slowly.

He shakes his head. "It can always hurt more, CJ." That's what he tells me.

We're quiet after that, just poking through the boxes. After a while the room is filled with the scent of fresh pancakes. Bacon, too. And something . . . cheesy, maybe?

"Smells like your friend is a hell of a chef," Grant says.

"I guess," I reply. "Jax was like a whole new person when he was cooking. Totally calm."

Grant turns to a new box. "That's pretty common with people with anxiety. When they find something they're good at, it's easier to deal with the other stuff. That's what it was with photography, for Ashlynne. People didn't seem so scary to her, I think, when there was a lens between them and her."

I pull my head fully out of the box. "Jax has anxiety?" I ask Grant.

"Doesn't he?" Grant tugs at another album. "Seemed obvious to me. I'm not a doctor or anything, but that scratching reminded me of Ash, for sure. With her, it was hair. Once her mom found this bald patch . . ." He makes a circle with his thumb and forefinger, nearly the size of two quarters.

It makes sense, I guess, about Jax. Only I wonder why he didn't just tell me he has anxiety.

I sit back on my heels, suddenly exhausted. I've only been through seven boxes, and there are about a million more. But Grant seems more energized than ever.

"You want to hear my favorite story about your mom?" he asks as he dives into a new box.

"Obviously," I reply.

"All right." He examines the albums one by one. "It's the dead of winter. I'm driving Ashlynne and Jennie June and some other girls around, and it's maybe only eight o'clock but it's *dark* outside, and the girls are just squealing in the back seat." I watch Grant's face as he talks, because I feel like this is a story I'm going to want to remember. "They must've been about eighth grade, not much older than you. Finally they tell me to stop in front of this one house, and all I gather is there's some boy in there one of them has a crush on."

I can see it, as he tells the story. My mom, giggling over a boy. I smile.

Grant adds another album to his pile. "So finally, I tell them, 'Look, we can't sit here all night, okay?' But even as I'm saying that, your mom gets out and comes up and taps on my window."

I press my palms to the floor, soaking in every word.

"So I roll the window down, and as soon as I do, your mom reaches in and blasts the horn, and I swear suddenly every house is lit up, everyone comes to their windows to see what's going on. And I'm trying to figure out what to do, when the lady whose house we're in front of comes storming down the driveway and starts shouting. *'Is there a problem here?'* Something like that. This lady is *mad*. But your mom, she just stands her ground—like she's so threatening, this little girl, and she says, 'Yeah, there's a problem. I asked your son to the school dance and he didn't give me an answer yet!'" Grant hoots with laughter at the memory.

I wait for him to finish, but he doesn't. He thinks the story's over.

"Well?" I say at last.

"Well, what?"

"Did the boy go to the dance with my mom? What was his name? What did he look like? Was he nice? Did they date?" I need more.

"I don't remember," Grant says, shaking his head. Then he sees my face and frowns. "That's not the answer you wanted, is it?"

"It's okay," I tell him. "I can ask her myself, when I figure out how."

"You really think this tether thing will work?" Grant says.

"All I know is, I asked Spirit for help, and they've been trying to tell me *something*." I pick up one more album, then another. Not what I want. "So as long as I don't mess up again, it'll work."

Grant makes his way through a whole new box before he asks, "Will you promise me something, CJ?" His voice is deep and quiet, like fog on a cold morning.

"Yeah?"

"If you do get another chance to talk to your mom? You take it. You talk to her every minute you can."

"I will," I promise. Then I rip open the lid of the next box. The album on top is labeled HIGH SCHOOL. "I think I found one."

Grant rushes right over and plops down on the floor beside me, and as soon as I open the album, a photo slides out. Lands right in my lap.

It's my mom—I can tell that much immediately. She's out of focus, but her curly hair gives her away. She's standing in a park or a yard, and there's this huge structure behind her—red brick with these strange bits of bent metal cropping out of it. They look like long, thin flower stems, but with bulby caps at the end.

"I remember that thing," Grant says, pulling the photo closer. "Oh, wow. That's a trip."

"What is it?" I ask.

"Well, it *used* to be a barbecue pit." He passes back the photo. "Then, if I remember right, your mom decided the barbecue pit was too ugly to exist, so without even asking her parents she filled it up with cement and built this weird mushroom sculpture inside it, right in their backyard." That's what the bulby flowers are, I realize. Mushrooms. There were some in the mural, too, on top of the dune. "I only saw it once. It was bigger than it looks in this photo. I'm pretty sure she made the whole thing out of aluminum cans and old bottles. Man, that thing was rough." He laughs.

I rise up on my knees. Suddenly I understand why Spirit led me here. Why they dropped this photo literally in my lap.

"Is it still there?" I ask. If anything will pull my mother back to Earth, it's this sculpture. I know it. I can *feel* it. There's no mistake this time. This is my mother's tether. "The sculpture didn't burn down, did it? With the rest of the house?"

Grant tilts his head then, like he doesn't understand the words I'm saying. "What do you mean, burn down?" he asks me. "Your mom's house is right where it always was. I drove past last week."

Every inch of my skin is tingling when I get it. *Of course.* The mural isn't here anymore because the pipes burst and ruined it.

The pipes in the wall.

Spirit's been trying to send me more signs this whole time. There is much more they need to show me, I realize, than a closet door.

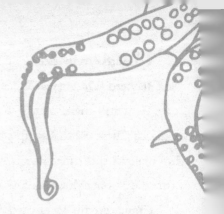

SIX

JAX WASN'T JOKING about the vinegar in the pancakes. They are definitely the fluffiest I've ever eaten. The coffee, however, remains undrinkable. Meg and Grant help me pick out some of the best photos of my mom so they can make copies to send me later. When we finally head out to the truck, around ten thirty, I'm half sad to leave.

The other half of me, though, is itching to get going.

"You're quite the cook, young man," Grant tells Jax, reaching through the truck window and across my lap to offer Jax a handshake. Then he focuses on me. "You sure you don't want me to come with you to check out the house?"

I set my messenger bag flat on my lap. "I think this is something I need to do myself."

Grant seems to understand, because all he says, his voice gruff, is, "Don't be *too* much like your mom, all right?" Then I get a handshake, too.

Meg makes her way over next, pushing an enormous red plastic jug through the window. "For the road," she says.

I unscrew the white lid. Take a big whiff. "More coffee," I tell Jax, and he does a really bad job not looking disgusted.

"I'm really sorry again," I tell Meg. "I shouldn't have said Ashlynne sent me."

And Meg surprises me then.

"Oh, Ashlynne *did* send you here," she says.

I open my mouth to correct her, but I don't get a chance.

"Whether you know it or not," Meg says, "that was our daughter directing you here." She's wiping at her eyes again, but she doesn't seem sad anymore. Not quite. "We've been sitting around wallowing for months, and then you two show up out of nowhere—Jennie June's daughter and a pancake-flipper all the way from Florida. It was exactly what we needed. Ashlynne's always been like that, finding ways to bring joy to the people she loves."

I'm about to tell her that, no, this has nothing to do with Ashlynne, it's all about my mom and her tether—but I stop myself before the words come out. Because who knows? Spirit works in mysterious ways. Maybe it was both.

Two minutes later, we're on the road. Although I wouldn't say Jax is exactly thrilled about the detour I want to take before heading back to L.A.

"We don't have time, CJ," he argues when I try to direct him to my mom's old house. 115 Chestnut, that's the address Grant gave me.

"Just this one stop, I promise. Take the parkway, coming up." I point out the sign.

When Jax sighs, I can tell he's giving in. But then he reaches for the cup holder. "Let's call your aunt, tell her we're gonna be late."

I whack the phone out of his hand.

"What the *heck*, CJ?"

I do my best to explain. "My mom was the one who told Aunt Nic the house burned down, right?" I look at the photo of the mushroom sculpture that Grant let me keep. "But she's *Spirit*. She obviously knew the house was still there. So there must've been a reason she lied to Aunt Nic. Maybe she didn't want Aunt Nic to go back, or there was something there that . . . I don't know. Once I know why Spirit's leading *me* there, I'll call Aunt Nic."

"But—"

"I won't let you get fired, Jax, I promise."

He doesn't answer that. But he does turn onto the parkway.

"Just . . . one favor, CJ?" he asks after we upshift together.

"Shoot."

"Whoever lives in this house now? Don't lie to them about why we're there, okay? I don't know if they'll believe you, about why you want to hang out in their backyard and look at a sculpture—that might not even still *be* there, by the way—but . . ."

"It'll be there," I say. And, just as importantly, "I won't lie." The way Meg looked, crying on Ashlynne's bed—I never want to make anyone look like that again.

We pass strip malls and gas stations—all places, I realize, that my mom and Aunt Nic probably knew growing up. It's mostly boring stuff, but I'm glad I get to see it.

So I'm sort of wrapped up in my own thoughts when Jax asks me, "How come you told Meg and Grant the truth back there? You didn't have to. You could've just bolted when you realized the mural was gone, and they never would've known you'd been lying. How come you owned up to it?"

I shrug. "If I hadn't've told them the truth, I never would've learned about my mom's sculpture, right? Or the house? We wouldn't be headed there right now."

"Yeah, but you didn't know that when you did it."

"So probably Spirit guided me somehow, I don't know."

I can tell Jax doesn't agree. "Or maybe you just felt bad for lying to such nice people, and you decided being honest was the right thing to do."

I don't bother responding. Jax is going to think whatever he wants anyway, no matter what I say.

"Why didn't you tell me you had anxiety?" I ask instead. "I probably would've been nicer to you if I knew."

He snorts at that. "Maybe I would've told you if you'd been nicer to me."

"Yeah, okay." So maybe he has a point. "Sorry," I say. "But do you? Have anxiety? That's what Grant thought."

"I mean, yeah." Jax keeps his eyes on the road while he answers. "But it's not a big deal. I just don't like new stuff. It's like there are all these *rules* for every place you go or every person you meet, and everyone knows them but me."

"Rules?" I say.

He sighs. "Like, okay, at that gas station before." He jerks his head over his shoulder, like he's pointing out the spot we stopped at earlier. "Some gas stations are the kind where you're supposed to pump your own gas, but at other ones a guy comes out and pumps for you, and you're supposed to stay in your car. But if you stay in your car and it's not the guy-pumps-for-you kind, then you're just sitting there for ten minutes, and then someone honks at you because they want to use the pump. And if it *is* the guy-pumps-for-you kind, at some of those places you tip, but at some other places you don't. And if you don't tip when you're supposed to, then you're a jerk, but if you do tip and you're not supposed to, then you're an idiot. And there's never, like, *signs* that say all that stuff, but somehow everyone but me always knows already. Every time I go somewhere new, or meet a new person, it's like I can feel the cells in my brain going into overdrive, freaking out just so I can look normal, so no one will figure out I'm the one person who doesn't know the rules. And the worst part is that I know people can *tell* I'm freaking out, and all I want to do is, like, run away so I can just breathe and reset and figure things out by myself, but then I know everyone would *see* me running away, and that would be even worse."

He's been scratching his arm again while he talks about it. He doesn't notice that I've noticed.

"That kind of sounds like a big deal, Jax," I say.

He shakes his head like he's going to argue, but then seems to change his mind. "School's the worst, because it's the same place every day, but the rules change all the time anyway, and you never know when it's going to happen. Sometimes it's teachers who change them, like new seating arrangements or whatever, but sometimes just other kids decide that one thing they were all doing the day before is now the *worst* thing you could do, and did they all, like, *text* each other or . . . ?" He clears his throat. Won't look at me. "I stopped going. I'd go to sleep every night thinking, 'Tomorrow, you are totally *not* going to have a weird freak-out,' and then the next morning I'd wake up and I'd just think, 'Well, what if I do?' And then I'd get anxious about getting anxious. And then I couldn't even make myself leave the house."

"So . . ." I'm beginning to see how he ended up on our crew. "Homeschool."

"Uncle Oscar told my mom about Cyrus, and she knew *you* were homeschooled—she didn't know about George

Watermelon, obviously, she thought you were, like, actually learning stuff." I stick out my tongue, and he laughs. "And, anyway, she thought maybe being around new people during the tour would be good for me. *Originally* I was supposed to work spotlight so I wouldn't be in the middle of everything, but . . ."

"Ah."

"Right. So." He drums his fingers on the steering wheel. "If this job falls through, my mom says she's gonna force me to go to regular school no matter what. I don't know if she's planning on, like, dragging me to the car and sitting on me the whole way there or whatever, but you don't mess with my mom when she decides she's going to do something. So that's why I can't lose this job." He takes a deep breath. "Now *you* think I'm crazy."

"I don't think you're crazy," I say. I feel like he's embarrassed, and I don't want him to be embarrassed. "You know what you need? When your brain's working overdrive like that and you want to run away? You need a distraction, so when you do leave no one will notice. How 'bout this? Next time you're feeling all anxiousy, I'll go up to the people you're trying to escape from and I'll flash my hands in their faces"—I demonstrate, pressing my hands open-closed, open-closed super fast—"and shout, *'Hey, everybody, look over here!'* And then you can run away."

"You're making fun of me," Jax says, but he's laughing.

"I am not! It would work! You just let me know when you need to escape."

"I'll do that," he promises. "How long till we get there?"

"About ten more miles," I say. Then, because we're passing a horse trailer and I can see a snout poking out of a slit in the side, I leap up in my seat and holler, *"HORSE!"*

Jax only blinks. Once. Twice. Three times.

"What?" I ask. "I'm playing Horse."

"I figured," he says.

"It's fun."

"You keep saying."

I sit back in my seat. Jax doesn't know what he's missing. "Just keep driving," I tell him.

. . .

"You sure Grant got the address right?" Jax asks when we pull up to the house. "This is . . . um . . ."

He doesn't need to say what he means by "um." The front lawn is so overgrown it's practically a forest, and the house itself is worse—paint peeling everywhere, one porch step rotted away. The whole building has a serious "Stay away" vibe.

"This is it," I say, yanking open the door. But when Jax moves to open his, too, I turn around. "Actually," I say, "you mind staying in the truck?" He squints at me. "To, like, be a lookout?" I nod toward his phone. "Call for help if you need to."

"If that's what you . . . want," Jax says slowly. I can tell he thinks he should go in with me. Which is nice of him, really. But I'm pretty sure this is one stop Spirit wants me to make on my own.

"Thanks," I tell him. And I hop out of the truck. Then I suck in a deep breath of cold air and make my way up to the porch, weeds prickling my ankles through my socks.

It'll be fine, I tell myself as I walk. Over and over. *It'll be fine. Spirit sent me.*

. . .

I try the front door first, but no one answers. The windows are grimy and the curtains are drawn, so I can't see anything inside. I turn back to the truck and shrug at Jax. He rolls down his window to shout at me.

"Ready to go back?" he calls.

"One more minute!" I tell him.

I stick my hands in my coat pockets, trying to squeeze some warmth into my fingers as I make my way back down the porch, through the weeds, and around to the backyard. As soon as I see the sculpture, I forget all about the cold.

It's definitely more beaten up than in the photo, but somehow all the rust and dirt and age have only made it more beautiful. Complicated and quirky and interesting, just like my mom.

Grant was right that the sculpture is mostly made out of cans and bottles, but as I get closer I see that there are some bigger pieces of metal in there, too. Long coiled stems rise out of the weeds, blooming into fat mushroom caps. A twisted mushroom garden. One of the mushroom caps has rusted right off—I find it hiding in the weeds below. When I pick it up, it fits perfectly in the palm of my hand, like it was meant to be there. I'm shocked by how heavy it is. The cap is icy cold, molded cement spotted with specks of colored glass.

This, I'm certain, is the reason Spirit led me all this way. I am holding my mother's tether.

I grip the mushroom cap in my bare hands, allowing myself to be overtaken by the emotional energy inside it.

Only, all I feel is cold.

I try again, gripping the cement cap even tighter. I sniff.

All I smell is the chill in the air.

I clench the tether to my chest, willing myself to sense her emotional energy. It must be in there. It *has* to be. I perk up my ears.

All I hear is . . .

Thumping.

Thumping?

I search for the source of the noise, and at last I find it. One branch of an overgrown holly bush is smooshed up hard against the back door of the house, and it's broken through a pane of glass. Inside, the wooden blinds are thumping against the window as the wind whistles through. One hand still tight around the mushroom cap, I pick my way through the weeds and discover that nearly the whole pane of glass is gone.

"Hello?" I call through the window.

It's dark inside. Still and quiet.

I look around, to see if this is where Spirit wants me to be.

All I hear is thumping.

I slip the mushroom cap inside my pocket, the weight of it tugging half my coat down. I pull my messenger bag over my shoulder and set it carefully on the bottom of the window-pane, in case there are any sharp shards of glass. Slowly and gently, I reach my hand through for the inside latch, hoping it will be like the one on our tour bus—one swift flick and it's unlocked.

One swift flick.

When I try the doorknob, it sticks for just a moment. But then I push harder, and suddenly there's the whole house in front of me, like it's just been waiting for me to step inside.

. . .

The air in the house is musty, like I've opened a bag of bread that's been sitting on the counter far too long. I try the switch on the wall, but no lights flick on. At least I can see okay, from the light streaming in through the blinds. Dust hangs thick in the air. I'd bet no one's lived here for years.

I make my way across the kitchen, eyes open for whatever it is I'm supposed to find that Aunt Nic isn't. There are still cookbooks lined up beside the fridge, dish towels draped over the oven handle, knickknacks on the windowsill. I pick up a small white picture frame to examine the photo, and I guess I'm not too surprised when I wipe a trail of dust from the glass and see two little girls smiling back at me—Aunt Nic and my mom.

These things are my mother's things. She and Aunt Nic, and me, too—we were the last ones to live here.

I leave the kitchen and step into the dining room. There's a piano against one wall. More framed photos. I want to sit on the couch where my mom must've opened presents on Christmas morning. I want to stand at the window where my mom might've spied on her neighbors. But I know what I need to see first.

The first bedroom at the top of the stairs is huge, with a four-poster bed made from wood so dark it barely creeps out of the shadows around it. Everything is put away, blankets folded crisp on the bed. It feels like a grown-up space—Grandma and Grandpa Ames's room, I'd bet, before they died. I move on.

The next bedroom is obviously Aunt Nic's, everything tidy. White wood dresser, white vanity, white wood headboard. No knickknacks. No photos. I open one dresser drawer, then another. Nothing inside.

The third bedroom, though, could not be more different. It's messy and lived-in and vibrant, even in the darkness. The walls are covered in posters of different bands and drawings and paintings and maps stuck up with thumbtacks. Oil paints and pencil cups are stuffed on the bookshelf. On the bed sits a teddy bear I recognize from photos of my mom as a kid. The dresser is crowded with *things*—a porcelain unicorn, a bowl filled with quarters, a messy stack of postcards. My whole body buzzes with confusion and excitement and nerves. I walk to the window and tug up the blinds, let the sunlight stream in. And as my eyes adjust to the light, I spot it, on the top shelf of my mother's open closet.

A box. Fat and orange, labeled JENNIE JUNE'S PRIVATE STUFF!

I cross the room to grab it. Remove the lid.

Inside is a beautiful mess of color. Paintings and sketches and doodles. Papers crackle between my fingers, brittle with chill and age, as I leaf through them. The sketch right on top is one my mom drew of herself—you can see the mirror in the drawing. Her hair is tied up in a messy knot and she's sticking her tongue out, scrunching her face. It somehow captures more than any photo I've ever seen of her.

I'm sniffling up cold tears as I rummage through the box, and I don't know why. This is amazing. This house, this box, *her*. Whatever their reasons might be, I'm so grateful Spirit led me here.

There are a couple portraits of my grandfather, who died when my mom was pretty young, and several of Grandma Ames, who left this world a year before I entered it. There are some of Aunt Nic, too, and people I guess must be my mom's friends—including a great drawing of Ashlynne gazing into the distance, like she's staring down the future. Another self-portrait of my mom, drawn in pastels, leaves my fingertips smudgy with color. And there are lots of random sketches in the pile—eyes, furniture, a puppy, people's hands in different positions. Mushroom doodles crop up again and again—the long, twisted stems with the bulby caps.

I'm still flipping through papers when I hear a door slam downstairs. Startled, I let the box slip from my fingers, and it falls to the floor, scattering papers and dust. "Hello?" I call as I scramble to pick the pages up. But there is no response. *"Hello?"* I try again.

Nothing.

My fingers are frozen as I pick up a drawing that's half wedged under the bed. It's a pastel portrait, rich with color.

"CJ?" comes a voice from the door, and I nearly jump out of my skin. "*There* you are." I look up. It's Jax. "You'll never believe," he says, excited. "I think I figured it out, about those mess—" His face falls as he takes in the sight of me, on the floor, frozen still. Staring at the portrait. "You okay?"

In response, I hold up the drawing. My hands are shaking, and not from the cold.

"How . . . ?" He frowns at the portrait in my hand, of the girl with the birthmark on her right cheek—the tiny brown heart-shaped cherish. "But, CJ," he says. "That's *you*."

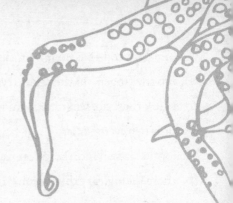

SEVEN

"I THOUGHT YOU said you were starving," Jax says as I lay out the pages from the box of JENNIE JUNE'S PRIVATE STUFF! We're seated across from each other at an old-fashioned ice cream parlor called The Cherry on Top. The chairs are shaped like half-peeled bananas, and the air smells like waffle cones. Jax wanted to head straight back to L.A., but I convinced him to stop for a snack first because I need a minute to figure things out.

I push my bowl of rocky road away to make more space for the drawings. "I'll eat in a second," I say.

Jax dips his spoon deep into his triple chocolate blast. "Don't let it melt too much. It's really good. You think they put espresso in their chocolate base? I think I taste espresso."

"You could ask them," I say, because I have slightly more important things on my mind. I rearrange two of the drawings on the table, like maybe if I get them in the right order everything will suddenly make sense.

It turns out there are a bunch of drawings of me in the

orange box. Me as an infant, sleeping. Me as a toddler, eating. I tap my fingers on the table, trying to figure it all out. "Do you think these are what my mom was hiding from Aunt Nic? How did they even *get* here?"

Jax is still mostly concentrating on his ice cream. "I'm sure there's a logical explanation," he says.

"Like?"

"Like . . ." He puts his spoon down to check out one of the drawings. A baby gazing up from a bouncy chair. "Well, maybe it's not actually you. Maybe your mom was drawing some other baby."

I shake my head and point to the baby's cheek in the sketch in his hand, and in all the other sketches, too. "Cherish, cherish, cherish. And anyway"—I take the sketch Jax is holding, put it beside my own, real-life face—"it *is* me. It looks just like me. Hair and nose and eyes and everything. Right?"

Jax presses his lips together. "Yeah," he admits. "Okay. But maybe someone else drew them, instead of your mom."

"They're all signed 'JJA,' my mom's initials." I shuffle through them again. "And they're all the same style, just like the mural she made in Ashlynne's room. So I guess it's possible that someone learned to draw like her, made these pictures of me after I was born, signed her initials on them, and then put them in this box in her old house. But that would be . . ."

"Weird," Jax finishes for me.

My mom must've drawn these pictures before I was born. That's the only thing that makes sense. Somehow, she knew what I was going to look like, and she put the drawings there for me to find, instead of Aunt Nic. "This must be what Spirit's been leading me to all along," I say. "Maybe I wasn't supposed to be looking for a tether at all." I still have the mushroom cap, weighing down my coat pocket, but as hard as I try I can't squeeze any emotional energy out of it.

"But then why send you a message in an octopus?" Jax asks. "And why 'take heed'? Couldn't they just send you your mom's address instead?"

I don't even bother rolling my eyes. "Spirit doesn't work that way, and you know it."

"Sure," Jax replies, and for a second it sounds like he's actually agreeing with me. Until he says, "But what if . . . ?" He lets his spoon clank into his ice cream bowl, and somehow I can tell that I'm not going to like whatever comes out of his mouth next. "What if none of this has anything to do with Spirit?"

"But the *signs*—" I begin.

"Look." He leans to one side to dig in his pocket, then pulls out his phone. "This is what I was trying to tell you before. Seriously, are you even going to *try* your ice cream?"

I do roll my eyes then, because, hello, can we *focus*? But just to shut him up, I take a bite of my rocky road.

"Whoa, this is *good*." I immediately scoop up some more.

"Right?" Jax grins. Then he scrolls through his phone. "I was thinking, in the car, that if that guy Gerald found an octopus message before you did, then maybe other people have found them, too. So I did an image search. And look." He hands me the phone.

The screen is filled with photos of octopus messages. Same as the one I found on my wrist. Same as the tattoo on Gerald's arm. Dozens of them. I scroll down. Hundreds. They're all the same sort of octopus, but they're not all stamped on skin. One is embossed onto the front of a hardcover book. One is burned into toast. Another's carved into a leaf, still hanging from a tree. And all of them have messages spelled out in the tentacles, one letter at a time. *NOT AT ALL*, one says. *LOOK LEFT*, reads another. One octopus, stamped on a bottle of clear liquid, commands, *DRINK ME*. The spookiest one is whittled under the eye socket of a human skull, and it warns, *I SEE YOU*.

"What . . . ?" I begin, but I don't even know how to finish the question.

Jax takes back his phone. "Once I realized that people were getting these messages all over the place"—he's typing quickly with his thumbs, trying to pull up something else—"I starting digging even more, to figure out where they were coming from. People have tons of ideas. But the one I think is probably right is that it's a group of magicians who do it."

"Magicians?" I scoop another spoonful of ice cream. "Like Harry Potter, wands and potions?"

"Harry Potter is a wizard," Jax corrects me. "And anyway, they're not *real* magicians. They're guys who saw ladies in half, that kind of thing."

"Um . . ."

Jax doesn't seem to notice how ridiculous I think his theory is. He's still typing. "There's this group of them. Or a club, or whatever. Le Char Mer." When he says that, I look up. He pronounces the word "char" with that soft *ch*. "It's French. It means 'the sea chariot.'"

I go back to my ice cream.

"The letters," he tells me, "when they're mushed together—*Char Mer*—it spells 'Charmer.' Like someone who casts spells."

I might finally be getting where Jax is going. "That's what Gerald said when I told him about the octopus on my wrist. He said I'd been 'charmed.'"

"Exactly." Jax is excited now, like he's gotten me to join his team. "So it *has* to be these guys, right?" He flips the phone to face me, shows me an image of about thirty mostly white, mostly male, mostly old people posing on a lawn in front of a huge mansion. "Le Char Mer Board of Directors," says the photo caption. "They're described as"—Jax reads the words off his phone—"'an elite society of professional magicians specializing in the unbelievable.' Apparently they have this huge mansion, where tons of magicians come from all over to put on magic shows for weird rich people. That's the first floor, anyway. On the *second* floor they have this, like, secret society. It's very mysterious. And lots of people think they're behind the octopus messages."

I definitely have not joined Jax's team. "O . . . *kay*," I say slowly.

"The mansion is in L.A.," Jax goes on, like that's going to convince me. "Not even twenty miles from the theater where your aunt's show is tonight. That can't be a coincidence."

"But I didn't find any of the messages in L.A. I got that stamp on my arm yesterday, in Santa Barbara. And anyway, the signs were from Spirit, not some weird magicians."

"But—"

"Maybe Spirit used those guys to *send* me the messages," I tell him. "I'll buy that. But it doesn't matter who did the stamping. It matters what the messages mean." I point to the drawings on the table. "That's the part I have to figure out."

"Well," he says, and I can tell he doesn't agree with me but is letting it go for now, "you know who might be a good person to ask about it?" He places two fingers over the image of the board of directors, zooming in on one corner until the entire screen is taken up by a single face. "This guy."

And when I see whose face it is, I nearly choke on my rocky road.

It's Roger Milmond. Aunt Nic's TV producer.

"But why would he . . . ?" I start. But then I discover I'm out of words.

Jax scoops up his last spoonful of ice cream and gets a sly look on his face. "You *might* just be able to convince me to take a short detour to go ask him," he says.

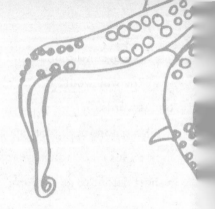

EIGHT

IF THE DRIVE to Bakersfield felt long, the drive back to L.A. is unbearable. "We should go faster," I tell Jax, my hand gripped around the gearshift. He's getting better with the clutch, but I still don't trust him to shift without me.

"You're the one who wanted to slow down," he says.

"That was before."

"Mmm," he *mmm*s. Which I'm starting to learn is his way of saying he thinks I'm being a moron.

I pull my atlas out of my messenger bag. I want to double-check that we're on the quickest route. After four painful minutes of driving at the exact same speed, Jax says, "Do you think your aunt knows her producer is in a weird magic club?"

"I don't know." I run my finger over the line for the 5. "I just want him to tell me how he knew to give me the message. Like, can he hear Spirit directly, or . . . ?"

"How can you possibly still think that message was from Spirit? You *know* it's from this Roger guy. We should ask him what he meant by 'take heed.' Maybe you're in danger or something."

"Mmm," I *mmm*.

"You're impossible, CJ. You've got clear evidence, right in front of your face"—he points to the phone in the cup holder—"and you're totally ignoring the obvious conclusion."

"Funny," I say, tapping the orange box in my lap. "I could say the same thing about you."

"Mmm," he tells me.

"Mmm," I say back.

We're quiet for a long stretch of highway. Dirt. Rocks. Rocks. Dirt.

"You know what I keep thinking?" Jax asks out of the blue. But he doesn't say anything I'd expect him to. "Your mom's friend Ashlynne must've been *ballsy*. I mean, if Grant was my dad, and he told me to stop dating someone, I'd ghost them so fast."

I laugh. "Yeah." But then my thoughts turn to Grant's voice when he was telling me about Ashlynne. "I just can't believe he stopped talking to his own daughter. Who cuts their own family out of their life like that?"

"My grandpa did," Jax says. "He ran away from home when he was younger than me. Never spoke to his family again."

"Seriously?"

Jax nods, eyes on the road. "He said he was better off without them."

"But they were his *family*."

Jax shrugs one shoulder. "Abuelo always said real family doesn't treat people the way his parents treated him."

I run my hand across the top of the orange box. "I just think it would be better to have some parents than none."

"Mmm," Jax says.

"Mmm," I reply.

And I guess that's that.

Well. Almost.

"HORSE!" I scream, because I've spotted one hanging out in an open barn next to an old farmhouse just off the road. "Did you see it?" I ask Jax after we've zoomed past. "Did you see the horse?"

He is looking at me like I have four heads. "This is *not* a fun game," he insists.

. . .

One thing about dead people—everybody's got them. Rich people, poor people, and every sort of person in between. So back in the day, when Aunt Nic still made house calls, we used to go to all different places. I've been inside homes of people so poor the bedroom walls were sheets, and I've been to estates where the furniture is so fresh and white, you'd swear no one in the house knows how to sit.

Le Char Mer is like nothing I've seen before.

"Whoa," Jax says as we stop at a red light and the mansion comes into view. We've been winding along Route 1, with the gorgeous blue of the ocean on our left and near-shear cliffs on our right, and there it is, this enormous white building with actual towering turrets at every corner.

Even the walk from the parking lot to the entrance is impressive. The path is lined with hedges carved into sea creatures—a seahorse, a dolphin, even a hedge shaped like an eel. When we finally reach the mansion, there's a marble fountain out front with an old dude in the center sporting a beard and a giant fork. His chariot, pulled by eight octopuses, floats on top of the bubbling water.

"Poseidon," Jax says as we pass by.

"Bless you," I reply.

He lets out a deep sigh. "No," he says, pointing at the bearded fork guy. "That's Poseidon. From Greek mythology. The god of the sea. Or, as you might call him in a report, Aquaman."

"All right, all right, I get it, you think I'm a moron."

"I just think you should go to actual school."

"*You* don't."

He does not have an argument for that.

The front door is massive, with hundreds of tiny sea creatures carved into the dark wood. Only a few dozen people are milling about in the lobby, but the room is dark and loud, so it feels crowded. The walls are a deep-brown wood, like the door, and carved with seascapes. Four darkened hallways branch off four different walls. A Roman numeral above the curved door-frame of each hall distinguishes it—*I*, *II*, and *III*. The doorway to the fourth hallway is blocked by a solid wooden door, and the marking above it is *X*.

The ceiling is frosty like sea glass and slowly shifts colors from blue to green and back again. Four more fountains burble around us. Being in this room makes me feel like I'm deep underwater. I can't decide if it's calming or terrifying.

Jax, who seemed totally fine outside with Poseidon, is back to scratching his arm. He sinks against one wall, eyes darting all around. I'm just thinking about how hard this must be for him, with all these new people in this new space, and how well he's holding it together—when suddenly the carving on the wall nearest his elbow, a long strip of seaweed, starts *swaying*, and then a wooden fish darts out and nestles into some wooden coral an inch farther along the wall, and Jax leaps away with a terrified yelp.

Everyone, now, is looking at him.

Scratch-scratch-scratch.

"You okay?" I whisper. "You want an"—I flash my hands at him, ready to help—"escape?" He shakes his head. When his breathing slows a little, I say, "You stay here. The walls are weird, but it's just mechanics." I run a finger along the piece of seaweed that moved before. There's a groove in the wood, and I can shift it back and forth if I push hard enough. There must be someone manipulating it from behind the wall, or from a remote control or something. "I'll see if anyone knows Roger."

Jax gives me a weak nod. I head toward the couple closest to me, a man in a dark suit and a maroon tie, and a woman in a long black dress and heels.

"Excuse me," I say. "Do you guys know where I can find Roger Milmond?"

The woman wrinkles her nose at me. "Roger Milmond?" she repeats.

"He's a TV producer. He works with my aunt. Monica May Ames. You ever hear of her?" I don't like the way this fancy lady is looking at me, in my puffy coat and ratty sneakers and messenger bag.

"Are you lost, sweetie?" The way she says it, you can tell she wouldn't care if I was.

I'm about to tell this lady where she can stuff her *"sweetie,"* but I'm interrupted by gasps and cries from the crowd. From out of nowhere, a flock of fat white doves comes swooping over our heads. They soar through the room toward the hallway marked *II*—and as they enter it, the hallway's dark floor suddenly ripples with light. All the well-dressed grown-ups in the room start laughing and clapping, like they can't believe they were just freaked out by *birds*. They gather themselves together and follow the doves down the hallway.

All except the woman in the black dress. She's too busy shrieking.

"Get it off!" she hollers at her husband, flapping her arms above her. "Dev, get it off of me!"

She's swatting at a dove, a single bird that didn't follow the flock and is now sitting calmly in her hair. I can't help myself. I let out a huge snort.

The dove looks at me then—I swear, it looks right at me—and it blinks. Just once, like it means something. And then the bird flies off, follows the others down the hall.

"That was disgusting," the woman spits, reaching for her husband's arm. And I must be getting better at this whole "take heed" thing, because I notice it.

"Where did you get that bracelet?" I ask the woman, reaching for her wrist.

The charms on her silver bracelet are mushrooms. Long, thin, with swoopy stems and big bulby caps. They look just like the ones from my mother's sculpture.

"*Excuse* me." The woman yanks her arm away.

"Where did you get it?" I ask again.

At first the woman only huffs at me, but then she looks around and seems to decide she wants to be nice, because she says, "My friend's gallery carries them." She half shows me the charms again, flipping her wrist over. "James Darek, that's the designer. He's made a few pieces, just for my friend."

Could this be another message from Spirit? Another sign I'm supposed to follow? Or is it just a strange coincidence?

"Where's the gallery?" I ask.

But the woman's husband is tugging at her arm to leave. So she only tells me, "Sorry, sweetie. They're sold out." And together they tromp off.

After the room is cleared of fancy people and birds, Jax looks much calmer.

"This place is the *weirdest*," he says, walking over to me. "How do you think we're ever going to find—?"

"You kids looking for Roger Milmond?" comes a voice. And suddenly there's a new woman in the room with us. She's wearing a long sparkly gold dress that hugs her hips, and her shiny black hair is pinned up at her neck.

"Uh . . ." I glance at Jax. "Yes?"

"Wonderful," she says. Her mouth is a straight line. Not a smile, not a frown. "Follow me."

And just as I notice that the door to the hallway marked *X* has vanished—it's not ajar, it's not open, it's just *not*—the woman heads straight in that direction. When she reaches the mouth of the pitch-black hallway, she turns her head to look at us.

"Well?" she says. "Are you coming, or aren't you?"

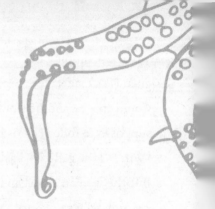

NINE

THE HALLWAY MARKED *X* does not light up as we walk through it. It stays dark, and gets darker, as we follow the woman in gold. It's growing so dark I bump right into the wall. All at once, the spot sparkles, lighting the path for a brief moment before fizzling back into darkness.

I touch the wall again, and the harder I press, the brighter the spot becomes.

"I see you've found our night-lights," the woman in gold says. She does not slow her pace. Jax and I rush to keep up, trailing our hands along the wall to light our way. As we move, the light catches the gold of the woman's dress, all the way down to the hem.

When we reach a grand staircase with a twisty iron banister, the woman pulls a pin out of her hair, long and skinny like a pencil, and her dark hair cascades to her shoulders. She stabs the hairpin down into the knob of the banister, making the knob light up like a streetlamp. The rest of the stairs begin to brighten, too, the glow traveling up the steps and the banister until the entire staircase is illuminated. Without bothering to check if we'll follow, the woman starts to climb.

My skin is tingling with curiosity, but beside me Jax looks like he wants to sink into the floor. I give him a hand-flash, making a question with my eyebrows. But he only shakes his head.

Together we follow the woman in gold.

The landing of the second floor is bathed in murky light, so it's easier to follow the woman as she twists and turns through new hallways. We walk for a long time, and just when I think she must be leading us in circles, she stops. I nearly trip over my feet trying not to plow into her.

To me, this hall looks exactly the same as all the others. But the woman presses an invisible spot on the wall, and an entire panel swings open, revealing a hidden room.

No, an *aquarium*.

I blink in the new light, taking in the sight of all the fish and coral and water. Every wall of this huge room, floor to ceiling, is glass, with a world of sea creatures behind it. The woman waves us inside, and as soon as we enter, the panel swings shut. Fish all around, no exits anywhere. In the center of the glowing room sit two old-timey couches, with a coffee table in between. The woman in gold is gone. It's just me and Jax, and the fish.

"Um . . ." I say slowly. Because as much as I would like to be freaking out right now, I feel like I need to hold it together for Jax. "So this is cool, right?" There's a large purple octopus behind the glass to my left, who *floops* his way lower in the tank until he is just above our heads. "Hey there, buddy." I tap on the tank to greet him.

And just like that, the octopus vanishes in a sea of cloudy blue ink. No sign of him anywhere.

"Whoa," I breathe. "That was—"

As the dark ink begins to clear, I see the octopus stuck to the glass, just inches from my face. And where each of the creature's tentacles meets the glass, a letter is formed in ink.

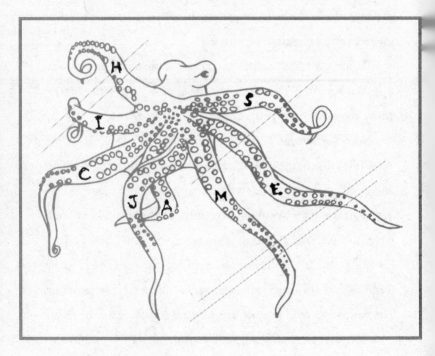

My skin tingles again.

"Welcome, both of you."

Jax and I spin around at the voice behind us. Although I'm certain there was no one else in the room a second ago, now Roger Milmond is stepping out of a watery corner. He's wearing a dark suit and fancy shoes. Somehow even the stubble on his chin looks more polished than yesterday.

"How'd you *do* that?" I ask Roger, gesturing toward the octopus, whose inky message is still pressed against the glass. Roger's a magician, I know that now, so while all this stuff is pretty creepy, I know it's just tricks.

My question makes Roger smile. "Seems to me you ought to ask the octopus," he replies.

So. Weird.

"It's good to see you again, CJ," Roger says when he reaches us. "And this is . . . ?" He looks at Jax.

"Jax," I reply, because I'm not sure Jax knows how to speak anymore.

Scratch-scratch-scratch.

Jax doesn't shake Roger's hand, which is maybe not the worst decision he's ever made.

Roger returns his attention to me. "So Nic sent her niece to yell at me, did she?" he asks.

"Huh?" Why would Aunt Nic want me to yell at him? "We came because of the message. 'Take heed.' That was you, right?" I turn again to the octopus in the tank. "I mean, obviously."

"Well." Roger folds his arms over his chest. "You two sleuths tracked me down all by yourselves? Impressive."

"We had help from Spirit," I reply. And when Roger tilts his head at me like he's confused, I say, "What is 'take heed' supposed to mean? Am I in trouble?"

Roger thinks that over. "Depends on how you define 'trouble,'" he replies.

Obviously I'm going to have to be a lot clearer.

"How did Spirit tell you to contact me?" I ask. "What am I supposed to be looking out for? And what do you know about my mom?"

With each question, Roger's eyebrows rise higher, until I worry they just might leap off his forehead.

"Why don't we have a seat?" he says when I finish. "We have a lot to discuss." He gestures toward the coffee table between the two fancy couches. "Care for a snack?" Even though I *know* the table was just empty, now there are three gold-rimmed teacups set on saucers, filled with steaming hot chocolate. There's a plate of cookies, too.

Scratch-scratch-scratch.

As Roger crosses to the farthest couch, I set a hand on Jax's shoulder. "Want to leave?" I whisper. Because as much as I want to stay and figure things out, I think it would be good if Jax still had two arms afterward. Jax only shakes his head, so together we sit ourselves down on the stiff couch across from Roger.

"First things first," Roger says as he leans forward to pick up his teacup. He takes a sip. "Good cocoa." He swirls the cup, then clacks it back into its saucer. "That message about taking heed was from me," he goes on. "No spirit told me to leave it for you. And I'm afraid I don't know anything about your mother."

My tingly excitement shifts quickly into disappointment, but I do my best to trust in Spirit. I need to follow the path they lead me down, no matter how twisty, and I'll get where I need to go.

"So why did you want me to 'take heed' then?" I ask Roger.

Roger studies my face for a moment, then glances into his teacup, as though trying to decide something. He downs the rest of his drink in one swig.

"I like you, CJ," he says. "You remind me of myself when I was a kid. I suppose that's why I was trying to warn you."

"Warn me about what?"

"CJ Ames," Roger says very seriously, "your entire world is about to change."

And just like that, I'm tingling again. I lean forward in my seat. But whatever I'm expecting to hear, what Roger says next is not it.

"How much do you know about what your aunt does?" he asks me.

It seems like an odd question, but I do my best to answer it. "I know she has the Gift," I say. "I know she helps people connect to their loved ones. I know she's helped me."

Roger nods, taking that in. "I thought you'd say as much." He gazes down into his empty cup before saying, "And do you know what it is we do here, CJ, at Le Char Mer?"

"Besides lure kids into creepy fish rooms?" I ask. I really wish this guy would get to his point already. "Jax said you guys put on magic shows."

"Indeed."

With that, Roger stands and strides to the far wall. When he waves his hand, somehow all of the fish and water and anemones behind the glass disappear, and what emerges instead is a view of the first floor of the mansion. A theater, I realize, when I rise from my seat—backs of heads, a stage in front. It's what you'd see if you were sitting inside the tech booth at the back of an audience. Onstage, a man in a suit gestures to a woman in a chair beside him—the same woman in the gold dress who led us here, her hair pinned back up against her neck.

"They can't see us," Roger says as Jax slowly joins us at the glass.

Like fish in an aquarium, the man and woman onstage go on with their business without paying us any attention. The man says something we can't hear, and the shoulders of the audience members rise and fall with laughter. But when the man claps his hands, the woman in gold disappears in a puff of smoke, and the chair along with her. I press my hands to the glass, mesmerized.

"Where . . . ?" I begin.

"Just watch," Roger tells me.

It takes a moment for me to spot it, but when I follow the crowd's pointed fingers, I see her—the woman in gold is floating above the audience in her chair, waving as she makes her way back to the stage.

When I turn back to Roger, I see he's sipping from his cup of hot chocolate again. I don't know when he refilled it. "Do you know what that magician and your aunt have in common, CJ?" he asks me.

"That guy's name is Nick, too?" I guess.

Roger takes another sip. "They're showmen," he replies, like that should've been so obvious. "They both put on a great performance, and charge people to see it. The difference is"—he pauses to swirl his teacup—"this crowd knows it's all an act."

"What Aunt Nic does isn't an *act*," I tell him. "It's a Gift." This isn't the first time someone's doubted my aunt. Lots of people don't want to believe what she can do—because it *does* seem unbelievable. But this is the first time I've had to explain it from inside a fish tank. "Ask anyone she's done a reading for, and they'll tell you. She knows things she never could've, unless she'd been talking to Spirit."

"And *there's* the trick!" Roger says, waving his saucer hand wildly. Suddenly his voice is booming, powerful, like he's the one onstage. "The amazing Monica May Ames can tell you the ages of your kids, the names of your bosses. Even the color of your car." He jerks his head back to the stage, where the man in the suit is showing an audience member the inside of his top hat. "Magicians have been doing the same sort of trick for centuries. It isn't hard to dig up information about a person before you meet them. And the internet's made it a whole lot easier. Give me your email address and I can tell you what type of cheese you had on your sandwich yesterday. Magicians call that sort of trick 'hot reading,' because the performer goes into the show already warmed up."

I'm not tingly anymore. I'm angry. "My aunt is not a performer," I tell him. "I've been with her when she's passed a person in the grocery store, who she's never in a million years met before, and she starts talking to Spirit for them, right there. She doesn't need tricks. She has the Gift. Now." I have no idea what Spirit wanted me to learn here, but they're going to have to find another way to tell me, because I'm leaving. "If you're not going to tell us anything useful, maybe you could at least show us how to get out of here."

"The exit's that way," Roger says, gesturing back where we came in. The octopus still has his tentacles suctioned to the glass. The first two letters in his message—*H I*—are starting to run, the letters growing longer and smudgier. "Press the brass plate on the floor."

"Great, thanks." But there's one more thing I need to know before I go, and Roger better give me a straight answer this time. "Why did you pretend to be a TV producer?" I ask. "Why did you have to get Aunt Nic's hopes up that you were making a show about her, when you obviously think she's some sort of phony? That was just mean."

It's Jax who answers for him.

"You *are* making a show, aren't you?" he says to Roger. "Only"—he still scratches his arm, but more slowly now—"it's not the sort of show Nic thinks it is."

Roger smiles in this way that makes me think he might be a supervillain, and we've wandered straight into his lair. If I didn't know Spirit was watching over me right now, I'd probably be mildly petrified. "Smart," he says to Jax. Then, to me, he explains, "I am a TV producer. But I may have . . . misdirected your aunt a bit. I'm working on a show that exposes her for the fraud she is. When I'm done with Monica May Ames, no one will trust her to read the phone book. Hopefully, they won't trust any other mediums, either."

I narrow my eyes at Roger. "Hey, Jax, can I see your phone for a sec?" I ask over my shoulder. "I need to call Aunt Nic now and tell her to come kick this guy's butt."

Roger only smiles what is definitely a supervillain smile,

while Jax digs in his pocket. "You're more than welcome to call your aunt, CJ, although I'll have to get Dana to escort you to the gardens first, since there's no cell service in the mansion." As I grab Jax's phone, I see Roger's actually right about that one. "But I do wish you'd give me a little more of your time. You might even want to help me with my little project. The major networks would be thrilled to land an interview with an insider like you, someone who could spill the beans about your aunt's tricks. There's good money in it, too."

I can't believe this guy thinks I'd turn against my own aunt just for some cash. "I told you. She doesn't *have* any tricks." I tug on Jax's nonitchy arm, and we head for the exit.

"Maybe you won't listen to me," Roger calls as we walk away. "But I hope you'll listen to someone else."

And then there's a new voice filling the room.

"Now, who's the one with the sister? Died of cancer?"

I whirl around. The wall that just moments ago gave us a view of the stage below is now showing me Aunt Nic, talking to *her* audience. For a sliver of a moment, I think she must be in the first-floor theater, too—until I notice Jax and myself standing right beside her. This is a recording.

"I'm getting a name," Aunt Nic continues. I can see traces of sea life swimming behind her face on the glass, which is maybe weirder than anything. *"Starts with 'M.'"* This recording is from

yesterday—the day Spirit sent me the first message that led me here. *"Marie, maybe, or Mary?"*

Roger stands in front of Aunt Nic's image, but he's not watching her. He's watching me.

He sips his hot chocolate.

"I'm Mary!" shouts the woman in the audience, jumping out of her seat, just the way I remember. And Aunt Nic rushes over, me and Jax right behind her.

Just like that, the recording freezes. A clown fish flits past Aunt Nic's nose.

"Funny how she knew that," Roger says between sips. "She *couldn't* have known Mary's sister died of cancer, right? Not unless she heard it from the dead sister herself."

I let out a growl. I know I should leave, but I hate that this jerk is gearing up the whole world to think such awful things about Aunt Nic.

"You really are dense," I tell Roger. "You think my aunt is finding dirt on every single person in her audience? We book five-hundred-seat theaters. You know how long that would take? She doesn't do that 'hot reading' stuff, or whatever you called it. She has the Gift. And she uses it to help people."

"I agree with you about one thing," Roger replies. "I don't think your aunt uses hot reading, either."

"Fabulous! So glad we're on the same page. Leaving now."

I'm busy searching for the brass plate on the floor when

Roger says, "Your aunt is a very clever woman, CJ. Far too clever, I'd say, to use a trick like hot reading. No. What she does—what I hope to convince the world she does—is called 'cold reading.' And it's much more sophisticated."

At last I find the plate on the floor—shaped, of course, like an octopus. And as soon as I stomp on it, the glass wall swings outward, and the real octopus in the aquarium with it. The first few letters of the creature's message are nearly vanished now. It's hard to make out anything besides *C J A M E S*.

I step into the dark hall, Jax right behind me.

"Your aunt doesn't dig up dirt about her victims beforehand," I hear Roger say as I go. "She manipulates *them* into handing their information over to *her*, without them ever realizing they're doing it."

And that's when I finally get it, what Spirit was trying to tell me with that first message. *Take heed.* Roger may have stamped those words on my skin, but no matter why he thinks he did it, I know better.

Spirit has been warning me about *him*.

I stomp back into the room, over to the frozen image of Aunt Nic holding Mary's sister's scarf. Spirit sent me here, I realize, to stop this creep from spreading lies. "You said Aunt Nic gets people to tell her information about themselves," I say. Jax slowly steps back my way, too, although he looks like he'd rather be anywhere else. "But she doesn't. This woman"—I flail my arm at the image of Mary—"Aunt Nic *knew* her name, right from the beginning. And she *knew* her sister died of cancer. And nobody told her that but the sister's spirit."

At that, Roger raises an eyebrow. "Did your aunt know those things, though?" he asks.

"You *heard* it." No wonder Roger doubts Aunt Nic's Gift. He's not even paying attention. "You *saw* it."

"Sure about that?" Roger tilts his head, and suddenly the frozen image behind him zooms backward in time. "Let's watch again."

And so we watch, once more, as Aunt Nic calls out, *"Now, who's the one with the sister? Died of cancer?"* And then, right after that, *"I'm getting a name. Starts with 'M.' Marie, maybe, or Mary?"*

Roger tilts his head to the other side, and the screen freezes again. Two blue fish chase each other around my aunt's hair.

"Didn't you see it that time?" I ask Roger—because he's staring at me like he's waiting for me to figure something out, when I'm the one who should be waiting for *him*.

"Didn't you?" he asks.

But Jax pipes up before I can answer.

"She said 'Marie' first," Jax says, looking at Aunt Nic's frozen face. *"Then* Mary."

"Big whoop," I reply. "Spirit can be hard to hear sometimes. Living people don't always speak super clearly, either."

"Yeah," Jax says slowly. "But that's a real common name,

Mary. Nic could've just been guessing. And"—when Jax looks at Roger then, he gets an encouraging nod—"it wasn't like she was pointing at the woman, Mary, when she said her name, either. She basically just shouted, 'Is anyone here named Mary?' and that lady jumped up."

I can't believe Jax is turning on me, too. "It wasn't a wild guess, Jax. I've seen Aunt Nic do that *thousands* of times. She's *always* right."

"Maybe," he says thoughtfully. Roger's busy beaming at Jax like he wants to give him a gold star, which is making me madder than anything. "But, okay, if you think about it, probably every person in that audience had someone who was close to them die, right? That's why they came. And cancer—that's like one of the most common ways people die. I mean, my grandpa died of cancer, and my mom's cousin, too. And so, yeah, the odds were probably pretty good that somewhere in that room was a lady whose sister died of cancer and whose name was Marie or Mary or Marjorie or something like that. And actually"—he pauses for just a moment as he thinks it through—"your aunt just said"—he does a pretty terrible impression of her voice—"*I'm getting a name that starts with 'M.'* She could've meant the sister who *died* was named that. She didn't say."

"Very astute, young man," Roger tells Jax, and I start fuming like I'm filled with steam. "In fact, if you watch a little closer"—Roger tilts his head again, and the video spins forward to the spot where we see Mary rise up in the audience—"you'll notice four other women"—he points out three figures deep in the back rows of the theater, and one not too far away from Mary—"who raise their hands when your aunt asks just such a thing. Four other women"—he points them out again—"who would just as happily tell her that *they* are the person the spirit is speaking about."

I squint at the figures on the glass. "But it doesn't matter if *they* think they're the ones the spirit meant," I argue. "Because they're not. If they were, Aunt Nic would've picked them instead."

Roger sighs, like I'm just not getting it. "She would've picked whoever she felt like," he replies. "Because she's not channeling any spirits at all. Your aunt is lying, CJ. Simple as that. And the worst part is, the very person she's lying to"—he jabs the image of Mary in the chest—"is helping her do it. This poor woman doesn't think she's telling your aunt anything. But your aunt is a very skilled manipulator, CJ. I've been following her for over a year. She got this poor grieving woman to tell her everything she needed to convince her that her dead sister was right there with them."

"She didn't manipulate anyone," I say. "I was *there*." I search my brain for a detail that will prove him wrong. "Aunt Nic knew about Mary's sister being super smart. I remember. And Mary never told her that. She just *knew*."

Jax, beside me, is nodding. First useful thing he's done in ten minutes. "I remember that, too," he says. "The lady was really impressed Nic knew that."

"Okay," Roger says, tilting his head again. The recording flips even further forward. "Let's watch."

"She was smart, your sister, huh?" Aunt Nic is saying to Mary. *"Used lots of big words?"*

"Sometimes, yeah," Mary replies.

"But she didn't like to show off," Aunt Nic goes on. *"Didn't want everyone else to feel bad, knowing they weren't as smart as she was. She was always looking out for other people."*

"Oh, yeah," Mary replies. Smiling. Big nods. *"Always."*

I turn to Roger just as he freezes the image again. "See?" I say. "She *knew*."

But he's still shaking his head like *I'm* the one missing something. "The first thing Nic asks is if her sister used lots of big words—and it's clear from the woman's reaction that her sister did *not*. It's only after your aunt gets a tepid response that she asks a follow-up question that fits a little better—if the sister was smart, but didn't like to brag about it."

"And she was right about that!" I don't understand how Roger can be watching the exact same recording as me but seeing something completely different. "The woman agreed. She was *thrilled* Aunt Nic knew that."

"She was thrilled about something," Roger replies. "She

might be agreeing with the fact that her sister was smart, or that she didn't like other people to feel bad, or that she cared about others. And what person *doesn't* think most of those things about their sister? The only thing we know for certain is that the sister *didn't* use big words, which is the only straightforward question your aunt asked."

Beside me, Jax is nodding again, but this time it's not me he's agreeing with. "Yeah, actually," he says, "I'd say that stuff about my sister, too, and I don't even like her that much."

"I think it's time we left," I say. I'm filled with hot, angry steam. How am I supposed to convince Roger to stop spreading lies about Aunt Nic when I can't even convince *Jax*? I head toward the octopus wall again and spot the woman in gold, waiting for us in the hallway. "I'm obviously going to let Aunt Nic know what you're up to," I tell Roger on our way out.

"I figured as much," Roger replies. But he doesn't look like he's mad about it or wants to stop me. Actually, he looks like he feels *sorry* for me.

I really hate this guy.

"Can I ask one question?" Jax says just as we're face-to-face with the octopus again. He turns to Roger, his voice a little steadier. "How'd you do that, with your cup filling up with hot chocolate, I mean?"

"It doesn't matter how he did it," I tell Jax, pushing him forward. "It looks cool, but it's just a dumb trick."

The look Roger gives me then, I think he's going to give *me* the gold star. "Exactly," he tells me. And then, even more annoying, "You're a smart girl, CJ. The truth is out there for you to find, if you want to see it."

"The truth is there for you, too," I reply. "If *you* want to see it."

At that, he smiles. A corners-only, sad little smile. I give him the same one back.

It isn't until the wall is swinging closed behind us that Jax and I notice the octopus again. I can tell Jax sees it too by the way he sucks in his breath.

Only the last five letters of the octopus's original message remain now, bold, inky blue against the bright water.

JAMES

As soon as we read the name, the wall closes completely behind us.

.   .   .

It's obvious Jax and I are avoiding talking to each other as the woman in gold leads us back through the weird mansion. But the second she deposits us in the gardens on our own, I tell him, "Look, I know Roger was getting to you in there—" Then I have to pause, because it's so bright outside that I sneeze, three times. "But I need your help again. I got another message from Spirit, and I think it's important." And as we cross back through the hedges toward the parking lot, I explain about the mushroom bracelet. "The artist's name was James Darek. *James*, just like the name in the octopus. And I swear, Jax, those mushrooms on the bracelet were *exactly* like the ones in my mom's sculpture. And I *know* you think this is all a coincidence, and you're worried about your job and everything, but I really think Spirit is telling me to look into this James guy, and—"

"I'll help you," Jax tells me. Which might be the most surprising thing he's said all day.

"You will?"

"The whole time we were in there," Jax says, "I kept getting this weird . . . feeling. Like someone was watching me or something, I don't know. And then that name in the octopus? James?" He's tapping the side of his phone like he thinks that'll make it pick up a signal faster. "James was my grandpa's name."

My eyes go buggy. "No way."

"Well, Jaime. James was the American version." He darts his eyes at me. "I thought maybe it was Abuelo's way of telling me that I need to help you out."

"Your grandpa sounds like a pretty smart guy," I say.

At that, Jax laughs. "He'd agree with you," he says. And then, whacking his phone one more time, he shouts, "Aha! A signal! *Whoa*." He brings the phone close to his face. "I've got fourteen missed calls from your aunt and six from Uncle Oscar. Oh, man, it's past two. They must be totally freaking out."

"I'll call Aunt Nic," I tell him, taking the phone. I need to warn her about Roger and try to buy us some time to work through this new message from Spirit without telling her *too* much. I flip open my messenger bag and hand Jax my tablet. "You look up James Darek."

The phone rings twice before someone picks up. But it isn't Aunt Nic on the other end. It's Oscar.

"CJ!" he answers. Oscar is never a happy person, but he sounds especially irritated right now. "Where *are* you? Your aunt is in a reading right now. She told me the *second* I got you I was supposed to make sure you're not in a hospital, and then yell at you. Are you in a hospital?"

"We're fine," I say. "But before you yell at me, I want you to know that it's not Jax's fault we're so late, it's mine. I practically dragged him here."

Jax's breaths are short and quick as he listens to my end of the conversation, but at least he's not scratching. Probably because he's too busy scrolling through search results on the tablet. I peek over his shoulder to see what he's found. It doesn't look like there's much, but Jax clicks on a website for a gallery that features some of James Darek's work. That might be a lead on how to reach him, I guess.

"Where's 'here'?" Oscar asks me.

"We're like, a half an hour from the theater. We're safe, I promise." I don't mention Bakersfield, and the Ezolds, and my mom's house. There will be time for all that later. "Listen," I say as Jax pings through more search results. "This is important. As soon as Aunt Nic's done with her reading, you have to warn her about Roger Milmond. That TV producer? He's not who he says he is. He's trying to prove to everyone that Aunt Nic is lying about being a medium. He's a real creep. Just tell her, okay? Soon as she's done?"

There is silence on the other end. At first I think I've lost the connection, but when I pull the phone away, I see the call's still going.

"Oscar?"

That's when Jax elbows me in the ribs. "CJ," he whispers. "I found him." He shows me the tablet.

The post on the screen is from a social media account, and it's time-stamped only fifteen minutes ago. *Back at work on the top-secret project!*

I raise an eyebrow like a question at Jax, and that's when he points to a location marker on the post.

The San Diego Zoo.

"The zoo?" I mouth at him. It's 150 miles from here. A two-hour drive, maybe, if you don't care too much about speed limits.

Jax just gives me a look like *I'm game if you are.*

On the other end of the phone, Oscar finally says, "CJ?"

I'd forgotten he was still there. "Yeah?"

"Just . . ." Oscar takes a deep breath. "Don't go searching for answers you don't want to find," he says.

I look back at the tablet, then at Jax's eager-but-terrified face. And I tell Oscar, "We'll be back in time for curtain."

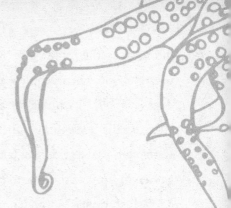

TEN

I HAVE NEVER felt as antsy as I do sitting in the passenger's seat on the road to San Diego. "Find anything?" Jax asks me after twenty minutes or so. He darts his chin toward the tablet.

"No photos of the guy, no nothing," I say. I sigh and slip the tablet back into my messenger bag. "James Darek has *one* social media account, which is the one we found, and there are only a few posts, mostly pictures of different types of mushroom art. I can't figure out how old he is, or where he's from, or anything."

I give up and stare out the window. At least the 405 is more scenic than the 5. "What do you think this guy has to do with my mom, anyway?" I ask, pulling the cement mushroom cap out of my coat pocket. For the millionth time, I transfer it heavy between my hands, running my fingers over those smooth, shiny bits of glass. Trying to feel my mom's energy. But I get nothing. "And what sort of top-secret project could he be working on at the zoo?"

"Maybe it's one of those guerilla art things," Jax answers. "You know, those guys who, like, plop a giant papier-mâché dinosaur in the middle of a Kmart parking lot overnight or whatever? So when people wake up, they're all, 'Whoa, what does it *mean*?'" I wrinkle my nose. I do not know about that. "It's usually something super weird, or making a political statement. Maybe this guy James is putting some mushroom garden in front of the zoo, to protest . . ."

"Mushrooms?" I wonder.

Jax shrugs. "Anyway, I bet he was a friend of your mom's growing up. I bet that's why their styles are so similar."

"Maybe," I say. But I'm learning to stop trying to predict where Spirit will lead me. "I just hope he's still there when we show up."

Jax's phone lights up then, from the cup holder between us. It's Oscar. He's called five times since we left the mansion.

"Reject it," Jax tells me, gesturing toward the phone. "If I'm fired, I'm fired. I don't want to find out about it till we get back to the theater. It'll mess with my driving."

"They're not going to fire you," I say, grabbing the phone to reject the call. I whip my thumbs through a text message. *We're fine! Talk soon!* "I told you, I'll explain it to them, I promise. I dragged you on this road trip—it's not your fault at all. They'll have to understand. I'll make them."

"That's really sweet and everything, CJ," Jax says. And he's using this voice like he thinks he's so much older than I am, but I decide not to be offended. "But they're not gonna care that it was your idea. I'm the one driving. I could've turned us around at any point if I wanted to. Still can. So if I get in trouble, I probably deserve it."

I study the side of his face while he drives. Really take him in. And I'm just about to tell him thanks, and how much it means to me that in all this craziness I know I have someone on my side, when, totally out of the blue, he looks right at me and shouts, *"HORSE!"*

It startles me so badly that I jerk my chest against the seat belt. And then I see where he's pointing, at the horse in the field off the highway up ahead, and I burst out laughing.

He grins. "Did I win the game?"

"I told you," I say, laughing, "you don't *win* Horse. You just—*HORSE!*" I spot another one, in the same field. And then several more. *"HORSE! HORSE! HORSE!"*

"HORSE!" Jax chimes in, pointing.

"No, I already claimed that one," I tell him.

"Nuh-uh. I was pointing to a totally different horse than you."

"How could you—? *HORSE!*" As we crest the hill, we see that the field is completely swarming with horses. *"HORSE! HORSE!"*

"HORSE!"

"HORSE!"

That goes on for some time. And I don't mind a bit.

. . .

The zoo is enormous. It's a bright, sunny afternoon, and the place is crowded. Everywhere I look, there are strollers. Parents holding kids' hands. Toddlers shrieking, gnawing on pretzels, startling pigeons.

Unfortunately, there is no protest mushroom artwork in the parking lot. Or—we discover, once we buy tickets and pass through the turnstiles at the entrance—anywhere we can see inside, either.

"So . . ." I say to Jax after we've been wandering awhile. "What do we do now?" I keep flipping the zoo map upside down and back again, like if I do it enough times I'll find a message from Spirit that says, *This way, CJ!* When Jax doesn't answer my question, I check over his shoulder at his phone. "Did James Darek post anything else yet?"

"Nope," he replies, just as the phone rings in his hand. It's Oscar. Again. Jax rejects the call, slipping the phone in his back pocket. "Maybe someone who works here knows something?"

I nod, because that's not the worst idea. "Want me to do the talking?"

I don't wait for an answer, since I know by now how Jax feels about strangers. Instead, I walk up to the first zoo employee I see, a woman in a navy polo shirt sitting behind a rolling cart piled with fossils.

"Excuse me?" I say as I approach, Jax lurking just behind me.

"Hello there!" The woman smiles broadly, clearly very excited to talk to us. I'm guessing most people don't spend much time with the fossil-cart lady, when they could look at real live animals instead. "Are you interested in learning about the evolution of the hoof?"

"Actually," I say, "do you know a guy named James Darek? He's an artist. He does, like, mushroom themes?"

The woman sets down her fossil, obviously sad that I don't want to chat about hooves. Of all the cart people we've passed so far, this woman definitely got stuck with the worst spot. She's sitting right on the edge of a blocked-off construction area where there's not much to look at but temporary plywood walls and a sign that says EXHIBITION IN PROGRESS!

"I do know James," she says slowly. And even though I asked, I guess I'm surprised. My legs twitch with excitement. "But I don't think I'm supposed to . . ." The woman trails off.

"Is he here?" I ask, jumping up on my toes. "We just want to talk to him. I think he knew my mom. My dead mom." I throw that last bit in for sympathy points.

The woman is darting her eyes around like she's not sure she should be speaking to us. "I'm just a docent," she says after a long pause. "A volunteer." She holds up the fossil again. "I can tell you anything you want to know about hooves."

Behind us, an elephant trumpet-snorts while a group of girls not that much older than I am snaps selfies and squeals.

I squint at the woman. "Look, I know we're just kids, but this is important."

Nothing. I get nothing.

I huff and turn around, ready to give up and try to pry info out of the hot dog guy not too far away. That's when Jax looks right at me, hunches his neck into the collar of his coat, and gives me his not-so-cool-guy smirk, along with a tiny shoulder shrug that I'm pretty sure means, *Why not?*

I spin back around to the lady. "Would you tell this guy?" I ask, jerking a thumb toward Jax. When the woman blinks at him, confused, I tell her, "Seriously? You don't recognize him? This is international pop sensation Jackson Gato."

She only shrugs, and I don't blame her. I'm more certain than ever that Jax did *not* get his sister free fro-yo.

"Anyway," I say to Jax. "Thanks for try—"

But that's all I get out, because suddenly I hear piercing squeals behind me. I turn to see the group of girls, who must've come up behind us just as Jax started acting "cool."

"No *way*!" one of them shrieks. "Are you *really* that guy?" And then I overhear another one saying she's seen his video—which is nonsense, obviously, because there is no Jackson Gato and there is no video—but before I can say any of that, the girls are totally fawning all over Jax, begging him for autographs and taking selfies with him, and they're *everywhere*, there must be at least a dozen of them, and then somehow one of the girls has actually ripped Jax's jacket right off his back, and he is freaking out, he is absolutely *freaking out*.

I flash my hands at him. A question.

With a quick bob of his head, he answers, *Yes, please*. His chest is heaving hard. I need to help him escape right this exact minute.

When I'm sure I have Jax's attention, I dart my gaze toward the blocked-off construction area right behind him, signaling, *That way*. Then, turning to the girls, I squeal louder than any of them. *"Oh, my god, it's James Darek!"* I screech, and I point way off, past the hot dog guy.

The girls turn away from Jax, just for a second. Just long enough for him to bolt for the construction area. By the time the girls look back and notice he's missing, he has slipped between two plywood boards and safely out of sight.

"James Darek went that way," I tell the girls, pointing around a far corner. "He's even more famous than Jackson Gato." And I watch the girls squeal off, two of them fighting over Jax's coat. I'm left alone with the woman behind the cart, who's clutching her hoof fossil, staring at me like *I'm* the weirdo.

"Whole lot of help you were," I tell her. And then, when I'm sure the coast is clear, I sneak inside the construction zone to find Jax.

"You okay?" I ask him. He nods. He is shaken but in one

piece. He scratches his goose-pimply bare arm. And then he points, straight ahead.

"Look," he tells me. And that's when I finally take in where we've found ourselves.

All around us, giant metal mushrooms are sprouting out of the ground, tilting and twirling their way into the sky. Some are stump size, some as big as small trees. The larger ones are miniature towers, with windy staircases inside and teeny windows for kids' faces to peer through. The mushroom jungle isn't finished, obviously. Two-by-fours and power tools litter the ground. Tarps cover several blobby structures. But what we can see of the exhibit is beautiful. I can imagine children scrambling and climbing over and through it all as parents laugh and snap photos.

"Neat, right?" comes a voice from across the site. It's a woman, short and bony in jeans and a puffy black vest with a hard hat on her head. "You the chairman's kids? Lila and . . . Sam, was it?"

"No, we're—"

"Wait till you see the full effect." The woman flips a switch.

"Wow," I breathe, just as Jax says, *"Whoa."*

Light. There is light everywhere. Each mushroom cap glows a different color. Yellow light, blue light, purple, green. It is radiant.

"Go ahead," says the woman. "Touch one."

I step forward into the exhibit and place my hand on the cap of a glowing-blue mushroom. The light embraces my palm, growing brighter around my fingers. When I lift my hand, the light disappears altogether, then leapfrogs to the mushroom just beside it. I slap at that mushroom cap, and the light hops away again.

"It's amazing," I tell the woman as she steps nearer.

"Be sure to tell your dad, will you?" she says. "Ask him to up my budget."

Jax gives me a look, and I know what he's thinking. Truth. Truth is best.

"We're not the chairman's kids," I say. "We're looking for the artist. James Darek. This is Jax, and I'm CJ."

The way the woman's mouth drops open then, you'd think I was some sort of spirit.

"Caraway June?" she says. Breathes the name out like air.

"I . . ." All I can do is blink at her. "How . . . ?"

But then I notice the tendrils of dark curly hair peeking out from under her hard hat. The features of her face, familiar and yet different. The same as in all my photographs, only older. And suddenly, she's smiling at me. Big as the sun. Like she's just so thrilled to see me.

"Mom?" I say.

ELEVEN

"OKAY," I SAY. "Okay, okay, okay, okay, okay."

"So you're feeling . . ." Jax begins. "Okay?"

"Well, obviously, *no*."

It's just me and Jax at the moment. After a good two minutes of me and my mom blinking at each other, not really knowing exactly what to say because how could we, someone started hollering at her about a mushroom exhibit emergency. So she's meeting us at the food court for lunch after everything is sorted. In the meantime, I'm in the gift shop helping Jax find a sweatshirt for his frozen arms.

Oh, yeah, and I'm totally freaking out, too.

"Are you *positive* that's your mom?" Jax asks, flipping through sweatshirts on the rack. He gestures back in the direction of the exhibit. "She's really alive?"

"I'm sure," I say. I've studied enough pictures of her that I could pick her out of a crowd of a million curly-haired ladies. But there was something else, too. A feeling. Maybe it was a mother-daughter bond, maybe it was an extra push from

Spirit, but whatever it was, it was real. "It's her. And she looked alive to me."

"So . . ." Jax stretches the word out like he's waiting for me to go on. When I don't, he asks me, "What are you, uh, thinking?" The way he says it, it's like I'm a balloon he's worried about popping.

"What am I thinking?" I repeat. I count off all the thoughts bumping around in my head. "Okay, so my mom's not dead. Which means she's alive. Which means she's *been* alive. Which means she's been living *somewhere* this whole time—and maybe I don't know where she's been, or why, but I know she's definitely never been Far Away. Which means my aunt was lying or confused or who knows what. Which means *Who the heck was Aunt Nic talking to that whole time?* Which means everything my mom told me, about boarding school, or the routes I was planning, or these shoes"—I kick out one foot to show off my gray sneakers, which I *thought* my mom and I once had a pretty good conversation about—"never even happened. Which means I never really met her, right? Only I must've met her, because she's my mom. Only I don't remember that at all. And did she draw those pictures of me because she *saw* me, like, she *lived* with me? Because if she lived with me, then Aunt Nic obviously *knew* she wasn't dead. Which means Aunt Nic *was* lying. Which means . . ."

I get a flash of a memory of Aunt Nic's hands in my wet

hair, massaging my scalp under the warm water in the motor home sink, while she passed down messages from my mom. Was Aunt Nic really lying when she said those words? What other words has she been lying about? And was Roger right, that Aunt Nic can't talk to *any* spirits, or was my mom's the only spirit she faked? All of a sudden, it's like every single thing I know about who my aunt is, who my mom is, who *I* am—it's all a lie.

I turn back to the rack of sweatshirts, because that's way easier to focus on than my world exploding. "Here," I tell Jax, yanking one off the rack. "This is your size, right?"

Jax wrinkles his nose at the sweatshirt, and as soon as he does I can tell why. The one I've pulled out is neon aqua, with a giant black silhouette of a panda and puffy letters that read, I ♥ THE SAN DIEGO ZOO! Not exactly Jax's style. But I guess I must really look like a popped balloon, because before I can put the sweatshirt back, Jax grabs it from me and says, "It's perfect. I love it."

"Shut up, no you don't," I tell him, moving to return it to the rack. "You don't have to humor me or whatever, just because my aunt ruined my whole life by making me think my mom was dead."

"I mean, yeah, that's the worst," Jax agrees. "But on the bright side"—he whips the sweatshirt from my hands—"you have *amazing* taste in outerwear. Now, if you'll excuse me, I'm

gonna go buy this, because I think it will look fantastic on me."
I snort. But okay, I guess it worked, because I'm smiling, just a little, now.

We're waiting in line to pay for the ugliest zoo sweatshirt in history when Jax says, "If you want to leave, you know, we can." His voice is soft, like he doesn't need everyone around us knowing my business, which is nice of him. Maybe that's the sort of thing his grandpa wanted him to help me out with. "I mean, this is a lot for you to deal with right now. So maybe we should just go find your mom and figure out a time for you guys to hang out, like, tomorrow, or next week, when your brain's had a minute to catch up."

I appreciate Jax looking out for my brain, but I shake my head. "My whole life," I tell him, "I thought my mom was dead, and now Spirit leads me right to her?" I stick my hand in my coat pocket. Feel the cool, rough cement of that tether, speckled with glass. "Nah, I'm sticking around to see what happens."

The person in front of us finishes up, and we step to the register. "Okay," Jax says. "But if you need an escape . . ." And he flashes his hands at me.

"Thanks," I say, and I smile. And while Jax is paying way too much money for his new sweatshirt, I make up my mind. Since Spirit led me right here, today, I'm going to make the most of meeting my mom. There will be tons of time to deal with Aunt Nic and all the awful things she did later—but for now, I'm just going to focus on the good stuff. My real-life mom, who smiled big as the sun when she saw me.

. . .

"Don't like mustard, huh?" my mom asks as we leave the Sabertooth Grill register with burgers on our trays. And then, as we're settling ourselves at a table, she says, "Check." Like she's making a list of things I like and don't so she can remember everything about me. Just that tiny word makes millions of happiness bubbles fizz up into my chest. *I'm sitting next to my mom,* I can't stop thinking. *My mom is alive. And she wants to know me.*

I am *humming* with happiness.

"And you really like mayonnaise," I note, eyeing the three tiny paper cups she's filled.

"On burgers, mayonnaise is good," she says. "But on french fries"—she slides me a paper cup of my own—"it's heaven. I promise." She says that last part with a laugh when she sees my wrinkled-up nose. "Try it."

So. I pluck a french fry off my tray and dip it in the mayonnaise. I'm pretty sure it's going to be disgusting, but it's the first thing my mom's ever asked me to do, so I do it.

It tastes *amazing.* "Oh, wow." Somehow the salt in the fry is a perfect match for the creaminess of the mayonnaise.

"Right?" she says, and she's smiling. It's a smile that says she can't believe how lucky she is that I stumbled into this spot, in this moment, and found her. I'm pretty sure my own smile says the same thing.

"I'm never eating fries with ketchup again," I tell her.

My mom claps her hands together. "Another convert!" She slides a mayonnaise cup in Jax's direction as he wedges himself into the bench beside me. "What do you think, sir?"

"I don't eat mayonnaise that's been squirted from a tub," he replies, and my mom lets out a hoot like she finds him just delightful.

I snag Jax's mayonnaise cup from him and dunk another fry. Fine with me if he doesn't want to try it. I'm sort of glad my mom and I have something that's just ours together.

"So," Jax says to my mom—and I guess I should take it as a good sign that my mom is one new person he actually wants to talk to. He unscrews the cap of his water bottle and darts his eyes at me before asking, "Why does everyone think you're dead, and who's James Darek?"

It's silent for a moment after that, no one talking, and I shift my butt uncomfortably on the metal bench. Because, I mean, okay, it's not like I wasn't wondering the exact same thing, but it seems a little rude, maybe, to just *ask* like that. What if my mom gets offended and leaves, after Spirit went to all this trouble to get us together?

But my mom just lets out another laugh—a whipping-back-her-head-and-showing-off-all-her-teeth sort of laugh. Which is a good thing for Jax, because if something he said made my mom leave, I'd make sure *he* was a spirit.

"So, enough with the small talk, huh?" my mom asks. That grin is still on her face.

Jax darts his eyes at me again. Picks up his water bottle but doesn't take a sip. "It just seems like important information," he says.

He *is* nervous, I realize. I can tell by the way his eyes flit all over when he's talking. Me, my skin is still tingling with happiness. My mom could talk to me about mayonnaise for an hour and I'd want to hear it all. *My mom,* I keep thinking. *My mom.*

"Fair enough," my mom says in response to Jax's question. She takes another bite of fry. "I guess the easiest answer is that James Darek is me. Although I'm pretty sure *somebody*"—she winks at me—"already figured that out."

I grin and dunk another fry. "Why'd you change your name?" I ask.

She shrugs, like the answer is so simple. "I started hearing rumors that Nic was going around telling people I'd died. I guess for her, it was a business decision, made her look more sympathetic, maybe, or more like a realistic ghost-whisperer, I don't know. Anyway, I was struggling a lot, back then, and I thought—maybe that's not the worst business decision for me, either. So I let people believe Jennie June was dead, and I started over as James. *J. Ames*. Nice, right? The 'Darek' part just had a ring to it. My career's skyrocketed since I changed it."

"So," I say slowly. Because my skin may be humming with happiness, but there are a million other emotions just under the surface, and I'm worried that if I let one sneak through they'll all come flying out, and then this nice buzzy happiness might buzz right away. "Aunt Nic just decided to tell me you were *dead*? For her *business*?"

Even though I've only just met her, my mom knows exactly how to calm the rising storm inside me. She reaches across the table and squeezes my hand, her grip warm and comforting. "Please don't blame your aunt, all right?" she says kindly. "There's so much I regret about what happened. The truth is, I had a rough time of it, after you were born. I was so young, and Nic always had a better knack than I did for taking care of people—you know my mother had Alzheimer's, right?"

I nod. "She died about a year before I was born," I say, but it's half a question. Because who knows if anything I think is true really is.

"That's right," my mom replies, and I let out a breath I didn't know I was holding. One thing about my life, at least, is true. "Our mother had a rough few years, so Nic left college to take care of her. She was a real saint to do it. So when you were on the way, I knew Nic would help me out, too. She was amazing. *Is* amazing." Suddenly my mom flashes her eyes at me, like she's just so excited to see me. "Just look at you, Cara!" she says. "You are *stunning* in blue, you know that?"

It takes me a second before I realize "Cara" means *me*.

"Uh, I go by CJ," I tell her. I feel weird having to tell my own mother my name. And I hate Aunt Nic even more for keeping me away from my mom so long that she doesn't know what to call me.

But the anger dies down as soon as my mom reaches out and tucks one of my stray curls behind my ear. "CJ's lovely," she says. "It suits you. You're a beautiful girl, you know." And in that moment, I'm so filled with happiness I'd swear I could float.

"Can I say the thing I don't get, though?" Jax asks. I can tell by the sound of his voice that I'm about to lose my floaty feeling. "How come you couldn't be James Darek *and* take care of CJ?" He still hasn't touched the hamburger in front of him. "What happened?"

I shoot Jax a *What's the matter with you?* look, but he doesn't even notice. "You can ignore him," I tell my mom. Floating. I want to be floating. "We don't have to talk about it if you don't—"

"No, I don't mind," my mom says. She gives my hand one more squeeze before reaching for her fries again. "I think the simplest answer is that Nic thought she could provide for you better than I could. And I can't say she was entirely wrong. I was never good at the sorts of jobs that get you paid." She lets out a little laugh. "This gig is bigger than anything I've ever done"—she waves her arms at the zoo around us—"but I'm still eating lettuce sandwiches three nights a week. But I always thought, as soon as I make something of myself, I'm going to get that girl back."

And just like that, I'm floating again. Soaring, really.

"You mean it?" I ask. The words are delicate, like tissue paper. "You'd really want to live with me?"

Sunshine on the beach, that's what my mother's smile is like. "I'd have to be out of my mind *not* to want that, my darling girl," she says. And I smile back. "I've been working so hard, CJ." My mom sets down her burger and leans in close to ask me, "Do you like the exhibit?"

Her eyes are eager as she waits for the answer. And when I say I think her mushroom jungle is pretty spectacular, her smile nearly grows bigger than her face.

My mom tells me all about the exhibit—how long it will take to complete, and what materials she's using, and how when the zoo contacted her she was "smack-me-on-my-butt bowled over!" Her face lights up bright as the sun while she talks about her work, so I keep asking questions, and she keeps talking. Meanwhile, my brain is buzzing, same as my skin. I'm going to live with my mom. No boarding school. No tour bus filled with liars. Just me and my mom. I wonder what her house looks like. Bright and sunshiny like her, I bet. I wonder what we'll eat for dinner, and what we'll do on weekends. Play board games, like me and Aunt Nic do sometimes? Probably something even better. Suddenly I picture us traveling. Mini-adventures, just us two. I'll navigate and she'll pick all the coolest, artiest spots I'd never think to visit.

"I've been working with the mushroom theme since I was a kid," my mom goes on, still talking about her exhibit. I do my best to tune back in, to focus. "I think I always liked the idea of life growing from decay and darkness. Mushrooms just *triumph*, you know?"

I love how passionate my mom is, about things I would never think to be passionate about.

I pull the cement mushroom cap out of my pocket to show her. "I found this today," I tell her. "In the backyard of your old house." Maybe the mushroom cap isn't exactly a tether, the way it normally works. But Spirit did use it to pull us together, now didn't they?

"Oh, wow." She takes it from me and cradles it in her hands, like it's a favorite pet she hasn't seen in ages. "You must've thought your mother was some kind of nutcase when you saw that barbecue pit, huh?"

"I thought it was incredible," I tell her seriously.

"I think *you're* incredible," she replies. And then—well,

it will take more than a cement mushroom cap to keep me tethered to Earth after that. "Just you wait, CJ," she says, pushing her tray toward me so I can eat more of her fries. "A few more years and I'll have saved up enough so we can finally be together for good, like we always should've been."

And just like that, I'm crashing again. *"Years?"* I repeat.

I don't realize I've started to cry until my mom grabs my hand again. "Oh, CJ," she says. "Oh, honey." Her face is as pained as I feel, and I hate that I've made her look like that. "Is she really so terrible, your aunt?"

I want to explain, about Aunt Nic's hands in my hair, making me care about her, making me think she cared about me. But all that comes out is a squawk.

"I'm so sorry, CJ," my mom says, and she's hugging me then, warm as her smile. "I wish I'd had someone else to turn to all those years ago. I really do, for your sake. But my parents were gone, and your father wasn't exactly in the picture." When she sees the question starting up inside me, she explains, "I'm afraid that's my fault, too. It was a short-lived love affair, and by the time I knew about *you* . . ."

One more tiny check in the "truth" column for Aunt Nic.

"But here you are now," my mom says. "And you're *perfect*."

That smile. I could get used to that smile.

I've honestly forgotten Jax is even sitting at the table with us until his phone rings. "Um," he says, checking the screen.

"It's your aunt." He says it like he's worried I might dump mayonnaise from a tub on him just for telling me. "You want me to answer it, or . . . ?"

"Just hang up," I snap. I never want to talk to Aunt Nic again.

"I mean," Jax says slowly. The phone keeps ringing, the same stupid song. "She's probably, like, worried about you?"

"Good!"

That's when my mom reaches for the phone. "Let me," she says. Before I can stop her, she presses the green button on the screen. "Nic!" she says into the phone, bright as sunshine. "Guess who?" There's a pause, and I don't know what Aunt Nic is saying, but my mom smiles as she tells her, "Cara found me." She reaches for my hand across the table, correcting herself. "*CJ*, sorry."

My mom squeezes my hand again, and I try to soothe the remaining bubbles inside me. Rage. Shock. Disgust. Jax keeps trying to meet my gaze, but I don't need to know how sorry he feels for me.

"She figured that one out on her own, Nic," my mom is saying. "She's a smart girl. Beautiful, too. Thank goodness she didn't get Dad's nose." Suddenly my mom seems irritated. "Well, I'm not the one who lied to her her whole life." Whatever Aunt Nic says then, my mom narrows her eyes to slits. "*That* was uncalled for."

"CJ," Jax whispers at me across the table. "*CJ.*"

I finally look over at him. "Yeah?" I'm trying to listen to my mom's end of the conversation, but apparently Jax has something super urgent he needs to share.

"Are you okay?" he asks me.

I only squint at him. I have no idea how to answer that question.

By the time I tune back in to the conversation, my mom is pulling the phone from her ear. She stretches it out to me. "Your aunt would like to talk to you," she says.

"What do you want?" I bark into the phone. My voice is a wolf. A *lion*. I hope it hurts to hear it.

"CJ," Aunt Nic says. She sounds sad, sorry even, but I know enough now not to believe anything that comes out of her mouth. "There's . . . a lot we need to talk about, obviously."

I do not respond.

"I don't want to do this over the phone. We'll talk when you get back here." Another pause. "This must be very confusing for you, CJ."

"I'm not confused at all," I tell her.

"Your mom's going to meet us after tomorrow's show in Oceanside. We can all talk. Together. We'll take as much time as you need, then head out to Phoenix the next morning. Sound good?"

"Not as good as knowing my mom my whole life," I reply.

Aunt Nic takes a deep breath. "Please tell Jax to drive safely, all right? I'll see you in a few hours. I love you so much, CJ."

I hang up the phone.

.   .   .

I do not want to leave. I do not. But my mother needs to get back to work, and anyway, she assures me, she'll see me tomorrow.

"You okay?" Jax asks me again as we climb the on-ramp to the freeway. It's the first thing that wasn't about shifting he's said to me since we got back in the truck.

"Yeah," I reply. Together we upshift till the truck is humming smooth and we're well on our way. "Why wouldn't I be? I met my mom today. And . . ." I stare out the window as the cars zoom by. Did I ever pass by my mom, on a highway like this, and not realize it was her? "I think I finally get it now."

"Get what?" he asks.

There's a new sort of bubble that's rising up in me, lighter and swifter and warmer than all the others. The tiniest bubble of hope.

"I know why Spirit sent me here," I tell him. "For real this time."

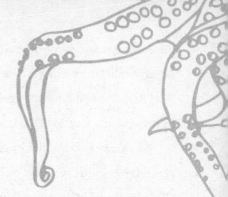

TWELVE

"ARE YOU SURE about this?" Jax asks me as I bite into my vanilla cupcake with thick chocolate frosting. One thing I can say about Jax—he has a knack for picking good dessert places. This one's called the Sweetest Thing, right outside of San Clemente, still an hour's drive from L.A. "You really want to try to live with your mom?"

"It's what *Spirit* wants," I clarify. "And anyway, why wouldn't I? Most kids live with their moms. And she said she's been trying to get me back my whole life. You heard that, right?" I never was supposed to go to boarding school. That was just another thing Aunt Nic made up. She kicked my mom out of her life to have me all to herself, and now she's kicking *me* out because she doesn't want to share the spotlight once she's a reality TV star.

Not that she *will* be a reality TV star.

Not that I'd want to live with her anymore anyway.

"I heard your mom say she never had the money to come get you," Jax replies, twisting his cupcake around on its little plate. He made a point of grabbing a knife and fork before we sat down, like he thinks he needs them to eat a cupcake.

"Right? Maybe we can get the zoo to give her a raise. I mean, you saw that exhibit. It's awesome."

Jax looks up from his cupcake—salted caramel with mango glaze. I thought it sounded weird when he ordered it, but actually it looks delicious. "But you just met her," he says.

"I just met you, too," I argue.

"Right," Jax says like I'm agreeing with him, which I'm not. "And if I asked you to move in with me, it would be weird."

"Oh, Jax," I say in a fake swoony voice. I clasp my hands under my chin like one of those ladies in old-fashioned movies who can't stop fainting. "I had no idea you had such *feelings* for me!"

"What I *meant* was," Jax says, darting embarrassed eyes at the couple glancing our way, "you hardly know anything about your mom. So how can you know if you want to live with her?"

"She's my *mother*," I tell him. I don't see why any of this is so hard to understand. "And anyway, if Spirit wants me to live with her, I don't have a choice, really. It's what I *have* to do."

Jax is frowning. "I think you always have a choice about your own life, CJ," he says.

I let out a huff. "You're not being super helpful right now," I tell him. "Didn't you say your grandpa wanted you to help me?"

Jax carefully peels down one side of his cupcake wrapper. "If that *was* Abuelo sending me a message," he says, "then he was probably telling me to *look out* for you." He stops peeling and meets my gaze. "Which is different from helping."

There is a smidge of chocolate frosting on my thumb. I lick it off.

"I just keep thinking," Jax says as he starts peeling again, "that you didn't talk to your mom your whole life because you thought she was dead. But she knew *you* were alive. So how come she never tried to talk to you?"

I roll my eyes. "She told us that. My aunt took me away from her, and then she lied to me about it." If it weren't for Aunt Nic, I'd be an artist's kid in San Diego right now. I'd wear blue every day, and I'd already know how great french fries were with mayonnaise, and probably a million other things, too.

"Maybe you should talk to your aunt before you get mad about it. Just hear her side of the story."

"You really think there's anything Aunt Nic could tell me that would make it okay that she lied like that?"

When he doesn't answer for a while, I think it might be the end of the conversation—maybe Jax will start discussing the baking soda in the cupcakes, or something equally boring. But he doesn't. Instead he says, "Abuelo used to always tell me about what it was like when he ran away as a kid, back in Quito. Like how for three days, he lived off of these little oranges, and how after he finished reading the book he'd brought with him he wrote his own stories in the margins so he wouldn't get bored."

I take a sip of water from my paper cup. I don't know why Jax is telling me this, but I can tell it's important, so I try to listen.

"And all that stuff was true, I think," Jax goes on, "but Abuelo always made it sound like this fun adventure. But then the night of his funeral, we were all up super late playing Cuarenta—that's this card game Abuelo loved. I don't think anyone wanted to stop playing, because once we stopped, the night would be over, you know?"

He pauses, and I nod.

"And after a while, my dad and my aunt started telling all these stories about Abuelo I'd never heard before, that were, like, *sort of* what Abuelo'd told me, but not totally. They said he hid in his neighbor's yard for a whole week, using a tarp for a blanket. And he got so sick from eating all those oranges, he never ate any again. Which, once they said that I realized, yeah. I'd never seen him eat one, ever. It was like my whole life, I'd heard one story." He suddenly tugs my half-eaten cupcake toward him, with the bite marks chiseled into the chocolate frosting. "And it was *true*, what Abuelo told me, but it was fluffy, you know? Pretty. Like chocolate frosting."

"Chocolate frosting?" I ask. Mostly I want my cupcake back.

"But the story my dad and my aunt told me"—he picks up

his cupcake, with the glaze—"it was *messy*. Definitely not as sweet. But it also . . . It seeped into all the little cracks I never noticed before." He turns the cupcake this way and that, and I can see the cake through the white-orange glaze, and the tiny dots of holes in the cake's surface. "It let me see more of what really happened."

When I'm sure Jax is finished, I point to the chocolate-frosted cupcake across the table and tell him, "I was still eating that." I half mean it as a joke, but Jax doesn't seem to think it's very funny. He slides the cupcake back my way.

"I just think," Jax goes on, "what your mom said today, about why she left—it seemed like a chocolate frosting sort of truth. And I think maybe you should wait for the mango-glaze truth before you decide anything for sure."

Here's what I think, though.

Jax Delgado may be four years older than me, but that doesn't mean he knows everything about my life, or my mom.

I reach for my cupcake. Chocolate frosting and all.

"I think this truth tastes just fine," I tell him. And I cram the whole thing into my mouth.

.   .   .

We don't speak much the whole way back to the theater. The only sounds in the truck are the whirring of the gears and every once in a while a *"Ready-and-clutch!"* But when we zoom past the theater, with the tour bus parked out front, I have to speak up.

"You missed the turn!" I tell Jax, moving in my seat to watch the theater shrink behind us. "Flip a U at the next light."

"Your aunt wanted me to drop you off at a diner," Jax says. "It's up here. She texted me while we were stopped for gas. She said if I dropped you off, you couldn't run away, and then you'd *have* to talk to her."

I harrumph into my seat. "I wasn't going to run away like your grandpa and live on *oranges*," I grumble. "I'm not doing anything"—I search for the word that Grant used before—"impetuous." I just need to keep my eyes open for another sign from Spirit. They'll tell me how to find the money my mom needs to take me in. In the meantime, I do not want to go to a diner with my lying aunt. "Just stay out of it, Jax. You're not my big brother. Turn around up here." He zips through the intersection. "Jax!"

"Why can't you just talk to her?" he asks. "Listen to what she has to say. Then make up your mind."

"Because she's a *liar*," I reply. I feel hot just thinking about it. Like anger is a feeling you can wear on your skin. "Do you not get that? Everything she's ever told me, my whole life, is a lie." I let myself laugh at her stupid jokes, I let her do my stupid hair, I let myself *care* about what she thought, and the whole time, she was lying. Everything was a lie. "So it doesn't matter what she has to say now, because it will just be more lies. You were the one who was so sure she was a crook, back at the mansion. And now you're totally on her side?"

"I just think, even if she's lying about stuff, maybe she has a good reason. And you've known her way longer than you've known your mom, so why not *listen* to her?"

He's scratching his arm.

"You don't want to go home," I say slowly, starting to piece things together. We're passing hotels, office buildings, a police station. All the while we're nearing the one person I'd give anything to avoid. "You want to keep working for my aunt so you don't have to go back to Florida, and if you think she's some horrible liar, then *you'll* feel bad. Right? Is that it?" He doesn't answer. "I thought your grandpa told you to look out for me."

"I *am* looking out for you, CJ." But he's still scratching his arm.

"You keep telling me that," I say as we whiz through another intersection. I see the diner, two lights away. "But you're the one who needs a twelve-year-old to rescue you."

Jax doesn't say anything else until we're turning into the diner parking lot. "I'm going to park right in front of the door," he tells me. "Then I'm going to wait until you walk in."

"You're being ridiculous," I grumble. "You can't even get back to the theater if you leave me here."

"I'll call Uncle Oscar to come help me," he replies calmly. For some reason that calmness makes me even more furious.

"If you don't pull out of this parking lot right this second," I tell him, "I'm going to make *sure* Aunt Nic fires you."

He finds a spot and shuts off the truck without even making it buck. I can see Aunt Nic at a booth inside. She jumps up and waves as soon as she spots us.

"Thanks for the ride," I tell Jax, scooping my messenger bag and the orange box off the cab floor.

"CJ!" he calls as I jump out.

But I only slam the truck door. Because there's nothing left for him to say.

. . .

I let Aunt Nic wrap me up in a hug when I walk into the diner, because I don't want to make a scene. But everywhere her skin meets mine burns like fire.

We slide into the booth's high-back maroon seats, and I set the orange box beside me, and my messenger bag, too. Feeling the bag's smooth leather makes me mad all over again—because it's such a perfect present, and I don't want to love something that has anything to do with Aunt Nic.

Luckily, the waitress comes over right away, so there are two more minutes of my life I don't have to spend talking to my aunt. Aunt Nic orders pasta primavera, even though it looks gross in the photo. I get french fries. "Can you put mayonnaise on the side?" I ask the waitress. And when Aunt Nic raises her eyebrows, I don't bother to explain.

The waitress slides our menus under her arm. "Do I know you from somewhere?" she asks Aunt Nic. Her name tag reads SYLVIE. "TV or something?"

Aunt Nic opens her mouth to answer, but then looks at me and pauses. "I've never been on TV," she tells Sylvie. "Thought I might be, but it looks like that's not gonna happen."

The waitress spends one more second blinking at Aunt Nic, then says, "Food'll be right out," and leaves to place our order.

"So," I say, slapping my hands on the table. "Why'd you tell me my mom was dead?"

Aunt Nic wraps both hands around her water glass, and when she pulls them away again they are wet with condensation. "I'm really sorry you had to find out about your mom this way, CJ. But I'm glad, at least, that the truth is out there."

"The *truth*?" I say with a sneer. "You told me my mom was drawn Far Away, that I could never talk to her again. You told me our *house* burned down." I blink at her. "Was that just so I wouldn't try to find her?" When Aunt Nic doesn't answer right away, I dig the cement mushroom cap out of my coat pocket, thump it on the table. "Your plan didn't work," I say.

Aunt Nic shakes her head. "Your mom was supposed to

clear her stuff out of that house, soon as we left, then I'd sell it. It was as good as . . ." She looks down at the mushroom cap on the table. "I'm sorry, CJ. I never should've lied about that."

"All you've ever done is lie to me."

Aunt Nic's face looks pained, like I've hurt her. Good.

"That's not entirely fair," she replies.

"Name one thing that hasn't been a lie."

"I love you," she says immediately. "I've always loved you."

"Well, you're sure great at showing it," I tell her.

Aunt Nic doesn't fight back, like I expect her to. What she says, her voice soft, is, "Do you remember when you were seven or eight and the motor home broke down? We had to stay for a week in Long Beach? Not too far from here."

I remember. That week was one of my favorites. We found a tidal pool and spent hours searching for starfish, even though it was January and frigid. We went up on the boardwalk way after dark, when everything was shut down, and ate pretend cotton candy and sang at the top of our lungs, because there was no one to hear us but the dolphins. Aunt Nic even helped me hop the gate on the Ferris wheel so we could sit in the bottom car, our feet dangling off the edge while we watched the dark waves crash on the shore. And I remember we were sitting like that, just us two, when it started to snow, right there on the beach. It never snows in Long Beach. Not ever. It was magical. I remember.

"Maybe," I say with a shrug.

"I tried to tell you that week," she says slowly. "About your mom. About everything. It was such a perfect night, that last day on the boardwalk, and I thought, 'Maybe once CJ knows, it could always be like this. No more wandering all over the place. We could get a little house and live right here in this town, and come up on the boardwalk every evening.' I wanted to tell you then. I really did."

"So why didn't you?"

She nudges her water glass back and forth across the table. Back and forth. "You were so happy," she says at last. And she smiles a sad little smile. "I guess I didn't want to ruin it."

But I think I know the real reason. Because if she had told me the truth that day, she knew I'd never want to see her again as long as I lived.

I'm about to say just that when our waitress comes over and plops our food on the table. "Sorry to interrupt, ladies!" she says, way too cheerful. "Enjoy your meal!"

Aunt Nic picks up her fork. "I think servers like to wait around the corner for the exact *worst* time to come to the table," she says, and she gives me a look like even though I'm so mad I'll have to smile.

I do not.

Aunt Nic sighs and sets down her fork. "I know you're mad at me, CJ," she says. "Of *course* you are. And I should've told you, only it kept getting harder and harder. And then with the reality show starting—when I thought there was a reality show—I was worried it was all building into this huge tower of lies. And I think I thought . . ." She picks up her fork again. "I told myself that if you were away at boarding school, away from all this"—she waves her fork around the restaurant, toward the theater, herself, everything—"then maybe it wouldn't affect you if the tower fell. Maybe you'd never find out about the lies, or if you did it would seem like so long ago that it wouldn't matter so much. But that was stupid." She stabs a noodle with her fork. "Obviously all of this has affected you more than I intended."

"But why did you take me from my mom in the first place?" My voice comes out cracked, like I'm sad instead of angry, which is not right at all.

Aunt Nic opens her mouth slowly, then closes it. Squints at me. "CJ," she says after a moment. "You just don't know what your mom is like."

"I *do* know," I reply. "She's nice. And she's funny. She's . . ." The way she lit up the whole zoo, just talking. Her sunshine-warm smile. "She's amazing."

"She is," Aunt Nic agrees. "She is all those things. She's also flighty and unreliable and incredibly frustrating. She'd leave for the grocery store to get you formula and come back six hours later with balloons. You did not need balloons. Sometimes she'd be gone for *days*."

"You didn't have to make her leave," I say. My voice is a whisper.

The look Aunt Nic gives me then, it's like she feels sorry for me. It makes me hate her even more.

"Your mother left on her own," Aunt Nic tells me. "I just told her she couldn't come back."

Which is precisely, of course, the moment our waitress pops over to our table and asks, "How're we doing over here?"

"We're *fine*," I grumble.

The waitress nods, but she doesn't leave. She's staring at Aunt Nic, like she wants to ask her something but can't get up the nerve.

Of course this is happening now. Of course it is.

"Let me guess," I tell the waitress. Sylvie. "You just figured out where you know her from." I jerk my head toward Aunt Nic.

Sylvie nods quickly, excited but nervous, too. Her hand is shaking around the wad of straws in her apron pocket.

"Yes," she says. "Yeah. You're that lady from the internet videos. You talk to people." She glances at the customers at the other tables, then leans in close. "Dead people."

Aunt Nic shoots a look my way before responding. "That's me," she says.

"Oh, I just knew it!" And while half of me is annoyed that Sylvie's interrupting what is clearly a super-intense conversation, the other half is grateful not to have to look at my aunt for a minute. So while Sylvie whoops like Aunt Nic is the greatest human in the history of the world, I focus on folding my straw wrapper into an accordion.

"Well, if you're hearing the voice of a bald man with a super-gut," Sylvie tells Aunt Nic, "I just wanted to let you know he's probably trying to get in touch with me." And then she gives a little laugh, like she's joking, only obviously she's hoping Aunt Nic will say, "Yes, he's right here," and do a reading at the table.

I fold my straw-wrapper accordion. Nice even creases.

Aunt Nic takes a sip of her soda. I can feel the heat of her gaze as she tries to make eye contact with me, but I'm not looking. At last she says to Sylvie, "Is he the guy making all the bad jokes?"

Sylvie drops her whole wad of straws on the floor.

"No *way*," she says.

I switch to folding up my place mat corners.

"He's telling me someone missed the funeral," Aunt Nic goes on. And immediately Sylvie starts crying.

"I couldn't go," Sylvie says between blubbering. People from other tables are definitely starting to pay attention now. "The plane ticket was so expensive and . . . Who misses their own dad's funeral?"

I fold those place mat corners, totally ignoring all of it.

"Your dad's saying it's okay," Aunt Nic tells her. "*Please tell her to forgive herself,* he says. *She's my little . . .* He's showing me something goofy, like, a piece of food? Some nickname he had for you." She squints at Sylvie. "What is that? A cupcake or a . . . ?"

I stop folding.

"A buttered biscuit?" Sylvie asks, wiping at her face. "That's what he called me sometimes. His 'little buttered biscuit.'" She laughs, like she knows it's ridiculous.

"That's it!" Aunt Nic hoots. "Oh, he's laughing so hard now. He loves you so much, honey. He says, *I'm so lucky to get to see the young woman you're turning into.*"

I can't take it anymore.

"My aunt isn't talking to your dad," I tell the waitress. But I look right at Aunt Nic when I say it—and I guess I'm pretty pleased with the way her mouth falls open. "She can't talk to any spirits at all. She. Is. A. Liar."

"Uh . . ." Sylvie starts, confused.

Aunt Nic blinks at her. "Sorry about this," she tells Sylvie, meaning me. "My niece is just having a little bit of a tough time."

Sylvie puts her hands in the air, like *None of my business.* "I'll let you guys alone. Sorry I bothered you. But"—she bends down to scoop up the straws, then grips Aunt Nic's hand tight in her own, straws and all—"*thank you.* Seriously. That was . . . You're amazing." And she rushes off, stuffing the straws in her apron

185

pocket with one hand and wiping her tears with the other.

"'Buttered biscuit'?" I ask Aunt Nic when she turns back to face me. She takes a bite of her pasta and says nothing. "You didn't know that was her nickname. You didn't even know it was her dad she was talking about until she said so. You're not talking to *any* spirits, are you? You never were. Roger was right. You didn't just lie about my mom. You've been lying about *everything*. That lady's dad . . ." I say, nodding toward Sylvie over by the register. She keeps glancing our way as she talks to two other waiters excitedly. "He probably *is* trying to talk to her. And whatever message he needs to pass on, you got in the way." My voice is fire, like my skin. "What if that woman meets a real medium now, who actually *can* hear her dad, and she doesn't believe them, because of all the lies you told her first?" I fold my arms tight over my chest, to keep myself from bursting into a million angry pieces. "It's one thing to lie to me, and to other people. But you're messing with *Spirit*. Don't you even feel the tiniest bit bad about that?"

Aunt Nic doesn't bother to argue. She's too busy darting her eyes around the diner, like she's worried about someone overhearing. "I didn't plan on doing this for a living," she says at last. Which is no sort of apology at all. "It just sort of happened."

"Do Oscar and Cyrus know you're a phony?" I ask. Was that what Oscar meant, I wonder, when he told me not to search for answers?

Aunt Nic clears her throat. "They believe what they want," she says. "They don't ask a lot of questions."

I'm so furious right now, my face burns. I'm mad at myself for defending her. I'm mad for all the people she's lied to for so long. And I'm mad, too, for all the spirits who haven't been able to connect with their loved ones because she got in the way.

"How do you just *happen* to lie about something like that?" I say.

"It didn't start out as anything so . . ." Aunt Nic searches the diner again, then lowers her voice. "Back in college, I was in this theater troupe, and we'd do this mind-reading skit." She pokes at another forkful of pasta, while I glare at her. I even hate the way she eats now. "We'd pick someone out of the audience, and I'd pretend to read their mind. I didn't try to be good at it, I just was. It was easy. I just had to ask the right questions."

"And then you forgot to tell them it was all made up," I continue for her.

Aunt Nic spears more pasta but sets the fork down on her plate. "After your mom left—"

"After you kicked her out."

"I knew we needed a change. So we took off in that horrible motor home, no idea where we were headed, no job prospects. And the first RV park we landed in—the very first one, I swear—this little old lady asks me if I know anyone who can reach her dead husband. She wanted to pay for a reading. So"—she picks her fork back up—"I told her I could do it."

"You lied," I say. I haven't touched my fries. They don't look nearly as good as the ones I had with my mom.

"I felt awful that first time," she says. She's really digging into her pasta now, like the most important thing she needs to do is eat. "But the lady was so happy afterward, thinking she'd reached her husband again, and I thought, 'Well, *is* it so bad? If it helps her?'"

The worst part, maybe, is that I know she's partially right. She does make people happy. I've seen it. She made Sylvie happy five minutes ago.

But I remember, too, at Meg and Grant's house, how the tiniest lie can hurt someone more than you ever expected. And if she can't hear Spirit at all, then obviously she has no idea how they feel about anything.

I'd be willing to bet they're not thrilled.

I catch sight of the mushroom cap on the table then, beside my napkin. "And the tethers?" I ask. "Do you just pretend to pull spirits back to Earth when you're holding a tether? How can you know if you're pulling the spirit down or not? Why even bother?"

"Oh, I just made that all up," she replies, and she stabs three more pieces of pasta. *Stab, stab, stab.* "If I can't get a good sense of someone, I say their loved one's been drawn Far Away, so they'll bring me something useful to work off of." *Stab, stab.* "You can learn a lot from the stuff these people bring in. It's—" She cuts herself off when she notices someone nearing our table.

Back when I was six, I broke my leg at an RV park pool. Cracked my tibia like a pretzel stick doing cannonballs in too-shallow water. I nearly passed out from the pain in the ambulance. Couldn't even walk on the cast for a week.

This hurts worse.

I know I should be focusing on what Spirit wants me to do—to find enough money that I can move in with my mom. But all I can think of is Roger telling me, *The truth is out there, if you want to see it.* I wonder how thrilled he'd be now if he knew what I've found out.

"Call 'im."

That's what Aunt Nic says. Just like that.

"Huh?" I jerk my head up, heart thumping in my chest— and the first thing I see when I do is an octopus. It's a ring, on the finger of a new waiter at the edge of our table. The creature's silver tentacles wrap the waiter's index finger all the way up to the knuckle.

I suck in a deep breath.

"What an unusual name," Aunt Nic is telling the waiter. Neither one of them is looking at me. "Is it German, or . . ."

The waiter's name tag, I see, says CALLUM.

"It's Scottish," the waiter says. "'Kal-um.' Uh . . ." He twists his octopus ring around his finger. "Sylvie said that you could, uh, talk to someone for me?"

Aunt Nic glances at me, like she doesn't want to make me more mad, but the truth is I'm not even paying attention anymore. Not to her anyway.

Call him.

It's another sign from Spirit.

. . .

It isn't till we're back on the tour bus that Aunt Nic asks me, "What happened with Jax today, anyway? Oscar wants me to fire him."

I climb the loft ladder to my bedroom, examining the walls as I go. Knowing that there are pipes behind there, carrying water, even if I can't see or hear them. Wondering what kind of monster would lie about seeing pipes they really couldn't. Wondering how furious the pipes would be, and what they'd want to do about it.

"CJ?" Aunt Nic calls up when I don't answer. "Did you have any opinion about Jax?"

And I only tell her, "Mmm," and shut the curtain on her.

Because I'm saving all my words for someone else.

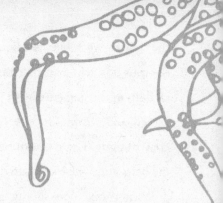

THIRTEEN

LAST TIME I was at the White Point Beach tidal pools with Aunt Nic, everything seemed bigger—the ocean was larger, the rocks were higher. Even the starfish seemed massive. Probably because I was so much younger back all those years ago when our motor home broke down, so compared to me everything else looked huge.

I guess things have changed a lot, since then.

By the time I hop off the city bus, it's well past dark, but the moon is round and huge tonight, and the floodlights in the nearby parking lot are more than enough for the few visitors to see by. I wrap my puffy blue coat tight around me as I pick my way down to the water's edge, the mushroom cap thumping against my hip. I know it's not a real tether—that maybe there's not even such a thing as tethers, if Aunt Nic really did make it up—but still, it's my mother's and I like knowing it's there. There are a few families down on the rocks searching for treasures with flashlights, and an older couple with tall hiking backpacks.

I tilt back on my heels as I wait. Every once in a while, I check

the time on my tablet, but I have at least an hour to get back to the tour bus before anyone misses me. Right now Aunt Nic will be deep in the audience, with Jax behind her trying to work the camera and the mics at once. I don't feel bad about ditching the crew tonight. There's nothing in this world that could make me help Aunt Nic ever again. I do feel a little bad that Jax is on probation—one more slip-up and he's straight back to Florida— but I tug my coat around me tighter and try to think about all the other beings, alive and dead, I'm going to be helping instead.

Roger is nearly twenty minutes late. When I finally spot him up on the bluff overlooking the water, I wave him down.

"I told you to bring a camera," I say as he joins me on the rocks.

"I must say, CJ," Roger replies, looking around, "of all the locations I've been summoned for covert meetings, this is by far the"—he sticks his hands in his pockets—"outdoorsy-est." Roger is not dressed for the beach. He's wearing black jeans and a dark bomber jacket, with black boots too nice to get wet.

"I wanted to make sure you couldn't pull any of your tricks," I tell him. "And I knew you liked fish."

He doesn't even chuckle. "Why am I here, CJ?"

"Get a camera, and I'll tell you. You said there was good money in it, right? If I say what I know about Aunt Nic? Well, I know she's a liar. And I think everyone else should, too."

Roger raises an eyebrow at me. "I convinced you?" he asks.

"This afternoon you didn't seem to hear a single word I was saying."

I look off at the fat, fat moon before telling him, "I met my mom." Then I glance back his way. "She's not a spirit, like my aunt said. She's been alive this whole time."

Roger doesn't move a muscle, not in his face or his body or anything. Just stands there on the rocks, watching me.

"I didn't get why I was supposed to find you earlier," I explain. "But I do now. Spirit wants me to help you, to expose Aunt Nic. All the signs line up, and everything works out perfectly." I count off on my fingers. "My mom gets her kid back. I don't have to go to boarding school. And Spirit gets to stop a total fraud from spreading lies about them."

Roger only rubs the stubble on his chin. This afternoon he was practically begging for my help, so you'd think that now that I'm offering it he'd be jumping up and down. But all he finally says is, "You must be pretty mad at your aunt right now, huh?" Which seems like a fairly annoying grown-up thing to say.

I let out a puff of air so huge it *fwoops* up my hair. "You think I'm just some dumb kid, don't you?" I ask. I reach up to readjust my headband.

"I think you believe a lot of things a dumb kid would believe," Roger tells me, his voice flat.

"That was mean," I answer.

"I thought you'd appreciate the truth. There are no such

things as 'spirits,' CJ. 'Far Away,' 'emotional energy' "—he puts air quotes around the words as he spits them out, like he can hardly stand the taste of them—"it's all fairy tales."

There are many things, I decide, to dislike about Roger Milmond. But probably the biggest one is the smug look he gets on his face when he's sure he's right. Like he's so sorry you have to be you and not him.

"Just because you don't believe in Spirit," I tell him, "doesn't make you smarter than me."

He looks out at the ocean and shakes his head slowly, exhausted from talking to me. "CJ, you know your aunt's a fraud. You said as much. So how can you think for a second that any other medium isn't? That there are any 'spirits' there to talk to in the first place?"

"Because I *know*." He wants the truth? That's it. "I've paid attention and I've seen the signs, things that just don't make sense otherwise. Spirit is there, whether you think they are or not."

"They're not," Roger says. "The Spirit world is an illusion, like a magician's trick onstage. And every medium is a liar, just like your aunt. It's that simple."

But here's what I know. Roger Milmond is standing on a craggy beach, on a chilly December evening, arguing with a twelve-year-old. "If it was that simple," I reply, "then you wouldn't need my help to prove it."

And for the first time all evening, Roger cracks a smile. "Well," he says, "you have me there."

"I'm ready for my interview anytime," I tell him. "And you better've been serious about the money."

He squints at me then. I think he's trying to figure me out. "There's money in a big interview, sure," he says. "But no one will hear what you're telling them unless they have a good reason to."

"So," I say, "get their attention first. Isn't that what you're good at? Fancy tricks? Fish tank walls and reappearing hot chocolate and octopus messages? Get people to listen, and then I'll tell them why they should."

Roger is giving me a look like I'm a cute puppy he found in a pet store window. "CJ," he says slowly, "when you came to me earlier, I told you everything I knew about your aunt. I presented you with scads of evidence about her lies. I could not have been more clear. And yet . . ." He stops, like he's waiting for me to finish the thought.

"I didn't believe you," I say.

"Bingo!" He tosses his hands in the air. "You didn't believe me because it was easier not to. You didn't believe me until you were shown something so undeniably true that you had no choice but to believe me. And whether I like it or not, that's human nature. This world would be a much better place if we were all purely rational creatures, but we're not. We're emotional. So we go along believing whatever suits us, until that belief runs us smack into a brick wall, and then we face the truth. What you made me realize today, CJ—and I guess it's my own brick wall I've been ignoring—is that if I want to convince people that your aunt uses cold reading to trick them, then I'll need to prove to *every single one of them*, without a shadow of a doubt, that she was lying directly to them. And that's just never going to happen."

The tide has been rising while we've been talking, and the rocks we're standing on are starting to get damp. I bend down, thinking I catch sight of something, a bit of movement. A hermit crab. I pluck it up by the shell.

"So thanks for the offer, CJ," Roger goes on, "but I think we truth-tellers can count this one as a loss." He glances back toward the parking lot. "Let me call you a cab, get you back to the theater."

"No," I say. And I feel calm. Because I know this is not how this ends. This is not what Spirit wants from either of us.

"No?"

I study the hermit crab. His tiny claws are flicking in and out of his shell, poking at the air. He's wondering, I bet, where he is, and why his world has changed so suddenly, and when it will all get back to normal.

I set the crab back down on the rocks, and he scuttles off to safety.

"I think you're right you can't prove Aunt Nic does cold reading," I tell Roger. I tug on the strap of my messenger bag. "But you're wrong that we can't prove anything."

And Roger just stands there, rubbing his chin, like *Go on*.

"What's that other kind of trick you were talking about," I ask, "back at the mansion? Where mediums dig up information about people beforehand?"

"Hot reading," Roger replies. "Although I believe I explained to you that it's definitely not what your aunt is doing."

I raise an eyebrow. "But her audience doesn't know that, do they?" And when Roger's eyes go wide, I unhook the latch on my messenger bag and slip out my tablet. "You told me all you'd need was somebody's email address, right, and then you could find out anything you wanted about them?"

"CJ," Roger says. "I'm . . . surprised." His hands are frozen in the air in front of him, like he *wants* to take the tablet but can't quite make himself grab it.

He also looks like he's deciding I might not be as dumb as he thought.

"You want the email addresses or not?" I ask.

He inches his fingers closer to the tablet. "Are you sure you want to prove that your aunt's been lying"—he picks over his words carefully—"by telling another lie?"

I look to the rocks, where the hermit crab found the place he was meant to be.

"If you see someone running straight for a brick wall," I tell Roger, "does it matter how you warn them?"

Roger takes the tablet.

. . .

When I wake up the next morning in the Oceanside Performing Arts Center parking lot, I hear the twittering of birds outside my loft window. I don't come down for breakfast with Aunt Nic, even though the coffee smells good, way better than Meg's. I don't ask to visit Jax at the hotel where he's staying with Oscar, because I don't care how the show went last night without me, or if Jax is still on probation, or if he's booked on the next flight back to Miami. Jax can look after himself. I don't come down till Aunt Nic is in the shower. That's when I snatch her phone from where it's charging on the counter and make two calls.

The first is to Roger, who assures me his crew of magicians has everything under control to capture the audience's attention at tonight's show. "All you have to do," he tells me, "is be on time for your interview tomorrow morning at the Cable 9 studios. Think you can do that? Explain to the nice lady interviewer how you discovered your aunt was using her client's email addresses to learn the intimate details of their lives. She'll hand you a big juicy check afterward."

"Of course I can do that," I tell him. "It was my idea."

I glance across the parking lot to where Jax's hotel looms in the distance. I know what he'd say if he knew what I was doing. But I also know that sometimes, Jax is wrong.

Next I call my mom, nervous bubbles fizzing inside me as I wait for her to pick up.

"Nic?" she answers. "What do you want?"

"Hi," I say extra softly, even though the shower is still running so there's no way Aunt Nic can hear. "It's me. Uh, CJ."

"Darling!" My mom's voice softens in an instant. "How *are* you?" But then, before I can answer, her voice goes all worried. "Don't tell me you're canceling on me tonight? I was so looking forward to seeing you again!"

"Oh," I say. "No. Nothing like that. Actually. I wanted to know . . . Can you come earlier? At six forty-five, right before the show? I can wait outside the theater. It'll just be me, I . . ." My words are tumbling out like water, but I still haven't gotten to the important part. "I want to come live with you," I say at last. And then all the words I was holding back gush out at once. "I know you were worried, because kids are expensive, but I can pay for everything myself, I promise. I'm about to get a bunch of money, so you don't have to worry about that anymore." When I stop talking, that's when my mom will respond. And I think maybe I'm not ready to hear what she has to say. Not quite yet. "I think it would be really great to live with you. I mean, that's what Spirit wants me to do anyway, and they kind of know everything, but I know I didn't talk to you about it before, and I know it's sort of a surprise and everything, but I was sort of hoping that—"

"CJ," my mom cuts me off.

Only she doesn't exactly say anything else.

"Um, yeah?" I ask after a too-long moment.

When she does finally say what she does next, I am filled with more bubbles of joy than I ever knew existed.

"You know I would be crazy not to want to spend every second with you, beautiful girl." That's what she says.

"Yeah?" I squeak. Because I need to make sure it's true.

"CJ," she tells me, "if you want to come live here, I'll throw you a *party*. Assuming . . . You sure you want to live with *me*? I do tend to hog the bathroom."

I laugh, because I have too many bubbles in me not to. "Positive," I tell her. Then, because I hear the shower shut off in the bathroom: "Six forty-five tonight, right?"

"Six forty-five," she confirms. "You got it, kid."

"Bye, Mom."

And I can hear the smile in her voice when she says, "'Mom.' I like the sound of that."

I'm back in my loft before Aunt Nic opens the bathroom door. And when she asks me if I'm sure everything's okay, I don't even have to lie.

"Everything is wonderful," I tell her.

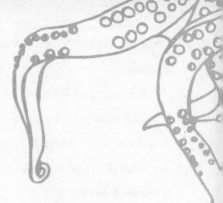

FOURTEEN

I DON'T KNOW what kind of car my mom drives, so every vehicle that slows down near the entrance of the theater parking lot makes all the bubbles inside me rise up to my throat. I swallow them down again after the red Mustang pulls back onto the street, using the parking lot to make a U-turn.

I can't check the time, since I gave my tablet to Roger, but it feels like I've been standing here for eons. The sky is dark. The air is cold. My shoulders are already achy from the weight of my messenger bag and backpack together—I packed my mom's orange box of artwork, and all the clothes I could fit. Aunt Nic can ship the rest of my stuff later. I stick my hands in my coat pockets for warmth, and the knuckles of my right hand knock against the cement mushroom cap. Another car slows near the entrance, then speeds off.

Where is she?

I wonder what sort of show-stopping reveal Roger has planned for this evening, and whether it's already begun. I wonder if Aunt Nic will be mad or sad or guilty once she knows

I helped ruin her career. I wonder if she'll ever try to talk to me again.

I wait and wait, but no cars turn into the parking lot.

The theater lobby is warm and bright when I step inside, and empty, too—except for the woman in the box office, who is very friendly. "You're Monica Ames's niece, right?" she asks me, a big smile on her face.

Behind the theater doors at the far end of the lobby, I hear the muffled rumble of Aunt Nic's voice. "Yeah," I say. "Can I use your phone?"

"I just *love* your aunt," the woman tells me as she ushers me inside the box office. "She's amazing."

I memorized my mom's number as soon as she gave it to me yesterday. I memorized her address, too, so I know the theater's only a short drive away. She should be here by now.

The phone rings once. Then twice. Three times.

Six.

"You've reached the one and only James Darek," her voice mail picks up. "Leave your message at the beep, and I'll think about calling you back!"

"Mom?" I say to the recording. "It's me. CJ. You probably didn't answer your phone because you're driving here. Aunt Nic never picks up when she's driving." I hear a roar of laughter from inside the theater, then applause. "I bet traffic's pretty bad. I was just checking that you're okay, because you're late."

Spirit wouldn't let anything happen to her, not after all this. "I mean, not too late. It's fine. Only." The woman beside me is doing a terrible job pretending not to listen. "It's fine." I make my voice as chipper as I can. "Okay, great, see you soon!"

I hang up the phone.

"I thought your mom died when you were a baby," the box office woman says as she takes back her phone.

"Nope," I reply.

Her eyebrows shoot up on her forehead.

"If you think *that's* shocking," I tell her, "then you'll definitely want to watch the news tomorrow morning. Cable 9."

I should wait outside, but it's cold. More laughter trickles in from the audience.

What is Roger waiting for?

I pick my way across the lobby and pull open the heavy door to the theater. The houselights are down on the audience, but the stage is bright, with Oscar's spotlight trained on Aunt Nic in her lime-green tracksuit. Jax is probably freaking out backstage, with only a few minutes left before he joins her down on the floor.

"And so your loved ones are gonna tell me things," Aunt Nic is explaining to the crowd, "and I'm gonna pass those words on to you, exactly how I hear them. Sometimes what they say won't make a whole lotta sense to me, so you might have to help me out a little." I've heard this speech a thousand times before. Why did I never question if any of it was true? "And just so you know, these spirits have minds of their own. Sometimes you wanna talk about Dad's will, but all he wants to talk about is his azalea bushes. So don't get mad at me if he won't shut up about gardening. I swear I find flowers just as boring as you do." That last bit gets a big laugh.

The bubbles inside me are bitter like poison. All these words I knew so well that always seemed silly or interesting or insignificant—now they just seem *mean*. Like my aunt carefully selected every single one so she could make her audience believe exactly what she wanted.

"Psst!" someone hisses at me. I look over, and there's a tech operator leaning his head out of the booth, his annoyed expression clearly saying, *Close that door already!*

My hand is still propping open the lobby door, letting in a sliver of light. I should leave. My mom will be here any second.

"Who's ready to talk to their loved ones?" Aunt Nic calls from the stage. The audience cheers wildly. The tech guy glares at me.

I step deeper into the audience, letting the door close behind me.

It doesn't happen right away. First, Aunt Nic reads for a couple who lost a close friend. Then she moves on to a high school teacher whose mother died when she was a kid. The whole time, Jax is right behind her, filming and swapping mics and actually doing a pretty decent job. He doesn't have any free hands to scratch his arm with, but from where I stand at the back of the theater, he doesn't look like he wants to.

I wonder how he can work for Aunt Nic when he knows she's lying. I wonder how Oscar can, or Cyrus. I wonder how Aunt Nic can even look in the mirror, let alone gaze into the high school teacher's eyes and tell her, "Your mom says you were always such a special girl."

I'm about to leave when I notice the flash on the projection screen onstage. Something unusual, just for a second. But as soon as I spot it it's gone, and all that appears on the screen is the live feed from Jax's camera, of Aunt Nic talking to the teacher.

"Your mom's telling me you have dreams about her," Aunt Nic is saying to the woman. "You worry about her, all the time, how she's doing now that she's passed. But she says, *Don't worry about me, kid! I'm fine! It's my job to worry about you!*"

An image flashes on the screen again. I catch it this time, though it's quick. It's a photo of the woman Aunt Nic is talking to, the teacher, only she's wearing a totally different outfit, standing in a totally different room. In the photo, she's happy and smiling, holding a book over her head the way you'd hold a trophy. And there's text underneath it, typed, like from a file of some sort.

Seat 4Q: Barbara Donovan, age 53, English teacher

As soon as they appear, the words and the photo flash away, returning to the regular image. I hear hums and murmurs in the audience, although it's clear lots of people missed it.

"Where's the big tree?" Aunt Nic is asking, unaware of the flashing screen behind her. "Your mom's showing me the big tree. She says you shared some happy memories there."

While the teacher, Barbara, is responding, that's when the screen flashes again. Another image, this one a post from online—a photo of Barbara hugging the woman I'd guess is her mother, and underneath it the words: **Can't believe it's been twenty-eight years, Mom! Miss you every day!** You can even see Barbara's friends' comments on the post: their likes and frowny-face emojis and well wishes.

Aunt Nic is still talking on the floor below. "Your mom says, *Memories are good, but real life is good, too.*" Another grainy photo flashes on the screen. A little girl icing cookies with her mom. Then another. Young Barbara hugging a black-and-white puppy. *"Don't forget to look forward, 'stead of always looking back."* More people in the audience are noticing what's happening now. On the screen, a tween Barbara does a handstand in a badly fitting leotard.

And all at once, the projection screen is bursting with words and images—the name of Barbara's husband, photos of her kids, the school where she works, the date of her last dentist appointment, and a receipt for a salad she purchased. More and more and more until it's coming too fast to take it all in, and the rustling in the audience is turning to shouts, and Aunt Nic is getting confused.

When she spots the screen, Aunt Nic's words freeze up inside her mouth.

But before she has a chance to react, there is a loud screech of feedback that pulls everyone's hands to their ears, and the images on the screen disappear. The theater—stage, audience, everything—goes black as oil sludge, and for just a moment, everyone is silent. When the lights snap back on, only the screen is lit up, and the image displayed on it is so startling that everyone in the room gasps together. Even me, although I probably should've expected it.

An octopus.

Of course it's an octopus.

It's only a shadow, really, a black silhouette, but it is huge and realistic and terrifying. And it's *moving*, slowly creeping its way down from the top of the screen, its tentacles spread wide.

Suddenly there's a voice in the air, as the creature moves.

"Seat 30N! Nicole Wythe!" It's Roger's voice, slicing through the black. *"Forty-six years old! Waitress!"* As soon as he calls the woman out, a spotlight finds her in the audience, illuminating her for everyone to see. This spotlight isn't coming from the spot bay, where Oscar works, but farther up the catwalk. One of Roger's buddies is up there, I'd bet.

"Deceased brother, Harry! Died of a heart attack!" Roger's voice booms on. Nicole Wythe shades her eyes and darts her head around, looking terrified, while on the stage the octopus slithers toward the bottom of the screen. From every corner of the audience, I hear whispers and mutters and hoots, people wondering what's part of the show and what it all means.

"Seat 83F!" Roger continues. *"Kyle Ng!"* And just like that, the spotlight blinks off of Nicole and lights up someone else. *"Twenty-three years old! Air force! Friend Dom died in a hiking accident!"*

At first I'm focused on the voice, the lights, the chaos—so it takes me a moment to realize that the creature on the screen isn't just an image after all but a shadow of a real octopus. Because there is a tip of a tentacle—an honest-to-goodness real tentacle—poking out from under the screen like a toe from a bedsheet. That tentacle grows longer and longer, and then there's another one. Two enormous, fat, slimy tentacles stretching themselves out toward the audience. But no one seems to truly take in what's happening until the projection screen hoists itself up several feet and thwacks back down hard on the stage as the knobby-headed octopus slithers his way through, black eyes gleaming. That's when the screams start, when the people in the audience jump out of their seats and clutch at their chests in panic. Some laugh and clap, thinking it's part of the show. Some simply remain still, mouths open.

This is it, I think. *It's happening.* Although I only half understand what "it" is—and I'm not quite sure if I'm terrified or excited.

The octopus thuds and flops his way toward the edge of the stage, bigger and faster than any sea creature I've ever seen or imagined. But just as the bulk of his body reaches the cliff of the stage—when it seems the only place for him to go is straight toward Aunt Nic and Jax in the fourth row—one of his tentacles curls up tight on itself, and then . . .

Puff!

It disappears in an inky-blue puff of smoke. Where once the creature had eight limbs, now he has only seven.

The crowd squawks as the smoke puff drifts upward, shifting into something. A shape. A letter.

The letter *T*.

As quickly as the first tentacle disappeared, the next three do, too—*Puff! Puff! Puff!*—replaced with inky smoke. The next three follow soon after—*Puff! Puff! Puff!*—and then the last, and the octopus's body along with it.

Puff!

The eight inky-blue puffs of smoke all drift toward the ceiling, shifting into eight different letters. The hazy letters rise several feet off the stage, bold and illuminated in the gleam of the stage lights. For the moment that they hover there, it feels like what's written in the air is the only message any of us will ever need to read for as long as we live.

T
    H
        E
           T
                R
                  U
                      T
                          H

We're silent, reading. Until something else pulls our attention away.

As the lights spring bright back to life on the theater audience, there's a tremendous burst like fireworks sparking, and from above hundreds of objects begin to tumble down toward us. Just like everyone else, I shriek and duck, covering my head—but the unfurling objects halt, midair, bobbing just above our hair.

Dangling over every member of the audience from the catwalk high above is a scroll of long brown paper. Three hundred scrolls bob over three hundred heads. Three hundred hands reach up to tug the scrolls down and examine them.

I scuttle to the nearest seat, where a whole family is investigating their scrolls. I read over the shoulder of the teenage daughter.

Photos.

Posts.

Personal data.

In the chaos, all I catch are snippets of words and phrases.

"*. . . wherever you are, Katie!*"

"*. . . never forget . . .*"

Anything this girl has ever thought or felt or posted online, Roger and his buddies have dug it up and made it public here. It seems they've found everything—where the girl lives and the car she drives and her SAT score and what she ate for dinner last night and her favorite movie and the current color of her toenail polish and how very, very much she misses her sister.

Well, I think, taking in the horrified sounds of the people all around me. *Roger sure made good use of those email addresses.*

And just as I think that, Roger's voice booms in the air once more.

"*Monica May Ames does NOT speak to the dead! She knows things about you, but not from any spirit. You gave her an invitation to collect these details about yourselves the minute you bought your tickets to come here. But tonight, you hold in your hands the truth. Believe it.*"

I'm so mesmerized by what Roger's done that when I notice Oscar darting across the stage where just moments ago we all saw an octopus, I can't understand why he's headed *toward* the audience. The crowd is so loud now, everyone up in their seats and shouting with confusion, that anyone with any sense would be running as far away as they . . .

Aunt Nic. And Jax.

Deep in row four, Aunt Nic and Jax are surrounded by confused, outraged people. And though I'm far away, I can see their frightened faces. They need to escape this crowd quickly, or it will be far worse than the swarm of teenage girls who surrounded Jax at the zoo.

I'm not filled with bubbles anymore. I am quivering jelly. *I did this*, I realize. *I put them in danger*.

But I don't have time to feel bad about it.

The aisles are filling fast now, and I can't get anywhere. Luckily Oscar is quicker than I am. He reaches Aunt Nic and Jax in row four and helps them climb over the blue-velvet seats, even as the people around them grab at them and demand answers. Oscar pulls them over one seat, then another—just one more row between them and a clear path backstage. I let myself breathe again as I watch Aunt Nic hoist herself up on the last chair. They are going to be safe. Whatever else happens, they are going to be safe.

And then Jax drops the camera.

When I see him jump down to retrieve the camera, I cry out, *"Leave it!"* But of course he can't hear me. Oscar is helping Aunt Nic down from the final row of seats, and without realizing that Jax has put himself back in danger, they take off into the wings. *"JAX!"* I scream. By the time Jax pops his head back up with the camera, it's too late. Oscar and Aunt Nic have gone. The crowd is all around him. And I don't have to see the look on his face to know that he's panicking, but I do see it, and I wish I'd seen anything else.

He is *terrified*.

I race for the tech booth, just a few feet away, and pull open the door. Maybe I started this, maybe it's all my fault—but maybe I can fix it.

"Whoa, whoa, you can't be in here!" shouts the tech operator, who's on the phone with someone, obviously freaking out about the chaos in the theater. "Get out of here!"

I don't listen. I storm to the center of the booth, where the wall of glass overlooks the entire theater. From here the tech operator can control most of the light and sound cues.

It would be a good place to cause a distraction.

I scan the control panel for the fader for the backup mic, ignoring the operator's *Stop! Stop!* signals—although lucky for me he's too distracted shouting at security on the phone to actually stop me. If there's one thing Oscar and Cyrus have taught me about working in a theater, it's how to avoid that deafening yowl of feedback. "One bad screech like that," Cyrus told me once, "will stop a show cold for a full thirty seconds."

Plenty of time for Jax to make his escape.

While I'm searching, I keep glancing up to check on Jax. A burly man is right in his face now, shouting and poking him in the chest, while a woman clings to Jax's arm and sobs. Several other people look like they're just waiting in line to shout at him or pummel him or worse. Jax has both arms wrapped around the camera. He keeps looking over his shoulder to where Aunt Nic and Oscar have sped off, but he doesn't need them—he needs *me*. I wave my arms over my head, trying to signal him through the booth window, and just as I finally spot the fader, he sees me.

Jax locks eyes with me through the glass, and I flash my hands at him. Once. Twice. *Don't worry,* I signal. *I'm going to save you.*

And Jax, well . . . Something changes in his face then.

He narrows his eyes at me, and slowly, he shakes his head.

No, he signals back.

I'm so surprised, I don't slide up the fader, not in time.

I'm so surprised, I watch, mouth open, as Jax straightens up, pushes away the burly man who's poking him, and hoists himself up on the seat back, camera and all.

"Hey!" the tech operator shouts at me. He's at my side now, off the phone. "You're the niece, aren't you?" I don't answer. I'm watching Jax. Climbing, dodging, escaping. All by himself. "We gotta get you outta here. I'll sneak you out the back."

And I do slide up the fader then, all the way to max—but by the time the feedback screeches the crowd into momentary stillness, Jax is already long gone.

. . .

There's still no sign of my mom when I burst out of the theater, but based on the look of the angry crowd that's gathering, there's no time to wait for her. Anyway, I don't need anyone to tell me where to go this time. Not even Spirit.

When the city bus pulls to a stop at the corner, I'm waiting, with money in my pocket. Clouds are covering the moon tonight, so it's extra dark as I tug my backpack straps up on my shoulders, hoist my messenger bag to my hip, and climb on board. I let the chaos of the evening shrug off me like a sweater tossed in the wash.

There are only two other people on the bus. All I can hear, as I find a seat, is the hum of traffic and my own thoughts.

I like the hum of traffic better.

Aunt Nic will be okay, I tell myself, and who cares if she isn't. Oscar will be okay, because nothing ever gets to him. Jax will be okay, obviously, because he doesn't need me to rescue him anyway.

I only did what Spirit told me to.

As I'm sloughing off my backpack straps, I spot one corner

of my tablet poking out of the half-zipped front pocket. I have no idea when Roger snuck it in there.

I pull the tablet out and flick it on, and sure enough, Roger's left a message for me. There on the screen is that same inky octopus image, the one I'm growing so familiar with. And written in its tentacles are eight letters, just for me.

FIFTEEN

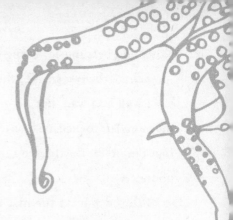

IT'S JUST SHY of nine o'clock when I pull the cord for the bus to stop. Then it's two short blocks to my mom's house. I pass a few folks out walking dogs, or taking out their trash. *My new neighbors,* I think when they nod and smile at me. I wonder what it will be like to live in a home without wheels. I wonder what it will be like to have a real mother, one with skin and bones and a real voice, hers alone. A winter chill whips past me, and I squeeze my coat tighter around me, the cement mushroom cap clunking against my hip. As I adjust my backpack and messenger bag, I can't help but feel buzzed through with excitement. *This is it.* I followed the route that Spirit laid out for me precisely, and now here I am, at the end of the journey.

Every house on the block is built exactly the same, one story high with tan stucco walls, pushed right up against the next one over, no space for driveways. But my mom's is covered in cheery Christmas lights, and the windows shine bright from the inside. Which is weird, I realize, because why did she leave all the lights on when she left to pick me up? I walk

closer and hear music blaring from inside. Which is weirder.

I climb the two steps to the porch and ring the bell.

I wait and wait, but no one answers. Obviously. Because my mom left to pick me up a while ago. She must be panicking that I'm not at the theater. I seriously need to get my own cell phone.

I flop down on the mat with my backpack against the door, to wait. But I've only let out a single breath before the door opens right behind me, and I tumble backward into the house.

"You must be CJ!" the woman in the doorway greets me.

Even upside down, it's obvious that this woman is not my mother. She is broad and tall, and dressed in a sequined black shirt and flowy black pants, with a dozen gold bangles clanking on one wrist. Behind her, I spy a whole room full of upside-down grown-ups having a very loud party.

I scramble to my feet, dust off my jeans, and say, "Huh?"

The woman laughs. "You're exactly how James described you," she says. Then she grabs my hand, her gold bangles clinking cold against my skin. "It's chilly out here!" Without asking, she pulls me inside and helps me out of my backpack and coat. I cling tight to my messenger bag, though, because I'm not letting this strange lady have *that*. "Dear lord, this is heavy," she says, hanging my coat on a hook near the door. "What do you have in here, rocks?"

"Cement," I reply, and she laughs again, like I'm just the most *delightful* thing.

"Everybody!" she announces, turning to the room. "CJ has arrived!"

And all these grown-ups in their grown-up party clothes burst into applause.

I am awfully confused.

"Um," I say, looking around. "Where's my mom? Why are all these people here?"

"Your mother didn't mention the party?" When I shake my head, the woman picks up a wineglass from the coffee table. "Sounds like James," she says.

It is in that moment that my mother bursts in from the kitchen, shouting, *"CJ!"* She is filled with such energy that the space around her seems to expand as she rushes toward me, the crowd making room for her as she slices through them. "You look *gorgeous*!" And she actually scoops me off the ground, twirling me full circle before returning me to my feet. She lifts up both my arms, showing me off to the wide room. "What did I tell you all?" she says over her shoulder, to no one in particular. "Isn't my daughter *stunning*?"

I feel a bit like one of the elephants at the zoo.

"You're so late, though!" my mom goes on. "We said six forty-five. I was starting to get worried. Is everything okay?"

I'm sure my whole face is scrunched up, which is probably

not very stunning. "You were supposed to pick me up at the theater," I say. I'm not trying to make her feel guilty about it, but that's the truth. And anyway, where *was* she?

My mom looks even more confused than I feel. "I told you I was throwing you a party, don't you remember, darling?" And when my face stays scrunched, she suddenly gets the most pained look on hers. "Oh, CJ, I'm so sorry. I must have really screwed up somehow. I'm new to all this mom stuff. You're going to have to help me out, okay?"

"I . . ." I'm not sure what I should be feeling. I thought she was going to come get me. I thought it would be just me and my mom. I sort of wish it *was* just me and my mom. Only, who gets upset when someone throws them a party?

"Anyway"—my mom squeezes my shoulders tight, and her voice perks up, happy—"you're here now and that's what matters!" And then she spreads her arms wide, so excited. "I'm so glad I finally get to show off my beautiful daughter! Now, let's get you some food, shall we? Did you drive here, with that boy?" She looks around, like Jax might be in the house, too.

"I took the bus." I wait for the part where I have to assure her that even though I'm twelve, I'm perfectly capable of taking a bus by myself after dark, but she skips right over that, which is kind of nice, actually.

"I bet you're *starved*. You like bacon?"

"Yes," I say firmly. Because this, at least, is one thing I know for certain.

"Fabulous. I made mini bacon quiches. I knew you'd love them." She leads me into the kitchen.

My mom is a whirlwind of energy as she loads up a plate of food for me, grabs me a ginger ale from the fridge. The whole time she's introducing me to her friends, laughing, chatting, joking. I feel a bit like when I used to play Ping-Pong at the RV rec centers we'd stop at, constantly having to dart my attention from one place to the next, to be sure I don't miss something.

"Amazing, right?" my mom asks me, about the quiches. I've already stuffed three in my mouth and there's no room for talking, so I only nod.

"Your mother *made* those," says a man with a too-strange mustache.

My mother waves the compliment away, then shouts to one of her friends across the kitchen. "Gloria! Come meet my fabulous daughter!" The woman rushes over with her husband or boyfriend or whoever, and they both give me enormous hugs, like we're old friends.

"It's so wonderful to meet you at last, Cara," Gloria tells me.

"CJ," my mom corrects before I get the chance.

Gloria smiles. "You were right, James. She's absolutely gorgeous." And without even bothering to ask, she runs her fingers through my hair, letting one of my curls spring back to my forehead. "Don't you wish you could have *hair* like this?" she says to the man next to her.

He swishes his drink in his glass. "I just wish I *had* hair," he replies, rolling his eyes toward his receding hairline.

I step back and adjust my headband. Plop myself down on a stool.

"Your mother tells us you're an artist, too," says the man.

"I am?" I ask.

"CJ's incredibly talented," my mom replies for me. But before I can tell her that's news to me, she claps her hands together like she's just remembered something important. "Okay, I can't wait anymore. CJ, I have to show you." And same as before, she grabs my hand and speeds away with me.

We dart past the crowd in the living room, into the hallway, me clutching my messenger bag to my side. "This is my room, the bathroom, linen closet, laundry," my mom says, and I realize that she's pointing out things I'll need to know because I *live* here now. My buzz of excitement returns. "And now . . ." We come to the door at the far end of the hallway, and she throws it open. *"Voila!"*

"Is this"—I can tell my mom's expecting a reaction, only I'm not sure what that should be—"your, um, art room?" There's an easel in the corner and huge scraps of cut metal piled up on a sheet in the open closet. There's a futon against the far wall, with stacks of boxes and books and who knows what on top. The air is thick with the smell of something strong—paint? Cleaner?

"Up until yesterday, it was my studio," she explains. "But I figure a teenager needs a space of her own. So now it's yours."

I'm trying to figure out the best way to tell my mom that I'm not *quite* a teenager, because I don't know if my mom doesn't know that twelve isn't teen, or if she doesn't know how old I am, and if it's the first thing, which it probably is, I don't want to be rude and make her think that *I* think she doesn't know her own daughter's age, because how bad would you feel if your daughter thought that? But while I'm busy with all that, it takes me a while to notice that my mom's face has gone droopy-sad.

"You don't like it." She says that like a fact, not a question.

"No!" I say, trying to explain. "I mean, yes. I do. It's awesome. I've never had my own room before, so this is great."

She squints at that. "Your aunt never gave you a bedroom? I thought she was loaded now."

"Well, I have a loft. But it's not the same. This room"—I look around, trying to find the best thing to say about it—"has a door."

I can tell she was hoping for more excitement, though, so I step closer to the futon, where five oil paintings in thick black frames hang on the wall. One is an owl with huge, huge eyes.

One is half of a hat. The others are mushrooms, painted in the same swoopy style I'm getting so used to. "Did you make these? They're great."

"Sometimes I dabble in oil," she says, like it's so easy to paint something. "I know the room is a mess, CJ. I'm sorry I didn't get a chance to tidy more before you got here. I wanted everything to be so special for you. But now that you're here, you can make it *yours*, right? I know you said you wanted to pay for things yourself, so we can pick you out a fabulous new dresser, and a cute bedspread, maybe a desk? And we'll put some of your artwork up on the walls, make it totally 'CJ.'"

"I don't have any artwork," I tell my mom. "I don't, um, paint or anything."

"Oh, I'm sure you have the art bug in there somewhere," she says, laughing again. "You're my kid, right? We'll put a paintbrush in your hand, and you'll make Picasso look like a hack, you watch."

For just a second, while my mom is straightening a stack of books on the futon, I close my eyes and try to picture myself in this house, this bedroom. Making oil paintings and eating quiche, and probably coming home from normal-kid school on the normal-kid school bus, walking past all the stucco homes. The thing is, I can picture every single part of this new life—but I can't picture *me* there. It's not how I thought it would feel, at the end of this journey Spirit led me on. I thought it would feel . . . Well, I don't know, exactly. But I thought it would feel different.

When my hand brushes the soft buttery leather of my messenger bag, I remember how, as soon as I opened up that gift box, the bag felt like *mine*, felt like *me*, in a way this strange house doesn't. And I'm mad that Aunt Nic gave me something that felt that way, when it should've been my mom who did. It should be my mom who knows me, and it's Aunt Nic's fault she doesn't. My skin burns with rage all over again, so I push the messenger bag to hang behind me so I won't have to see it. Still, I can't quite bring myself to take it off.

"Okay," my mom says after a minute. "We'll have tons of time to make this place work. For now, we should rejoin the party, hmm?"

We're walking back through the hall when something catches my eye that didn't before. I stop dead in my tracks.

"Whoa," I say.

It is another oil painting. But this one's not of mushrooms.

"You like it?" my mom asks. "It's you."

"I *know* it's me." In the painting my face is bathed in light, curls framing my face as I hold a black-and-white cookie in one hand. The tiny heart-shaped cherish is perfectly placed on my cheek. I'm grinning like a maniac. It's a very good painting. Only . . . "Did you paint this last night?" I always thought oil paintings took forever.

My mom laughs. "Hardly. I made that one, oh, a year or so ago? Worked on it for a good month, probably."

"But you just met me yesterday."

"I worked off a photo I found online," she says. "I saw it and I thought, 'My Cara is a truly gorgeous child. I *must* paint her.' It's good, right? Looks like you." She's darting her eyes from me to the portrait, to check her work, maybe.

"You found the picture online?" I say. My insides are buzzing again, but I'm not sure with what. Because I recognize it now, the image. My mom cropped Aunt Nic out, for her painting, but the original photo was one of the two of us together. It was taken after a baker Aunt Nic did a reading for gave us these incredible cookies as a thank-you.

My mom nods. "There are all sorts of photos on Nic's website. Some of them are very good. Who does her photography?"

I know there are photos on Aunt Nic's website. I help Cyrus post them. I know, too, what else is on the website.

"We did a show in El Cajon last year," I tell my mom, "right after Tucson." The tour schedule is posted on the home page of Aunt Nic's website. You can't miss it. "We were thirty minutes from here." Buzzing. I am buzzing. "The year before that, we hit up Hillcrest. That's even closer."

My mom is half listening. She's still looking at the painting. "The chin's a little off, I think. I'll have to do a new one, now that you can model for me."

Jax said it yesterday, only I didn't want to hear him. He said that even if I thought my mother was dead this whole time, she knew *I* was alive. Aunt Nic was never hiding me away. My mom could've found me, easy. She could've come to get me anytime she wanted.

"Why didn't you ever come to a show?" I ask her. "Didn't you want to see me?"

"Oh, CJ!" My mom turns fully away from the painting then, to look at the real-life me, and her eyes are big. Hurt. "Of *course* I wanted to see you. I was *dying* to see you, darling. But your aunt . . ."

"Right," I say. Feeling stupid I asked. Feeling guilty I made my own mother look the way she looks now. "Right." That's what I told Jax, even. I *knew* that.

"Let's get some dessert," my mom says, wrapping an arm around my shoulder. "Harvey's rhubarb crumble is to die for."

As she leads me away, I take one last backward glance at the portrait, suddenly remembering why I'm grinning so big.

That cookie—the amazing one the baker gave us—there was only one left, and I offered to split it, but Aunt Nic said I could have the whole thing myself. She said seeing me that happy was worth missing out on half of any cookie.

"You coming, CJ?"

I turn back to follow my mom.

. . .

The rhubarb crumble is pretty good.

And I get to talk to my mom about lots of things, even more than we talked about at the zoo. Her latest cooking experiment, and what it was like to grow up with Aunt Nic, and more about her exhibition.

But she keeps having to bounce between me and her friends and do things like restart the music when it stops playing and clean up a spill in the kitchen.

I wait and wait for her friends to leave, but they don't. I think it's been ages, but when I look at the clock not even two hours have passed. I pull out my atlas just for something to look at, tracing the route I've zigzagged the past few days. It's several hundred miles, all added up, but it feels like even more.

"And what kind of art do *you* do?" asks some man I haven't seen before, who's settling beside me on the couch with a dessert plate. Aunt Nic is off helping someone find ice. Who can't find ice?

"Huh?" I ask, looking up from my atlas.

"Your mother says you're quite an artist. What medium do you use?"

For a second, I hang up on that word, "medium," because I think he means somebody who talks to the dead, like Aunt Nic. Or somebody who Aunt Nic is *pretending* to be, anyway.

But then I realize he means "medium" like the kind of materials an artist uses in her work—oil paints, pastels, metal.

"Pig intestines," I say so he'll get up and leave me alone with my atlas.

He does not.

"Pig intestines?" I can tell this guy's never actually spoken to a kid before, and he has no idea how seriously to take me. "Really?"

"Oh, yeah. I like to smear 'em all over the canvas with my bare hands. It smells awful, but once it dries, you should see the *color*."

The guy sticks out his lip, considering. "How modern," he says at last.

A woman I haven't met yet offers me a wink. "Don't mind him," she says. "He doesn't get 'jokes.'" She puts air quotes around the last word, and I can't say I know why. "I'm Lucia."

Lucia seems nicer than the pig-intestine guy, and anyway, I have no one else to talk to, so I say, "CJ," even though I realize she probably already knows that.

She nods politely, and then, like she's trying to make conversation, she asks me, "What does 'CJ' stand for?"

"Caraway June." Lucia gives me the *that's unusual* eyebrows I'm pretty used to getting after I tell people my full name. So I give her my usual short-version explanation. "My mom gave me my first name, after the seed. Then my aunt gave me my middle name, after my mom."

"Hold on," I hear my mom call from halfway across the room. She rushes my way. "*Nic* gave you your middle name? Is that what she told you?"

"You picked June?" I ask my mom. I guess I shouldn't be totally surprised that the story behind my name is a lie, along with everything else.

"What, I'm gonna let someone else name my own baby?" My mom makes space for herself next to me on the couch, then tucks one of my curls behind my ear, the way she did at the zoo. I love when she does that. "You want to hear the story?"

I set my atlas in my lap. "Of course," I say. It's my name, after all. My story.

"So the nurse hands me this tiny, wrinkled thing, right?" my mom begins. I glance at the grown-ups around us. Some are busy with their own conversations, but some are suddenly paying attention, like anything my mom says is worth stopping to listen to. "And honestly"—she raises a hand in the air—"all I could think when I saw this baby was, I didn't know they *made* them that ugly."

She laughs, and most everyone else does, too. Lucia and the pig-intestine guy and Gloria and the mustache weirdo and at least a dozen others.

I do not laugh.

This one woman, who's wearing a single feathered earring, must notice me not laughing, because she leans across the back of the couch to put a hand on my arm, and she tells me gently, "All babies are ugly, you know, right when they're born." Like I must be so upset or something, that my mom said that.

I shrug my arm away from her.

When my mom catches sight of my face, she suddenly goes serious. "Oh, CJ!" she says, all sorry—but there's a hint of laughter still in her voice. "I didn't mean that to sound cruel. You've turned into a stunning young lady. But good God, when you were born, you were so skinny and shriveled, and hair like you wouldn't believe. I'd thought of all these baby names, for months, but I just couldn't bring myself to call you any of them. That's the truth."

She must be bad at telling stories, I realize. Aunt Nic uses words for a living, so she knows how to stretch them and squeeze them, how to use them to make you feel good. My mother, that's not her job. So she's just telling it badly.

"And then Aunt Nic gave you the caraway pudding," I say, to help her out. "And you realized that I looked like a little seedling. So that's what you decided for my name. Caraway."

"You named your daughter after pudding?" the pig-intestine guy asks.

My mom wraps an arm around me tight. "I did. I looked at that pudding, and I looked at this *thing* in my arms, and I said, 'I don't have a baby, I have a seed!'"

The woman with the earring is the only person who doesn't

seem to find the story hilarious. She doesn't put her hand on my arm this time, but I think she's trying to comfort me with her words when she says to my mom, "It must've been overwhelming, I'm sure, becoming a mother so young."

My mother takes a long sip from her wineglass while she thinks that one over. "It was hard," she says after a moment, a deep breath in, then out, "for someone like me, with so much life to live. It was hard putting all that on hold, for a baby."

What I think then, I wish I didn't. What I think then, I wish I could unthink. Only, thoughts don't work like that.

I liked my mother a lot better, I think, *when she was a spirit.*

While my mom and her friends take up a new conversation, I turn back to my atlas, trying to squash the thoughts in my head and the buzzing in my belly. *All these routes,* I think, studying the lines on the map before me. *So many ways I could have traveled.* And I wonder why Spirit chose this route for me, of all the millions out there.

That's when the doorbell rings.

"Another guest!" my mom shouts happily. She's already rushing across the room, reaching for the doorknob. "Welcome, welco—" She stops short as the door swings open, and she sees who's on the mat.

It's Aunt Nic.

SIXTEEN

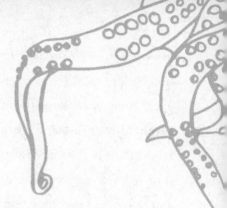

WHEN I SEE Aunt Nic on the doorstep, it's like I'm suddenly a cannonball. Without any thought in my head, I shoot off the couch and straight into Aunt Nic's arms. Her grip is warm, safe.

"Oh, Ceej," Aunt Nic says, breathing deep into my hair. "Thank god you're here. What the hell were you thinking?"

As quickly as I became a cannonball, when I hear Aunt Nic's voice, I morph right back into CJ Ames. And CJ Ames is *mad*.

"I was thinking," I say, pulling sharply out of the hug, "that I was *leaving*, to come live with my *mom*." I wave my arm, trying to point to my mother, but I accidentally point to Lucia. I wave the other arm.

That's when my mom drapes her arms over my shoulders in a behind-hug. "We're fine here, Nic," she says. "No one needs you to swoop in and save the day."

"No one needs . . . ?" Aunt Nic's eyes are bugged out bigger than the time that repair guy tried to charge us four hundred dollars just to rotate our tires. "Jennie June, do you know what

I've been through the past few hours?" She turns her attention back to me. "The theater was a *nightmare*, CJ, and no one could find you. I thought something had *happened*. And then I realized your messenger bag was gone, and your backpack, too, and the police said to stay put, but then I saw you'd called your mom on my phone and I was praying I'd find you here and no one had murdered you." She takes a breath. "Of course, then I saw you'd called Roger, and I wanted to murder you myself." I think she's joking. "Did you help him, with that stunt tonight?"

I am cool as ice when I tell her, "It was my idea."

And I can't say I feel bad when I see her face go all splotched-out rage. "Holy hell, CJ, I'm dead in this business now, you know that, right?" she cries, arms waving. Then she blinks at me, like she's figuring out the answer to her own question. "Of course you know that. That's why you did it." She lets out a giant breath, and her whole body relaxes a little, like just holding on to that air was causing her so much pain. "That was pretty cruel, CJ."

I think she's expecting me to apologize. But I don't.

But I don't do exactly what I expected, either.

"You called the police?" I ask her, my voice small.

Aunt Nic just closes her eyes for a moment, her chest rising, then falling, under her coat. "Of course I called the police," she tells me.

My mom hugs my neck a little tighter. "Well, you didn't need to do that. CJ was here with me, right?"

I nod. But I can't take my eyes off Aunt Nic.

"Why don't you answer your *phone*?" she growls at my mom. "I called you fifty times."

My mother only snorts. "I didn't hear it, Nic, sheesh. CJ and I are busy celebrating. Now, if you're done yelling at everyone, you're welcome to take your coat off and stay for a while in my home." She gives my shoulders a squeeze. "*Our* home." Then she pulls away and gestures toward the kitchen. "Mini quiche?"

. . .

Fifteen minutes later, Aunt Nic and I are sitting on the couch together in silence. My mom's friends are pretending to mind their own business or are too busy with their own conversations to care about us, who knows. My mom is in the kitchen getting Aunt Nic some food, although I'm starting to doubt she plans on coming back.

I'm looking at the floor. I'd bet Aunt Nic is, too.

Finally, Aunt Nic says, "How did Roger *do* that tonight, with the octopus?" She shifts on the couch to face me and tucks one leg under her butt. "It looked so real. I was *petrified*—I thought that thing was gonna eat all of us!"

She's being funny, but I know she's still mad at me. She's using her words to lull me in, just to snap at me when I least expect it.

I cross my arms over my chest. "I'm not sorry," I tell her. "About helping Roger. You shouldn't lie to people. You can be mad at me forever, and I won't care. I'll always know I did the right thing."

Aunt Nic just sighs, big and deep.

"I am mad at you, CJ," she says after a moment. "Furious, actually." She takes another deep breath and lets this one out slow. "But I'm more relieved than anything. Because the nastiest trick you pulled tonight was running off without telling me where you were going. A million giant octopuses couldn't scare me as bad as that."

I spend a long time adjusting my headband, even though my hair is just fine. I don't want to be lulled in by her, not again.

"I think it's octopi," I say at last.

She does not respond.

Even though the room is filled with people and music, it feels much too quiet. So finally I ask, "Is everyone okay? Jax and Oscar and . . . ?" I pick at the skin around my thumbnail, not looking at Aunt Nic again. "I thought Roger would just *say* stuff. I didn't think it would be *scary*. I didn't want . . ." Someone could've gotten hurt, that's what I haven't been letting myself think about. That if that happened, it would've been my fault. Even if I was only doing what Spirit told me to, I still think it would've been my fault.

"Oscar and Jax are on their way to Chula Vista," Aunt Nic replies. "Or maybe they're there now—I should call them. Oscar found an RV park that has vacancy for the tour bus tonight. I took a car here, to find you."

"Chula Vista?" I ask. That's only ten miles from here. "Why are they staying there? We're booked in Phoenix tomorrow."

At that, Aunt Nic laughs again. Only this laugh has a bitter ring to it. "We're not booked anywhere, CJ. Wasn't that your whole plan? Venues canceled, the whole rest of the tour."

"Oh." That's all I can think to say. I mean, I *knew* exposing Aunt Nic would ruin her career, obviously. I guess I just didn't think about what things looked like, once it was ruined.

"Anyway, Chula Vista seemed like a good place to hide out for a few days. Things got pretty ugly at the theater. We needed to get out of there."

"But Jax is okay?" I say. I didn't think it was possible for my voice to sound so squeaky.

"Jax is okay," Aunt Nic assures me. "He's pretty strong, that kid. Clumsy. But"—she scratches her cheek—"good head on his shoulders."

Just then, Harvey, the guy who made the rhubarb crumble, decides to lean over the back of the couch and interrupt. "Hey, this is you, isn't it?" He shoves a phone under Aunt Nic's nose. I can't see the image playing on the screen, but I can hear the sounds of Roger's voice calling out personal information like he did tonight in the theater, and shrieks and hollers as I'm assuming an octopus appears and disappears onstage.

Aunt Nic darts her eyes at me. "Yep," she tells Harvey. "That's me."

"You're totally going viral." Harvey says this like it's the greatest news a person could ever receive. "Half a million views in the past two hours. That's more than the squirrel who can do the monkey bars. You're famous!"

"Goodie," Aunt Nic replies. Then she leans into me. "Who is this guy?"

"He makes a rhubarb crumble that's to die for," I explain, and she snorts.

When Harvey leaves to show everyone else the video, Aunt Nic asks me, "What the heck is this party, anyway? Why are all these people here?"

"It's for me," I say. "To celebrate."

"Celebrate what?"

Suddenly I realize why Aunt Nic came here. It wasn't just to make sure that I was okay, or to get mad about tonight, either. Of course it wasn't. And when I realize that, I'm on fire all over again. "To celebrate *me*," I tell her. "Because I *live* here now. This is my *home*, and I'm staying here, and you're not going to take me away. I'm not going to boarding school. You can't make me. You're not my mom. *That*"—I point to the kitchen—"is my mom."

Aunt Nic doesn't talk for a long time. She only scratches her cheek, looking at the floor.

I wait.

"I'm not going to make you go to boarding school, CJ," she says at last. "And I won't make you live with me, either. Not if you'd rather be here."

I feel like my heart should be lighter, hearing that, but it isn't. I don't know why.

"Look, Ceej," Aunt Nic says when I don't respond. "All I want in the world is for you to be safe, and for you to be happy. I've screwed up in a lot of ways, and I know that. But if it's best for you to be with your mom for a while, I get that. We can . . ." She blinks a few times, thinking. "You still have a lot of stuff, right, back at the tour bus? Tomorrow I'll take you to pack up. Your mom can come, too, if she wants. I'll pick you up first thing, and we'll all go over together. How does that sound?"

I guess I'm surprised. I guess I thought, after all this time keeping me to herself, Aunt Nic would fight harder before letting me go.

"How do I know you're not just lying again?" I say. And I'm not sure if I'm angry or sad when I ask it. Maybe I'm feeling some totally new emotion that humans haven't named yet. "You lied about everything else."

I think Aunt Nic's going to shout at me then, but she doesn't. Instead she says, "Yeah." Like I've said something that makes a lot of sense. "I'm really sorry, CJ."

It is then that a woman I haven't met yet approaches the couch, dragging a man behind her who's much shorter than she is. "I don't mean to interrupt," she says, even though she obviously does. She inches a little closer, smiling as she peers more closely at Aunt Nic. "It *is* you, isn't it? I told my husband, I said, 'That's her! That's the psychic!' I've seen you at your shows. You're *amazing*. Tell Brent." She pushes her husband forward a little. "Does he have any spirits with him right now?" The woman swirls her hand over her husband's head, like she thinks that's where his loved ones probably hang out.

If I had to guess, I'd say this woman has not seen Harvey's phone.

"You are her, right?" the woman asks, because Aunt Nic's not saying anything. "The medium?"

Aunt Nic clears her throat. "Sorry," she tells the woman, shaking her head. And she looks at me before she says, very clearly, "I'm not a medium."

I'm surprised she says that. Really. Because I thought Aunt Nic didn't know how to tell the truth.

But still.

It's a chocolate-frosting sort of truth, isn't it? It's not a lie, but . . .

I shrug at Aunt Nic like *Say whatever you want. What do I care?*

"Oh," the woman says. She blinks at Aunt Nic like she's still unconvinced, but what's she gonna do? "Well, sorry to bother you."

She's tugging her husband away—until Aunt Nic reaches out for the woman's arm.

"Actually," Aunt Nic says. She looks at me again. "The truth's a little more . . . complicated." And for the next five minutes, while I stare at the wall, the floor, the edge of the couch, Aunt Nic holds on to the poor woman's arm and tells her everything. I mean, seriously, *everything*. Her acting troupe in college. Me being born. My mom not dying. Our busted-up motor home. The woman at the RV park. The tour bus. Cold reading. Roger and the octopus and all of it.

"And that," Aunt Nic finishes at last, "is why I can't do a reading for your husband. Or anybody."

"Wow," the woman says slowly. This was clearly more information than she was looking for. "Okay. Thanks." And without another word, she tugs her husband away at last, making a face at him like *That lady is SO WEIRD.*

Aunt Nic slouches into the couch when the couple leaves. I think she wants me to be impressed or something, that she finally grew a conscience.

"You gonna explain all that to every person who recognizes you?" I ask her. Being honest for five minutes doesn't make up for a whole lifetime of lying.

"Maybe I should get it printed on a T-shirt," Aunt Nic replies. "Save a lot of time that way." Then she checks her phone. "Jeez, it's *late*. I need to call the police, tell them you're safe." She looks up at me. "You must be tired. Does your mom have somewhere for you to sleep tonight? Like a bed or something?"

"I have a whole bedroom," I tell her, icy, because she thinks my mom doesn't even know how to be a mom. "And anyway, I'm not tired. I'm at a party. My party."

Aunt Nic opens her mouth like she wants to argue with me, then closes it. She puts her hands on her knees and stands up. "I'm going to find a quiet place to make a phone call," she says.

And even though her being next to me on the couch made me mad, her walking away makes me madder.

. . .

All right, so I actually am pretty tired.

While Aunt Nic is letting the police know I'm not dead, I find my mom gabbing in the kitchen and tell her I'm going to bed. She swirls me around and calls me fabulous and tells me there's sheets and pillows in the linen closet. I head to my new room, change into my pajamas, and clear all the stuff off the futon. Fold it out flat and make up the bed with the sheets. Tuck myself in.

I'm fine.

When the door opens, a soft, slow crack, I bolt upright. Then I toss myself back quick, before my mom can see how excited I am she came in to say good night. I'm *twelve*, for Pete's sake.

"CJ?"

It's not my mom. It's Aunt Nic.

"What do you want?" I ask. I don't say it nicely.

She sighs.

"Do you mind if I crash in here tonight?" she asks. "I can't get a car, and your mom said I can sleep on the couch, but . . ." She darts her eyes toward the living room. "I don't think those *artists* ever plan on leaving." I don't say anything. "I'll sleep way over here on the floor, okay?"

I still don't talk. She can do whatever she wants. I'm fine.

She's shoving aside a box of art supplies to make room when I tell her, "There's blankets in the hall closet." I don't ask why she can't get a car. Aunt Nic once got a car to pick us up in an actual swamp. "And an extra pillow, too."

"Thanks, CJ."

I guess I'm not too mad she'll be sleeping in this room with me, just for tonight. The owl painting above the futon is kind of creeping me out.

"What's going to happen to Jax and Oscar?" I ask after Aunt Nic returns with the bedding. Just enough moonlight is seeping through the shades that I can see her stretched out on the floor, ten feet from where I'm lying on the futon. "Since the rest of the tour is canceled, I mean? Where are they gonna go?"

I hear Aunt Nic shift under the blanket. "Oscar's a pro. He'll land at a theater somewhere. With Cyrus, I bet. Those two go way back. It might be good for them, staying in one spot for a while. Jax . . ." She lets out a breath. "I guess he'll go back to Miami. Back to his old school."

I curl up tight on the futon, wrapping my arms around my knees. But I can't squeeze the squirminess out of my stomach. I wonder if Spirit is watching me right now. I wonder if they're thinking this all turned out just how they planned.

"What about you?" I ask.

The room is filled with silence. I lift my head off my pillow to check if Aunt Nic's asleep. She's not. She's lying on her back, staring straight up at the ceiling as she talks. I can see the whites of her eyes.

Finally she turns to look at me in the dark. "Don't worry about me, CJ. That's not your job. Just worry about what's best for you, okay?"

I curl up my legs a little tighter. I want her to be madder at me. It would make it so much easier for me to stay mad at her.

"I can't go with you to the tour bus tomorrow morning," I

tell Aunt Nic. Because as long as I'm pressing her for the truth, I should probably be honest, too. "I'll go with you, to get my stuff, only I can't go tomorrow morning. I have to go to this television studio and do an interview, about what happened last night, how I helped . . . expose you."

"Oh, CJ . . ." Aunt Nic sits up.

"I'm going to do it, no matter what you say." I forgot to tell my mom that I need a ride, but I'm sure she'll drive me, when she knows what it's for. "I have to do the interview so I'll have the money I need to live here. You can't stop me."

I see Aunt Nic's eyes, blinking in the dark.

"Do you want me to stop you?" she asks at last.

I don't answer.

She stays still for a long time, and I do, too, as we look-but-don't-look at each other in the black room. Then she rises to her feet, and I think she's going to try to hug me or something, but she doesn't. "You go to sleep, okay, Ceej? I need some water." And she softly opens and closes the door.

. . .

" . . . asking your daughter for rent money now?"

That's what I hear that pulls me out of bed. It's Aunt Nic, and she is loud. And angry. I make my way to the door, then down the dark hall, to hear more.

" . . . not fair at all," my mom is saying back. I inch closer to the living room, pressing against the weird portrait of myself to listen. "I didn't ask CJ for money. Of course I didn't. She said she wanted to help pay for her own things. Was I supposed to turn her down? Food's expensive. And furniture. And, I don't know, school stuff. She probably needs school stuff."

"She's a *kid*, Jennie. You don't take money from a kid. You need money to help keep her here? You ask me. Or you get a better job." There are still people at the party, but they're starting to make their way to the door now. "You can't use CJ like this. She's your daughter."

I poke my head around the corner just in time to see my mom death-glare at Aunt Nic. They're so wrapped up in fighting they don't notice me in the shadows of the hallway.

"Are you really mad CJ wants to help out with her own expenses?" my mom spits at Aunt Nic. "Or are you just upset anyone would pick me over you?"

Aunt Nic starts rubbing her face then, like she's so exhausted. I get the feeling they've been fighting this argument for a long, long time.

"Jennie, I'm *thrilled* you're getting to know CJ. She's . . ." Aunt Nic rolls her head to the ceiling, and for a second it looks like she might cry. But then she pulls herself together. "She's awesome. She's worth getting to know. It's just . . . I am so worried that you're going to blow this. You don't know the first thing about being a parent, and I can't stand the thought of that girl getting hurt again."

It's the "again" that I get stuck on. Which time before is Aunt Nic talking about?

But my mom seems focused on something else.

"I could've been her parent her whole life, Nic," she snaps back.

Aunt Nic lets out a growl so loud then that the stragglers in the doorway don't even bother to wave goodbye.

"I gave you a *million* opportunities to see your daughter!" That's what Aunt Nic shouts at my mom.

"You kept her away," my mom argues. She sounds younger, all of a sudden. Like a little sister, I think. "You didn't want her to know me. You wanted her all to yourself."

"Oh, please," Aunt Nic says. "You could've come anytime you wanted. You *knew* that. You could've come *five years* ago when you said you were going to. We waited for a *week*, Jennie. I had to tell the poor girl our motor home broke down."

I slip down the wall, all the way to the floor.

Long Beach. The Ferris wheel. One of my happiest memories, and my mom could've been in it, too.

Only she chose not to.

In the living room, my mom is still arguing. "You'd told her I'd *died*," she says. "How was I supposed to show up out of the blue after you told her that? Who *does* that, Nic? Who lies like that to a little kid?"

Aunt Nic swallows hard. Her voice is mean, but her face is pained. Broken.

"Someone who can't bear to tell that little kid that her mom doesn't want her anymore," she replies.

And then she flicks her eyes to the hall and sees me on the floor.

I scramble to my feet and race back to the bedroom so she can't see my face. I don't want her to see my face, because she'll know, in an instant, how much I want to cry. And I'm not going to cry.

"CJ." Aunt Nic reaches me before I'm able to shut the door on her. "I'm sorry," she whispers into my ear as she scoops me up and cradles me right there in the doorway like I'm a little baby. I am crying. I can't stop. "I'm so sorry, seedling. I'm so, so sorry."

Seedling.

My heart catches on the name. It's what my mom always called me, when she was a spirit. Only it wasn't ever my mother at all. It was Aunt Nic.

It was always Aunt Nic.

I let her rock me for a long time, and I don't even care that I'm crying. And then, when I'm certain there are no tears left to worry about, that's when I ask the question that's weighing heavy like a rock in my stomach.

"Didn't you mind?" I say the words softly. Like even though I know I can't cry anymore, maybe I'm not so sure I want to hear the answer anyway.

"Mind what?" Aunt Nic asks. Just as soft.

The words are hot, but I push them out.

"Putting your life on hold," I say. "For a baby. For me."

I had far too much life to put on hold for a baby. That's what she'd said. That's what my mother had said.

"Oh, CJ."

And when Aunt Nic pulls back to look at me, I know. I'm certain I know the answer, but she says it out loud anyway. Because Aunt Nic has always been good with words. She's good, I guess, at a couple things.

"You are my life," she tells me.

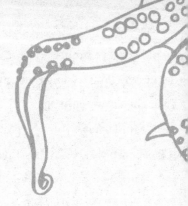

SEVENTEEN

AUNT NIC FINALLY falls asleep, her breath relaxing itself into a steady rhythm as she lies beside me on the futon. But I stay wide awake, all night, and I think. By the time Aunt Nic's phone reads 5:27 a.m., I am sick of thinking.

I find two guests crashed on the couch when I slip into the living room in my socks, Aunt Nic's phone in my hand. Plates and glasses and napkins are littered everywhere. There's no sign of my mom. Probably in her room. I tiptoe to the bathroom.

"Nic?" Jax says groggily. It takes him seven rings, but he finally answers. "Are you okay? Is CJ—?"

"Jax, it's me," I tell him. "I'm fine." I examine my face in the bathroom mirror. Puffy eyes. Greasy curls. "I'm fine."

"Hold on, okay, CJ? I . . . Give me a sec." Jax sounds like he's thinking himself awake. I hear rustling, then a door creaking open and shut, then after a bit, Jax's voice again. "Sorry. I didn't want to wake Uncle Oscar. We slept on the tour bus last night. That foldout couch is *sweet*. Anyway, I'm outside now. What's going on? It's early. Are you really okay?"

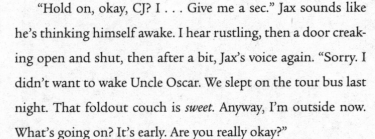

The stuff that's been jumping around in my head all night—it's hard to put into words. But I guess I must take too long to answer, because Jax says, "Hello? CJ? You still there?"

"I'm here." I stick my finger under the dripping faucet, let the water plop cool onto my skin.

Drip.

Drip.

"What if none of this was supposed to happen?" I ask Jax. And Jax takes a long breath, like he knows this is about to be a *conversation*.

Drip.

Drip.

"What if I messed up what Spirit was trying to tell me?" I say. "What if . . . ?" *Drip.* "What if there aren't any spirits at all?"

Drip.

Drip.

"Jax?"

"I'm here."

"Well?" *Drip.* "What do you think?"

Drip.

"I don't know, CJ."

That's what Jax tells me.

"That's not helpful."

That's what I tell Jax.

He laughs. "Yeah," he admits. "But . . . I mean, I really *don't* know. Some days I think spirits are probably just something we invented so the world makes more sense. But then other days . . . It did seem real, all those signs that led us to your mom. And there are times I'd swear Abuelo is here, watching and helping me out."

Drip.

"So how are we supposed to know what's right?" I ask.

Drip.

"Maybe it doesn't matter," Jax tells me.

Which is obviously wrong.

"Of course it matters!" I say. "I mean, if Spirit is real, and they're telling me what to do, then obviously I need to *know* that. Because how else am I supposed to do what they want?"

"You do everything everyone wants you to, CJ?" Jax asks me.

But he already knows the answer to that one. So he asks me something else.

"What do *you* want, CJ?"

The faucet drips for a long time while I think about that.

Drip.

Drip.

Too many drips to count.

But at last I think, just maybe, I have an answer.

"Hey, Jax?" I say.

"Yeah?"

Drip.

"How would you feel about rescuing me for a change?" I ask him.

. . .

I leave two things in the bedroom before I tiptoe outside to meet Jax.

The first is a note for Aunt Nic. Exactly where I'm going. Exactly what I'm doing. I'm not sneaking off this time. I'm just doing something on my own.

The second is my mom's orange box from the house in Bakersfield. Those drawings were never mine to have. They always belonged to my mother.

But the mushroom cap, the cement one from the sculpture, that I keep, tucked into my coat pocket for luck. I'm growing to like the weight of it, like no matter what, it's there to keep me rooted to something real.

I'm only outside a few minutes before Jax pulls up in the truck. As soon as I open the door, he offers me a coffee cup. There's another one in the cup holder.

"It's from the registration lobby at the RV park," he says as I take the cup. "It's about nine thousand times better than Meg's."

"Thanks," I say, sliding into my seat. And then, as I shut the door, "And, you know, thanks."

"'Course."

I point Jax in the direction we need to go, and he pulls back onto the road. It isn't until we're merging onto the highway that I realize.

"Wait, *how did you drive here?*" I ask him. Okay, I shriek it.

Jax has got his right hand on the stick shift, working through the gears like it's no big deal. I haven't helped him once since he picked me up.

Jax raises his eyebrows, like he's so proud of himself.

"No way," I say.

"Way."

"Well, look at you, Jax Delgado. You're, like, a real driver now."

"Yeah," he says, a laugh in his voice. "I totally mastered it, right? Just in time to go home."

"Oh."

Suddenly I feel like a real jerk.

"No, CJ, I was joking, I . . ." He points his elbow in my direction, hands still on the wheel. "Ignore me—it's fine. Well, it's not *fine*, but it's not your fault. Well, it *is* your fault, but . . ." He trails off.

"Jax?" I say softly.

"Yeah?"

He is watching the road. Not me. Maybe that's what makes it a little easier.

"I'm really sorry. About your job, and about not listening when I should've, and about thinking you were looking out for yourself when you were just trying to help me. You were right, obviously, about my mom and the signs and everything. And . . . well, I'm sorry." He doesn't answer for a long time, though, and I can't take it anymore. So I say, "You're thinking I'm a horrible person, aren't you?"

And to that, Jax only replies, "Mmm."

I can't help it. I laugh.

Jax laughs, too. Just a little.

"You okay?" I ask. I should've asked earlier, but maybe I was afraid to hear the answer. "After last night, I mean. That was really scary, with the crowd. You must've . . . Are you okay?"

Still watching the road, he says, "I'm okay. It was scary, but . . . Anyway, it's good to know that I can rescue myself sometimes."

"You going back to Florida?"

"I've got a flight out this afternoon." He starts to scratch that arm. "My mom . . ." *Scratch-scratch-scratch.* "We talked a lot last night. It was good, I think. I told her I need more help, that it's not so . . ." He pulls his hand away from the scratching and grips the wheel tight. "I can't count on other people to rescue me all the time, you know?" He looks at me quick. "But I also know I can't do it by myself all the time, either. I think she gets it. She said she'd help me look into therapy or alternative schools and stuff."

"That sounds good," I tell Jax.

"Yeah."

"You'll be back in time for the Christmas boat parade," I say helpfully. "You can protect your stuffing from Mari."

"Yeah."

But I can't tell if he's happy about that or not.

"Anyway," I tell him, "I'm still sorry."

"You should be," he says. But he laughs again, after he says it.

"Ooh, next exit!" I tell him, pointing. He switches lanes.

"Okay, so." He drums his thumbs on the wheel. "Now might be a great time to tell me where we're actually going, don't you think?"

In response, I point to the building that's just appeared over the crest of the highway. The sign is lit up bright in the not-quite-dawn sky.

"There," I tell him.

Cable 9 news.

. . .

"You're early." That's what the receptionist in the studio lobby tells me. She looks at the computer screen in front of her, then back to me and Jax. "I don't have you scheduled for makeup for another half hour."

The building is huge, with glass all around. The floor is white marble. There's a fish tank built into the wall by the reception desk, but it's a normal-size one, not ridiculous like Roger's.

"I'll wait," I say, trying to be polite. The receptionist nods us toward a row of chairs, then picks up her ringing phone. We sit.

"So," Jax says, still sipping his coffee, even though it must be frozen by now. I told him he could wait in the truck, but he insisted on coming in with me. "You're really going to do this interview, huh?"

I shrug. "I have no idea what I'm going to do."

The truth is, I thought maybe everything would become clear to me once Jax picked me up in the truck. But it didn't.

The truth is, I thought maybe I'd know exactly what the right thing to do was when I got here, but I don't.

The truth is, when you don't have anyone telling you which path you need to take, sometimes it's awfully hard to figure it out for yourself.

I kick my toe against the white marble floor. "Here's what I'm not sure about," I tell Jax. Then I take a deep breath, trying to get the words out the clearest I can think them. "I don't think what Roger and I did was right. What we said about Aunt

Nic, I mean, that she's a phony. Because it was partly true, but it was a lie, too, the way we said it."

Jax nods and sips his coffee, just listening.

"But I don't think what Aunt Nic's been doing is right, either, and I think it's okay that people know that." He nods some more. "I just feel like if I *do* go through with the interview, then I'm saying Roger is right. But if I *don't* do the interview, I'm saying Aunt Nic is. And they're both totally wrong." I frown. "I was wrong, too."

"So . . ." Jax starts as he flicks at the plastic lid of his coffee cup. "Why not go in there and say all of that?"

"The mango-glaze truth?" I ask, and he smiles.

I kick the floor again. I remember that woman at my mom's party last night, when Aunt Nic fessed up to everything, how bored she got halfway through all the truth Aunt Nic had to tell her. I remember, too, at the creepy fish mansion, when Roger tried to tell me things I didn't want to hear, and I only got angry. Mango-glaze truth may be more real, but chocolate-frosting truth is a whole lot easier to swallow.

"You think it's better to tell people a half-truth they'll actually hear?" I ask Jax. "Or a whole truth they won't?"

Jax lifts his coffee to his mouth without sipping, then lowers it again. "I think," he says, jerking his head toward the clock on the wall behind the receptionist, "you have about twenty minutes to decide."

I sigh. I know this is my decision to make, but still. It would be awfully nice if someone made it for me.

"One thing I'll say?" Jax tells me, and I sit up a little straighter in my chair. "This person who's doing the interview?" He nods his head down the long hallway. "She's probably expecting you to tell the story you and Roger came up with before. If you tell her another story, she might not like it." I nod. I'd thought of that. "If she doesn't like what you say in your interview," Jax goes on, "then they might not put it on the air." I'd thought of that, too. "And if they don't air the interview"—he flicks his cup again—"you probably won't get any money."

I blink at the fish tank on the wall. "Yeah."

"I thought you needed that money to live with your mom."

"Yeah."

Maybe, I hope, watching the fish in the tank, there's still time for me to get another sign—from Spirit, or anyone else out there in the sign-giving business. Maybe if I just pay enough attention, a miniature octopus will pop up inside the fish tank, with a miniature message in its miniature tentacles, and tell me exactly what to do.

I wait and wait.

"You okay, CJ?" Jax asks me.

I'm staring right at the fish tank when I say what I do next. Because I still wish there'd be a sign, even though I know there won't be. Even though this is one decision I can make all on my own.

"I'm not going to live with my mom," I say. It feels good, actually, to say the words out loud.

In the reflection of the fish tank glass, I can see Jax nod. One short bob of his head. "And the signs from before?" he asks. "That you thought were pointing . . . ?"

"I'm not going to live with my mom."

I already have a home, that's what I know now. I've had a home my whole life.

And just as I'm thinking that—I swear, that exact second—I hear the lobby door *swoop* open, frigid air filling the room, and from behind comes a voice shouting, *"CJ!"*

I whip around, and there's Aunt Nic. Not a sign or a spirit or anything, just a real person who runs at me and squeezes me into a hug like she thinks I've been on Mount Everest instead of just a few miles away like I wrote in my note, and she says, "Will you *stop running off*, you wretched child? You're going to make me go gray, and I will *not* look good with gray hair."

And I let her hug me, hard. And I hug her back. And then, because she needs to know, I say, "I'm here for my interview. And I might say some things you don't like."

Aunt Nic opens her mouth to respond, but the receptionist interrupts her.

"Miss Ames?"

Both Aunt Nic and I look up.

"Sorry," says the receptionist. "I meant CJ. We're ready for you now. I'll take you back."

Aunt Nic still has her grip around me, from that hug. Which is why her voice is so clear in my ear when she tells me, "It's your story, too, CJ. Say whatever you need to say. I'll be right here when you're done."

I pull away and turn to the receptionist. "You ready?" she asks me.

Jax gives me a tiny nod of encouragement. Aunt Nic gives me one, too.

"Ready," I say. And I follow the receptionist down the hall.

"So," she asks as we walk, "what is it you're here to talk about today, Miss Ames?"

I don't have to hesitate at that.

"The truth," I reply. "The mango-glazed, messy truth."

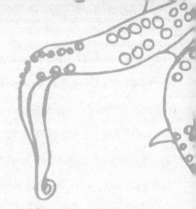

EPILOGUE

"**I SWEAR THEY** told us we only need a dime-size drop of shampoo," Aunt Nic says, leaning my neck back gently over the kitchen sink. The water is deliciously warm as it hits my scalp, and Aunt Nic works the wetness through all my curls. "But that seems ridiculous. Doesn't that seem ridiculous to you, CJ? Maybe I need to take you in with me to class tomorrow and tell that teacher, 'See these curls? *This* girl needs a dollar's worth at least!'"

I laugh, eyes closed, as I enjoy the feeling of Aunt Nic's fingers working through my wet hair. So far, Aunt Nic's first month of beauty school is going about as well as my first year of regular school did—"a little rocky." But I settled in, eventually, so I know she will, too.

I did try Plemmons, for a whole semester, but boarding school and I didn't get along too well. After that, Aunt Nic and I spent a while hopping around here and there, dipping our toes in new towns like they were pools we were nervous about taking a full-on swim in. Aunt Nic says it's hard to stop being a nomad, after so long on the road. But when our Toyota honest-to-goodness broke down in Long Beach, in front of an apartment building that just happened to have a two-bedroom for rent with a view of the Ferris wheel, we decided it didn't matter if it was a sign or chance or what—this was the spot for us. And nearly a year in, it seems to have stuck.

The weirdest thing that happened after my interview was that Aunt Nic's career did kind of blow up for a while—but not at all in the way any of us expected. After my interview got picked up nationally, and the whole world got to hear me explain the mango-glaze truth about everything, Aunt Nic had more requests for bookings than ever before. Theaters all over the country, bigger venues than she'd ever played. For whatever reason, there were some folks who believed in Aunt Nic's Gift *more* after that. Even after Aunt Nic did her own interview, confirming every detail of my story, there were *still* people who didn't want to hear it. People who said she'd absolutely spoken to their loved ones already, whether she knew it or not. People who said she must've been paid to lie, or gotten brainwashed, or who knows what.

Aunt Nic turned all those offers down.

"I'll get to talk to plenty of people once I'm a hairdresser." That's all Aunt Nic will say about her old career. "And probably most of them will be alive this time."

Roger still works at Le Char Mer, last I heard, but he hasn't made any new reality shows. He wasn't exactly happy with me when I went on TV and called him a liar. I called myself a liar, too, but I don't think that's the part that made him mad. I'm still deciding what to do with the interview money. Aunt Nic says it's mine to use for whatever I want, but it doesn't feel right to spend it on myself. Most days I think I'll donate it to some sort of charity for people who are grieving, or people who've been lied to, or both.

Anyway, I'm still deciding.

Aunt Nic ends up putting five dime-size dollops of shampoo into my hair before she gets a good froth. "I'm going to rat you out to your teacher," I tease her. "You'll get a D-minus in shampooing."

"I'm gonna find a new niece to help me with my homework," Aunt Nic replies. But even with my eyes closed, I can tell she's grinning.

I move on to more important matters. "Did you find any pudding for a backup?" I ask.

"Oh, so you trust my cooking as much as you trust my shampooing, hmm?" Aunt Nic says. But she's joking again. Obviously. Because she knows I do *not* trust her cooking.

Last month, Jax said he had his choice of recipes to master during "Custard Week" at his new culinary school, and he picked caraway pudding. The one he made looked super fancy— I saw photos—but he also found a "completely foolproof" recipe and mailed us a copy so we could make it ourselves for my birthday. But I walked through the kitchen when Aunt Nic was working on it yesterday, and I'm positive that couldn't possibly have been what it's supposed to smell like.

"Anyway, yes," Aunt Nic says as she rinses the last of the shampoo out of my hair. I guess they don't have a coin-size limit on conditioner, because she squeezes an enormous blob into her hand. "I did find a backup pudding this morning. Whichever one looks the *least* like something a penguin barfed up, we'll try after your mom calls, how's that sound?"

"Sounds good," I say.

In a lot of ways, my mom is about the same alive as she was when she was a spirit. We're just an hour-and-a-half drive from her now, so she visits when she wants to—she'll join us for trips to the beach, or the movies, or we'll head to her place for dinner. We went to the grand opening of her exhibit at the zoo last year, and it was *amazing*. And we get to talk a lot, pretty much whenever I want. Which, mostly, is okay. It's not how I ever thought things were supposed to be, when you have a real-life mom instead of a spirit one. But mostly, I think there probably isn't any such thing as *supposed to*.

When she's all done with the rinsing, Aunt Nic sits me up and grabs a towel. Just as I open my eyes, she is looking at me, her head tilted to the side. The smile on her face is warmer than the warmest water.

"You know, seedling," she tells me, "you *look* fourteen."

I watch the last of the water swirl down the drain, and I think about the pipes that the water is swirling into. I'm pretty sure—the same way I know the pipes exist even when I can't see them—that Spirit exists. It feels right to me, so most days, that's what I think. But I also know that even if Spirit isn't real, even if there's no one to send me signs and tell me where to go, I'll be just fine.

I know where I'm meant to be.

Aunt Nic is wrapping my hair up tight in the towel when I spot the postcard on the kitchen table, under the cement mushroom cap that we use as a paperweight. "It came this afternoon," she tells me when she sees me looking. She lifts up the paperweight to remove the card from the top of the mail stack.

I know, without even reading it, that it's a postcard from Jax, because on the front is a photo of a horse. A warm smile works its way onto my face as I flip the postcard over. Sure enough, on the back, Jax has written a single word.

HORSE!!!!!!!

Sometimes, that's really all a person needs to say.

FAR AWAY
Discussion Guide

1. CJ is great at navigating by using maps, finding routes along roads and highways. And yet she struggles to find a way forward in her own life, hitting any number of metaphorical roadblocks and potholes. Do you think there is a connection between these two abilities (or inabilities) of CJ's? Why or why not?

2. CJ has grown up believing her mother died, but still feels a powerful connection to her—enough so that she goes on a wild road trip just to find a way to keep that connection strong. Why is that so important to CJ? How does our connection to our family members—those we grow up with and otherwise—shape who we are?

3. Aunt Nic chooses to tell CJ that her mother has died, even though she knows otherwise. What reasons does Aunt Nic have for this decision? Do you think she made the right choice? Why or why not?

4. Jax is a character who lives with anxiety. Why do you think the author chose to give Jax that challenge? How does that impact his actions, decisions, and influences as a character?

5. When CJ does finally meet her mom, her excitement turns to disappointment before too long, as James doesn't wind up meeting her expectations. In what ways did James live up to the picture of her that CJ had carried in her mind, and in what ways did she fall short? Should CJ have known that her mother might not actually be the perfect person she'd imagined her to be?

6. Why does CJ decide to team up with Roger in the end? How do you think she feels about that decision after the fact? What does she learn from it, and what impact does that have on how she thinks about her own situation and Aunt Nic's choices?

7. CJ's mother is an artist, and she spends her time creating things designed to bring out emotions in the people who come across them. In what ways is what James does similar to or different from what Aunt Nic does? Is one sister's work more "real" than the other's?

8. Roger tells CJ, "We go along believing whatever suits us, until that belief runs us smack into a brick wall, and then we face the truth." How do CJ's beliefs evolve over the course of the novel? Why do you think it can be difficult to change another person's mind about something they believe? Have you ever had to question one of your beliefs? If so, how did you go about searching for answers?

9. In the end, CJ decides that she's better off sticking with Aunt Nic, and forgives her for not telling her the truth about her mother. Why does CJ make that choice? What do you think you would you have done in her position?

10. CJ spends a good portion of this book looking to Spirit for signs of what she's meant to do and where she's meant to go. Ultimately, do you think she finds the answers to those questions? If so, do you think she's guided by Spirit or by something else?

11. In this book, many characters keep secrets from one another, telling half-truths or even flat-out lies. At one point, Jax makes a comparison between chocolate-frosting truth (fluffy and pretty) and mango-glaze truth (much more messy). Do you think it's ever okay to keep secrets and tell lies? What factors might impact your decision here?

Turn the page for
a sample of Lisa Graff's

LOST IN THE SUN

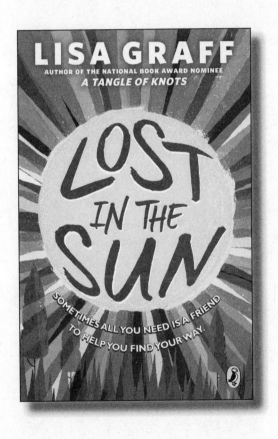

ONE

IT'S FUNNY HOW THE SIMPLEST THING, LIKE riding your bike to the park the way you've done nearly every summer afternoon since you ditched your training wheels, can suddenly become so complicated. If you let it. If you start to think too hard about things. Usually, when you want to go to the park, you hop on your bike, shout at your mom through the window that you'll be home in an hour, and you're there. You don't think about the pedaling, or the balancing, or the maneuvering of it. You don't consider every turn you need to make, or exactly when your left foot should push down and your right foot should come up. You just . . . *ride*.

But suddenly, if you get to thinking about things too hard, well, then nothing seems easy anymore.

When I'd left the house, with my baseball glove tucked into the back of my shorts, and my ball in the front pocket of my sweatshirt (next to my Book of Thoughts, which I wasn't going to take, and then

I was, and then I wasn't, and then I did), the only thought in my head was that it was a nice day. A good day for a pickup game in the park. That there were sure to be a few guys playing ball already, and that I should get going quick if I wanted to join them.

And then I got to pedaling a little more and I thought, *Do* I want to join them?

And just like that, the pedaling got harder.

Then the steering started to get hard, too, because I started thinking more thoughts. That was the problem with me. I could never stop thinking. I'd told Miss Eveline, my old counselor back at Cedar Haven Elementary, that, and she'd said, "Oh, Trent, that's silly. Everyone's *always* thinking." Then she gave me the Book of Thoughts, so I could write my thoughts down instead of having them all poking around in my brain all the time and bothering me. I didn't see as how it had helped very much so far, but I guess it hadn't hurt either.

Those guys had been playing pickup all summer, that's what I was thinking on my way to the park. I'd seen them, when I was circling the field on my bike. Just popping wheelies, or whatever. Writing down thoughts, because what else was I supposed to do? At first I'd waited for them to ask me to join in, and then I'd figured maybe they didn't know I wanted to, and now here I was wondering if I even wanted to play at all. Which was a stupid thing to wonder, obviously, because why *wouldn't* I want to play? I hadn't swung a bat the entire summer, so my arm was feeling pretty rusty. And what with sixth grade starting in three short days, I knew I better get *not* pretty rusty pretty quick if I wanted to join the intramural team. Because the kids on the intramural team, those were the guys they picked from for the real team in the spring, and the competition was tough, even in sixth. That's what my brother Aaron told me, and he should know, since he landed on the high school varsity team when he was only a freshman. The middle school team, Aaron said, that's where you learned everything you needed to know for high school. Where you practiced your fundamentals. Where the coaches got a feel for you.

But here I was, the last Friday before sixth grade began, not even sure I was up for a stupid pickup game in the stupid park.

This is what I mean about having too many thoughts.

So like I said, it was tough, getting to the park. It was tougher still, forcing myself through the grass toward the field. The grass was only an inch high, probably, but you'd've thought it was up to my waist, what with how slow I was moving.

When I got to the edge of the field, sure enough a bunch of the guys were there, my old group, warming up for a game. A couple new guys, too, it looked like. And all I had to do—I *knew* that all I had to do—was open up my mouth and holler at them.

"Hey!" I'd holler. I could hear the words in my head. "Mind if I join you?"

But I couldn't do it. It turned out opening my mouth was even harder than pedaling. Maybe because the last time I'd opened my mouth and hollered that, well, it hadn't turned out so well.

So what was I supposed to do? I dumped my bike in the grass and flopped down next to it, and just so I didn't look like a creeper sitting there watching everyone else play baseball, I tugged out my

Book of Thoughts and started scribbling. I guess I was glad I'd brought it now.

This one wasn't the original Book of Thoughts. I'd filled up that one in just a few weeks (I don't think Miss Eveline knew how many thoughts I had when she gave it to me). I was on my fifth book now, and somewhere along the line I'd switched from writing my thoughts down to drawing them. I wasn't a super good artist—I never got things on the page exactly the same way I could see them in my head—but for whatever reason, I liked drawing my thoughts better than writing. Maybe because it felt more like a hobby and less like the thing the school counselor told me to do.

Anyway, I drew a lot these days.

After a while of drawing I decided to look up. See how the game was going. See if any of the guys were about to ask me to play (not that I was sure if I wanted to). They didn't look like they were, so my eyes got to wandering around the rest of the park.

I saw the side of her face first, the left side, while she was walking her fluffy white dog not far from where I was sitting on the side of the baseball field. I didn't recognize her at first, actually. I thought she might be a new kid, just moved to town. Thought she had a good face for drawing.

Big, deep, round brown eyes (well, one of them, anyway—the left one). Curly, slightly frizzy brown hair pulled back away from her face. Half of a small, upturned mouth. She was dressed kind of funny—this loud, neon-pink T-shirt blouse thing with two ties hanging down from the neck (were those supposed to do something? I never understood clothes that were supposed to *do* something), and zebra-print shorts, and what looked like a blue shoelace tied into a bow in her hair. The kind of outfit that says, "Yup. Here I am. I look . . . weird." But that wasn't the first thing I noticed about her—her weird outfit. The first thing I noticed was that the left side of her face was awfully good for drawing.

Then she tilted her head in my direction, and I saw the rest of her.

I recognized her right away. Of course I did. Fallon Little was a very recognizable person.

The scar was thin but dark, deep pink, much darker than the rest of her face. Raised and mostly smooth at the sides, with a thicker rough line in the center. The scar started just above the middle of her left eyebrow and curved around the bridge of her nose and down and down the right side of her face until it ended, with a slight crook, at the right side of her mouth. That was where her top lip seemed to tuck into the scar a little bit, to become almost part of it.

Fallon had had the scar for as long as I'd known her. She'd moved to Cedar Haven back in first grade, and she'd had the scar then. Some people thought she'd been born with it, but no one knew for sure. If you asked, she'd tell you, but you knew it was a lie. A different story every time. Once I'd been sitting next to Hannah Crawley in chorus when Fallon described how she was mauled by a grizzly while trying to rescue an orphaned baby girl.

(Hannah believed her, I think, but Hannah was pretty dense.)

Fallon Little saw me looking at her, from across the grass.

And she winked at me.

Quick as a flash, I turned back to my notebook. Not staring at Fallon Little and her fluffy white dog at all.

Drawing. I'd been drawing the whole time.

Still, while I was drawing my thoughts on the paper, I couldn't help wondering how I'd never noticed the rest of Fallon Little's face before. It was like I'd just gotten to the scar, and then stopped looking.

Like I said, it wasn't a terrible face.

I guess I was concentrating on my drawing pretty hard—I do that sometimes, get lost in my Book of Thoughts—because when I finally did notice the baseball that had rolled into my left leg, I thought it was the one from my pocket. Which didn't make a whole lot of sense, obviously, because how would the baseball jump out of my pocket and start rolling *toward* me? Plus, *my* baseball was still in my pocket, I could feel it.

But sometimes my thoughts didn't make a whole lot of sense.

So it wasn't my baseball, obviously. It came from those guys in the field. Which I figured out as soon as a couple of them started walking over to retrieve it. Jeremiah Jacobson. Stig Cooper.

And Noah Gorman.

Noah Gorman didn't even *like* sports, I knew that for a fact. I used to be the one who dragged *him* to pickup games, so what was he doing here without me? Not that I cared. Not that it mattered if Noah wanted to spend all his time with *Jeremiah Jacobson*, the biggest jerk in the entire world.

Jeremiah Jacobson was pretty scrawny (my brother Aaron could've snapped him like a toothpick—heck, give me another month and *I* could do it), but he acted like he was the king of the whole town. His parents owned the only movie theater in Cedar Haven, so he never shut up about how he and all his stupid friends could get in to all the free movies they wanted. Free popcorn and sodas, too. Even candy. I heard that there were pictures up behind the counter of Jeremiah and all his friends, so the high school kids who worked there would always know not to charge them. It might've been a lie, but you never know. Maybe that's why Noah was hanging out with him now—for the popcorn.

Anyway, it didn't take a genius to figure out that when those guys came to get their ball, they weren't going to ask me to join the game.

"Hey, you," Jeremiah said, as soon as he was within hollering distance. "Give us back our ball."

Seriously, that's what he said. "Give us back our ball." Like I had *stolen* his idiotic ball or something, instead of him practically chucking it at me, which is what happened. Didn't even use my name either. Trent Zimmerman. We'd lived in the same town since we were *babies*. And it was a small town.

Well.

As soon as he said that, I got that fire in my body, the one that started like a ball in my chest, dense and heavy, then radiated down to my stomach, my legs, my toes, and out to my neck, my face, my ears. Even all the way to my fingernails. Hot, prickly fire skin, all over.

I snatched the ball out of the grass and clenched it tight in my fiery hand. Then I stood up so Jeremiah could see just how tall I was.

Taller than him.

"This is my ball," I told him as he and the other guys got closer.

That was a lie, obviously, but they were ticking me off. And when I started to get ticked off like that, soon the fire would be up to my ears and down to my toes, and well, then I wasn't exactly in charge of what I said. "Go find your own."

I didn't look at Noah. Who cared what he thought about anything? He was hanging out with Jeremiah Jacobson. His thoughts didn't matter anymore.

Jeremiah cocked his head to one side. "You serious?" he said. "That's our ball. Don't be a turd." Only he didn't say "turd." "Give it back."

"Yeah," Stig said, "give it back." Stig Cooper was the fattest kid in town. Dumbest, too. Not to mention an enormous jerk.

Noah stood just behind the two of them, shrugging at the ground, like he didn't really care if he got the baseball back or not.

"Make me," I told them.

I think Stig might've actually tried to fight me, and even though he was thick like an ox, I bet I could've taken him easy. Quick and mean, that's what Dad said about me when he was teaching me how to defend myself. He meant it as a compliment.

Stig didn't get the chance to get pummeled, though, because Jeremiah Jacobson, for all his faults, was a lot smarter than Stig was, and he could always find a way to get to you that didn't involve punching.

My Book of Thoughts. I'd left it in the grass, like some kind of moron.

"Hey, look," he told the other guys, snatching the book off the grass, "I found the little girl's *diary*." And he held it over his head and started flipping through the pages. Even though I was taller, I couldn't grab at it, because Jeremiah's bodyguard, Stig, kept blocking me. "The little girl's an *artist*," Jeremiah said as he flipped. Stig hooted like that was the funniest thing he'd ever heard, and Noah Gorman didn't laugh and he didn't help with the bodyguarding, but he didn't go away either. The ball of fire in my chest was getting hotter and hotter, till I almost couldn't stand it. But I couldn't get that notebook.

Then all of a sudden, when Jeremiah had flipped through maybe five or six pages, he stopped flipping. He didn't give back my thoughts, though. Instead, his eyes went wide at me and his face went long and he said, "What's *wrong* with you?"

Well.

"Give it back," I said, still trying to pummel through the Wall of Stig to get my notebook. "It's mine."

"What's in it?" Stig asked.

Jeremiah went back to flipping. "He's like, sick, or something," he said. "It's all messed-up stuff."

It's not messed up, I wanted to say. *It's just my thoughts.* But of course I didn't say that.

"It's all, like, people getting attacked," Jeremiah went on. Still flipping. "A guy getting eaten by a shark, a guy smushed under a tree, a guy falling off a building."

It was a tightrope, like in the circus. The guy was falling off a tightrope, not a building. I knew I was no great artist, but that seemed obvious.

The grass on this end of the park must've been super fascinating, because that's what Noah was staring at.

9

"What's wrong with you?" Jeremiah asked me again.

It was the kind of question you really couldn't answer.

"Leave him alone."

Well. *That* was a voice I hadn't expected to hear.

"Go away, Fallon," Jeremiah told her. Like he was in charge of the whole park.

She stood right in front of him with one hand on her hip, her fluffy white dog yanking at its leash. She didn't look afraid of him in the slightest. "Not until you give Trent his notebook back." Her little dog yapped.

The fire was up to my hairline now. "I'm *fine*," I told her. I didn't need a *girl* defending me.

"Go away," Jeremiah told her again. "This has nothing to do with you."

"Yeah," Stig agreed. "This has nothing to do with you."

Noah looked like he was going to write a love poem to the grass, it was so interesting.

"It does too have to do with me," Fallon argued. Her dog yapped again. (I really wished he'd take a chunk out of Jeremiah's leg. But it wasn't that kind of dog.) "Those are drawings of me."

"What?" Jeremiah said, flipping his gaze from the pages to Fallon and back.

"*What?*" I said, even louder.

"Yeah," she said. "I asked Trent to draw some theories about how I might've gotten my scar, because I don't remember. Amnesia," she explained, as though we'd even asked. Her little dog yapped. "So he made some pictures."

Jeremiah looked at the notebook one more time. A drawing of a guy standing at the very tip of an exploding volcano. "Is that true?" Jeremiah asked me. "You drew all these pictures of *her*?"

On the one side of me was Jeremiah Jacobson, standing with his bodyguards, holding my Book of Thoughts. And on the other side was stupid, nosy Fallon Little and her yappy dog. And what was I supposed to say? Those drawings *weren't* of Fallon, that was for sure. But if Jeremiah and Stig and Noah knew the truth, they'd think I was even sicker than they already did.

"Yeah," I said. "That's what it is." And while Jeremiah and Stig were busy hooting with laughter, and Noah was still focused on his love affair with the grass, I managed to snatch back my Book of Thoughts and stuff it safely into the front pocket of my sweatshirt. "Take your stupid ball," I told Jeremiah, tossing the baseball at him. He caught it easily.

Fallon was grinning big, like she'd helped me out so much. "You boys can leave now," she told them.

Jeremiah just rolled his eyes. "Tell your girlfriend there's something on her face," he told me. And then he and his bodyguards walked away.

When they were safe back on the field, I jumped onto my bike and was ready to pedal my way home when I heard Fallon say, "You're welcome, by the way."

I didn't turn around. "I didn't say thank you, by the way," I grumbled.

I could almost *hear* her shrug. "You owe me one now."

"Whatever," I replied. I pushed my right foot down hard onto the pedal.

"Trent?" she said.

I sighed and stopped pedaling. Did turn around, then. "I'm going home," I told her.

She didn't seem to care about that. "What are the drawings of, really?" she asked. She had scooped up her yappy white dog and was staring at me now, those two big brown eyes, one on either side of that deep pink scar.

"None of your business," I replied.

She nodded, like that was true. Her little dog yapped. And I pedaled away for real. "See you later, Trent!" she called after me.

"See you," I told her. But I didn't mean it.

The pedaling home was hard, harder than it had been on the way to the park, because my whole body was fire now, all over. I couldn't believe I'd let anybody see my Book of Thoughts. That was just mine, and no one had ever looked at it before, not even Miss Eveline at school. *Stupid*, I told myself, with every push of the pedals. *Stupid, stupid, stupid, stupid.*

Those drawings weren't of Fallon and her lame scar. I wished they were. I'd rather have thoughts about that. Instead my thoughts, every page, the whole five volumes, were all about nothing but Jared Richards.

The kid I'd killed in February.